LOVER
HUSBAND
FATHER

THE AFTERMATH

ELSIE JOHNSTONE
GRAEME JOHNSTONE

Lover, Husband, Father, Monster
The Aftermath

Copyright © 2015 by Elsie Johnstone, Graeme Johnstone
G. & E. Johnstone
978-0-9925059-6-7

Part One

JENNIFER

The wretched bikie lay in the middle of the road in the pouring rain, yelling for help, complaining about his legs.

I wanted to yell back, 'If you can feel them, then they're fine. Now get off the road and let us get to the airport!' But that was never going to happen. Not now. Events had been set in train. Police were being summoned, an ambulance siren could be heard further down the motorway, the bikie's blood was mixing with the rain, a ruby river running into the gutter.

The elderly couple that had sideswiped him were out of their ancient Mercedes hysterically chirping away in an Irish dialect that neither I nor anyone else had ever heard before, all the while making useless up-and-down flapping movements with their arms. I was highly agitated as I visualized our flight to freedom vanishing into the clouds without us on board.

And it is all Stuart's fault! Had it not been for him interfering and insisting on coming to the airport to say goodbye to Molly we would have bade our farewell at home and arrived in time for a latte before our flight. I know he did it on purpose, just to make me suffer, and I hate him for it.

Now, Kevin has just told me in no uncertain terms that I am not helping the situation and to bite my tongue. That really annoys me, my own brother turning against me.

'Whose side are you on?' I snapped. He dismissed my question with a shrug, adjusted the buds attached to his phone and retreated into himself and his music.

The pandemonium on the road outside our car increased. Suddenly, I became aware that Stuart's door had been opened. I assumed that he was getting out to help. That's the type of person he is, the sort who likes to take control.

Maybe he would try to calm the dithering couple. Perhaps he would enlist some knowledge gleaned from the first aid lectures of his days in the Boy Scouts. If all else failed then he was sure to take charge by directing the traffic. I had seen it all before, so I sat fuming silently in the front seat praying that this mess would be cleaned up and we would make it in time to catch our flight, or any flight for that matter, and escape Dublin forever.

THE SON - STUART HOARE (JUNIOR)

When we were in the front room, and Mam told us all that stuff about leaving us and going to London to live with her boyfriend and Molly, Da got really angry. I was frightened. I have seen him cross plenty of times but he has never been as mad as this. Shaking! Red in the face! Angry!

It was really confusing and scary and my little brother started to cry. I couldn't do that so I just stared into the fireplace and watched the gas flame. We both felt really bad because it was probably all our fault. I should have tried harder at school and Richie should have at least have tried out for the football team, but he wouldn't because it was at the same time as his drama class. Da said he was a wuss.

THE SON - RICHIE

Mam and Tommy are taking Molly with them and flying off to London to live and we will never see them again. And Da will look after us and take us to school before he goes to work and make us do our homework and Nanna Mary and Grandma Moira are going to do the cooking. Mam says she will come back and visit us a lot, but you can never really trust grown-ups to do what they say.

What I don't get is that Mammy is the one who is always cuddling us and telling us what good boys we are and how much she loves us, while Da never does anything like that, he just looks angry and yells at us, and now it is Mam who is going away while Da is staying. If she really loves us as much as she says she wouldn't leave us, would she? It's just not fair.

STUART

I was seething. The bitch had totally blindsided me, not only with what she did but also with the sneaky way she went about it, recruiting everybody to take her side, including my own mother. She had isolated me completely and that really hurt.

How could they side with the lover and not the husband? To even consider that the best option for Molly would be to take her away from her own home and her own biological father to live with some stranger?

Jennifer had trashed my love for my own children and made me out to be the baddie, when all I had ever done for the past fifteen years was to devote myself to our family and work hard to give them everything. That lousy long-haired loser from London has already betrayed Jennifer once before and yet she has the nerve to take my little girl away from me to live with him in a foreign country. They set me up a treat.

Now I was stuck in the car with her going on and on in the front seat, blaming me for the traffic accident for God's sake, blaming me for them being late, blaming me for everything. As if she was blameless herself. It takes two to tango! She hates me and I hate her. Even Kevin, her favourite bother, had told her to shut up but she wouldn't. Nag! Nag! Nag! Yakkety yak!

I looked at Molly and stroked her hair. She was my beautiful baby and was being snatched away from me. Fury surged, coursing through my veins, a raging river of resentment.

It was hot in the back of Kevin's new car. I couldn't stand the sound of Jennifer's voice. I had to get away from that whining and whinging before it made me vomit. I opened the back door, took Molly with her little dolly from her car seat and stepped out into the fresh air.

We began to play the Drop Molly, the game we often played together.

JENNIFER

It was several minutes before I realised that Molly was gone. I turned around to tell her what a good little girl she had been for sitting so quietly, only to discover her seat was empty!

Stuart must have taken her with him when he had got out of the car. 'He's done a runner with my baby girl,' I thought. A shocking notion entered my head. 'He's taken her and is going to hide her in a deserted farmhouse somewhere so that I can't have her.' I had to get out of that car and get my daughter back.

My adrenalin levels soared as I frantically clawed at the door's unfamiliar fittings. Time stood still. Every nerve in my body tensed as I battled with the new-fangled handles that were embedded, almost flush with the side panel. I finally found the lever and pushed the door open and clambered out, looking desperately around for Stuart and my daughter. Yes, there they were, on the other side of the car, on the far side of the road. Next to the railing overlooking the motorway.

But what was that horrific sound coming from below? The piercing screech of brakes, the sickening thud of metal on metal, the shattering of glass.

With the retching smell of smoking rubber wafting up into my nostrils, I raced to where Stuart was standing. He had his back to me, his hands outstretched as if he was praying to the Holy Spirit. His eyes stared straight ahead, zombie like, his expression hardened and steely.

Molly was not with him.

Something was wrong. Terribly wrong.

I tried to push him aside to find out where she was but he was an immovable stone statue.

I screamed. But no scream emerged, just a weird, rasping sound. Once, twice, thrice! Finally, the sounds came together as one. 'My little girl! My beautiful little girl! Where is she?' That was what I was trying to say, but all that came from my throat was one horrible banshee-like noise.

My primitive scream galvanized Kevin into action. He dropped his phone and discarded his earphones as he scrambled out of the car and rushed to where I was standing.

Rain, blood and terror mixed with noise from the motorway below as the nightmare began.

Kevin grabbed me by the shoulders and tried to shake me out of it.

'Hush Jen! Shhhhh! Jennifer, calm down! What is wrong, Jen? Tell me what is the matter.'

I couldn't speak. Ignoring Kevin, I turned and pointed at my husband, the marble mad man. Then I began to pound into him with my fists.

'Where is Molly?' I screamed. 'What have you done with Molly?'

He ignored me, standing solid and resolute, unmoved. Then his gaze shifted slowly from an undisclosed point on the horizon to the motorway beneath.

My glance followed his to the scene of carnage below. The southbound traffic had come to a crunching halt, piled up, all skewwhiff. Merciful Lord, Molly was down there somewhere!

I froze and stopped pummelling him as inhuman screams flowed like a river of molten lava from my throat. My heart went cold, my legs buckled under me and I turned and sat down with a thud on the cold wet ground that soaked into my clothes. A surge of warm yellow pee mingled with the rain and slid into the gutter.

Somehow the boys appeared by my side as Stu and Kevin disappeared, leaving us a confused and disoriented little trio sitting together on the asphalt. My sons cuddled into me, frightened and cold.

This horrible, inescapable nightmare had us in its vortex, pulling this way and pushing that way, spinning us in ever increasing circles. There was no escape.

'Molly,' I whimpered. 'Molly.'

KEVIN

I had been a reluctant participant in this whole shebang, but Jennifer is my sister after all, and so when she asked me to come over to her house and protect her while she told Stuart that she was leaving him, I thought that if this was the path she had chosen then the least I could do was to support her. It didn't sit well with me, all the same. I don't like getting caught up in other people's domestic situations, but I knew he had been violent towards her in the past, so what could I do?

On the journey to the airport, Jennifer had been niggling poor Stuart all the way, sniping at him from the front seat, blaming him for everything. I even began to feel sorry for the poor beggar. After all, she was getting what she wanted. The least she could do was to be civil. Either that or not say anything at all. So I plugged into my phone and tried to ignore it. But it was her scream that galvanised me into action.

To be perfectly honest with you, I've never heard anything like it. It eclipsed the music coming through my earphones, sounding like a wild animal caught with its foot in a trap. I didn't know what she was saying, it was like another language entirely, but I immediately got out of the car and ran towards her because I instinctively knew that something was horribly wrong.

There was Stuart with his arms outstretched over the side of the bridge, like the high priest at a pagan ritual sacrifice, just standing there motionless. But there was no Molly! Oh my God. Don't tell me she had gone over the edge! I looked down at the carnage below, as dazed drivers got out of their shattered cars to survey the mess and the traffic began to form into a tailback.

She couldn't possibly have survived that.

T O M

A few minutes after we came to a halt, I saw Stuart get out of the car with Molly, and not knowing much about children assumed it was for a toilet break. I continued absentmindedly drumming my fingers on the steering wheel to a tune running through my head at the time when, realizing something odd had happened, I opened the car door, told the boys to stay where they were and began walking quickly towards Jennifer.

The boys took no notice of what I said and responded to their mother's screams as well. They ran so fast that they got there before I did and flung themselves onto the ground next to her. Jen seemed oblivious to everything around her. Richie kept tugging at his mother's sleeve crying, 'Mam, what's wrong? Mammy, what's the matter?'

The three of them clung together like magnets in the rain and the dirt, repelling the outsider - me.

Kevin arrived at about the same time, took in the horrible scene and reacted instantly. He grabbed Stuart and pushed him forward. 'Is that Molly down there? Is that our Molly? Come on, we have to go to her. Come on, Stu! Come on!'

He ran ahead and Stuart turned to follow, but spotted me standing on the sidelines. I remember thinking, 'How in the hell have I got myself into all of this?' And I recall not getting much time to ponder an answer as Stuart marched up to me and said something like, 'Enjoy your fucking freedom now.'

I have absolutely no memory of what happened after that.

STUART

There. That should jolt "Little Miss Do What I Want Without Considering Anybody Else" back into the real world. That'll make it clear to her that if I can do something like this to Molly then I am capable of doing anything to her and the lads.

Ha! Won't be so much fun going off to London with drummer boy now! In war, sometimes one has to make a sacrifice for the common good and it is unfortunate that Molly has to take the hit for the family.

A violent, horrendous scream interrupted my thoughts. It was Jennifer hoeing into me with her fists. 'Where is my baby? My beautiful little girl! What have you done to my baby?'

'*Your* fucking baby? Don't you mean *our* baby?'

I grabbed her by both wrists and pushed her back up against the barricade. 'Remember this! What ever has happened down below, it's your fault. You did this.'

She looked up and, spat in my face. Oh, how I would have loved to have given her a decent thump across the head, but I felt an urgent clap on my shoulder and turned to see Kevin urging me to go with him.

'Stu! Stu! Is that Molly down there?' he was shouting. 'Is it our Molly? Come on, Stu, we've got to go and help! Come on! Oh, Jeezus, I hope she's all right,' he prayed. 'Oh, Mary Mother of God, please make her all right.'

He began to run and tried to pull me with him, but I resisted because I became aware of the two shocked and puzzled faces of my lads.

'Calm down,' I said to Kevin. 'She'll be okay. She'll be fine.' And then to the lads, 'It's all right, Junior,' I whispered. 'It's okay. Daddy will sort things out.' I put my hands out to my sons to offer protection and comfort and assurance, but a shrill voice broke my attention and the link.

'What have you done? You are the devil himself!' shrieked the elderly woman from the car that had hit the motorcyclist. She had left her husband to attend to the stricken rider - who I noticed was *still* moaning - and decided she would enter our family dispute.

'What have *I* done?' I queried, turning on her, my face just a few centimetres from hers. 'I've done nothing! I was playing our game, that's all I was doing. Playing our game!'

She put her hand to her mouth mumbling, 'I don't think it is a game.' Then, deciding that it was perhaps best to mind her own business, she backed away to sort out her own predicament.

I turned to follow Kevin down to the motorway but not before stopping for just one more moment. Out of the corner of my eye I spotted lover boy hovering around like a lost soul and decided to give him a little lesson in the realities of life. I summoned up my old judo skills, took a deep breath and landed him a beauty, right on the side of the nose. I felt my right hand collapse his lower eye socket.

Well, there's something. It seems I haven't lost my touch!

JUNIOR

It had been a crazy trip anyway. We followed Uncle Kevin all over Dublin and Tommy kept swearing under his breath about how fast he was going and what an idiot he was. Kevin took us charging up a little alleyway and Tommy knocked over a rubbish bin. It was funny, but Tommy didn't think so. He swore.

When we stopped for the accident he banged his fists on the wheel and said, 'Now what's the fuckin' matter? We'll miss the fuckin' plane.'

We didn't really take much notice because we were both playing our games and we don't like him anyway. I was getting very close to my best score ever when I heard Mammy scream. Tommy told us to stay in the car, but who is he to tell us what to do? We got out and ran to Mam anyway.

Then Da hit Tommy right on the snout and made him bleed and disappeared with Uncle Kevin and Mam was crying and we couldn't find Molly. They were telling us it was going to be all right. But I knew it wasn't going to be because Molly was not there anymore and they were all looking worried. Adults think kids are dumb, don't they?

STUART

Kevin instinctively made his way back along the overpass to find a spot where he could get down on to the motorway embankment. Having not lost much of his flexibility or fitness from his playing days, he hurdled the fence easily, leapt onto the grassy slope and landed cleanly. But due to both his anxiety and the sheer angle of the earthworks, he plunged almost out of control down through the knee-high ground cover and stringy saplings before reaching the roadway and regaining his balance. I followed suit but was more circumspect, easing myself over the fence and carefully picking my way slowly down toward a scene of utter devastation.

What a sight. A driver obviously distracted by the event had hit the brakes at the crucial moment, deviated from his line, lost control and turned sideways. The car behind would have had no time whatsoever to take evasive action and smashed into him, creating an even bigger target for those following. The combined mass of half a dozen cars or so had careered on under the flyover, finally coming to a halt about seventy or eighty metres further down the road. I could see one was on its side, one was on its roof and several were badly battered, just like those spectacular American raceway accidents you see on the television. Steam and smoke was rising everywhere. Jammed up behind them in three neat rows were several cars that had avoided the major pile-up but had rear-ended each other. The cars near where we stepped onto the road had stopped in the nick of time, some only a few centimetres from each other, and were now forming a stationary tailback of concerned and angry drivers.

We headed down the motorway towards the point of major impact, assuming that that was where Molly was likely to be. God knows, I thought, she must surely be dead. A sickening feeling began to overwhelm me. What have I done? But then we were interrupted by shouts. 'Over here!' came a stricken voice. 'Is she yours? Over here, then!' and our gaze turned towards the centre of the motorway, directly underneath the edge of the flyover.

There was a group of people, in varying states of panic, agitation and concern, standing in the median strip, the two metre-wide pit formed by metre-high concrete barriers that run the length of the motorway.

'Stu, Stu, she must have fallen in there!' shouted Kevin, picking his way through the three lanes of stalled traffic and rushing up to the group.

'Out of the way! Out of the feckin' way, we're family,' he urged as he hurdled the barrier and landed lightly on his feet in the strip. The crowd obliged, parted and closed in around him as I puffed and panted after him. I heard Kevin's anguished incantation, 'Oh, Molly, Molly, oh Jeezus, Molly.'

'Please, please,' I said. 'Let me through. I'm her father.' I worked my way to the front of the group where a middle-aged woman was on her knees, cradling Molly's head. I could tell that she was experienced - a nurse, a doctor maybe, something in the medical line - trying to do her best in the situation. She held two fingers to the side of Molly's neck. 'There is a pulse, but it is very weak,' she said. 'That ambulance had better get here soon.'

Molly was lying on her back, her eyes closed, looking peaceful. Apart from a bruise on her right temple, she was just like the little Molly who had been cuddled up next to me in the car a few moments before. Her tiny chest was moving up and down at a rapid rate.

I edged closer. The lady looked up and said, 'Can you please keep back, sir? She needs air.'

'I'm her father,' I said, affronted that she was trying to deny me access. Repentant, she indicated for me to come closer. 'Perhaps you could hold her and reassure her? She'll hear your voice and won't be so frightened.'

I hesitated, unsure what to do, when a tall, burly chap in a greatcoat standing at the back of the group blurted, 'How the feck did this happen? How the hell did a little girl end up down here, from way up there?' He pointed to the flyover bridge, but continued to stare menacingly at me with piercing blue eyes. 'Hey? So, you're her father, yes? Then how the feck ..?'

He clenched his fist, but his wife put her arm through his and whispered, 'Not now, darl, not the right time.'

'It was our little game,' I said.

'Game?' he said, trying to disentangle himself and approach me. I could see this was not going to end well.

Suddenly I got a whiff of tobacco and realized salvation was at hand and I could create a diversion. I hate smoking, knowing what effect it has on me from the few times I tried it as a teenager in a failed endeavour to become part of the in-crowd. But desperate times require desperate measures.

I turned and spotted the smoker, a man in his sixties with a grey beard and a moustache tinged at the edges in yellow. 'Could I have a cigarette, please?' I said.

He produced a packet of Mayfairs and offered me one. 'I thought you'd be a Marlboro man,' I said, trying to make light of the moment as he struck the match.

The initial blast of nicotine was soothing but after two more puffs, I felt a surge of dizziness and vaguely remember trying to keep my balance before the lights went out.

RICHIE

In the car ride to the airport Tommy tried to talk to us but he was having trouble keeping up with Uncle Kev. It was funny when we hit the rubbish bin and he didn't talk at all after that. When we got out of the car, we sat with Mammy in the gutter while Da and Uncle Kevin went to see where Molly was and afterwards a nice lady looked after us and gave us her phone to telephone Nanna Mary and tell her to please come and get us.

Da hit Tommy but I don't think that Mammy knew that because she didn't say anything. They took us to an ambulance and because we were so cold that our teeth were chattering a man in a green uniform put some blankets around us. I was glad when Nanna and Daideo came to get us and brought us back to their house.

We had spaghetti bol for tea.

A WITNESS ON THE FLYOVER - MARGERY BOURKE

The traffic stopped on the flyover because of the motorbike accident four cars in front of me and didn't look as if it would flow again for a while. So I changed from the driver's seat, took my knitting into the back seat and began adding to the fabric, eyes wandering, taking in the scene, as it was a simple pattern.

I saw it all. A gentleman in a car about two back from the accident opened the back door and got out, leaned in and unclipped a child whom he took in his arms, kissing the top of her head as he did so. I thought it was sweet so I continued to watch.

He walked with her to the edge. I thought he was going to show her the traffic on the motorway beneath. You know how kids love to watch the cars and trucks disappear under the bridge. He stepped back and held her a little above his head and let her go catching her at the last moment. She giggled and squirmed. 'That's nice,' I thought, 'a dad playing with his daughter to amuse her.'

He did it again. And again! He did it four or five times on the pavement. They were having a great old time.

Then he walked back to the edge of the bridge and held her in his hands out over the safety rail.

I didn't want to look but was compelled. This was taking the game too far! I held my breath. He dropped her. He made no attempt to catch her.

I tried to tell the grandmother who came to collect the two boys what I witnessed but she brushed me off. The Garda took my details and said they will be in touch. I do know what I saw!

WITNESS NUMBER 1 ON THE MOTORWAY

It was all very confusing. Traffic and chaos everywhere! Slowly, the overall awfulness of the situation began to dawn on everybody. The little girl had somehow ended up in the median strip of the motorway and caused an appalling pile-up of vehicles.

Everybody was horrified, and as we looked around, we were lost for a solution. How did she get there? Did she run onto the road? Did she fall out of a car? Did she come down from the flyover? Did that man who had been standing up there at the railing have something to do with it? Parents let kids wander anywhere these days.

We could not, would not, dare not, countenance the most awful conclusion of all. That someone would have done this on purpose. We simply did not want to go there.

WITNESS NUMBER 2 ON THE MOTORWAY

The first fellow came rushing down the embankment flat chat, nearly falling arse over head and tearing his jacket in the process. He was very distressed, poor chap when he reached the group surrounding the little girl. Apparently he was her uncle.

Then the father wandered down like he was on a Sunday stroll, ever so casual. He sort of pushed his way to the front of the crowd and stood there looking, just looking. Never made any attempt to cradle his daughter or anything like that and when someone had a bit of a go at him, blow me down with a feather if he didn't turn around and cadge a cigarette. Unbelievable!

PAUL SMITH

I was on my way to the airport, pretty pumped because I was flying out to Buenos Aires and from there, taking a ship from Punta Arenas to Antarctica to complete my thesis on 'The Ability of Young Penguins to Retain Warmth in a Cold Climate'.

I had allowed myself plenty of time so wasn't particularly worried when an accident caused a delay in traffic on the flyover. I had just picked up a fabulous new camera that morning and so I grabbed the opportunity to have a bit of a play with it. I took it out of its packaging, quickly scanned the manual and began shooting.

I was a bit concerned about being intrusive so I opened the car door and discreetly filmed, panning the collision scene between the bikie and the Mercedes slowly, adjusting the focus, zooming in and out and trying the different lenses. It was a bit high tech compared to what I was used to, but I bought it because I knew I would need some good quality stuff to illustrate my report.

There was another kerfuffle on the motorway down below, but eventually the traffic dispersed, the northbound lanes were clear and I made it to the airport just in time to take my flight, which was a good thing because LAN only flies out a couple of times a week.

JENNIFER

I sat on the wet sidewalk with my legs in the gutter, a stranger's overcoat hung loosely around my shoulders and a tartan car-rug draped over my knees. A female emergency worker in a luminous yellow vest leaned over me, stroking my hand and speaking in a reassuring voice. 'Jennifer, can you stand up, love? Let me help you. The ambulance is here and they want to check you out. You've had a terrible shock and you need to be seen to.'

'Molly, where's Molly? Molly, Molly, Molly!' I sobbed. 'Where's my Molly?'

I repeated that chant over and over in my comatose state, saying her name, unable to comprehend the enormity of what had just happened.

'Is she still alive?' I pleaded. 'Is she badly hurt? All those cars, the noise …'

'Mrs Hoare, the good news is that she did not land on the road! She landed on the median strip. The ambulance has taken her away and you can be sure that everything possible will be done for her. The Garda will take you there as soon as they get a car up here.'

As I tried to take all this in, the lady helped me up and led me and my two lonely, confused boys to the ambulance. The boys! My poor boys, having to go through all of this.

A kindly older woman took them into her care and, and under her instructions, they phoned for my parents to come. Stuart Junior was acting his usual stoic self with his arm around Richie, comforting and reassuring him. 'Mammy's all right, Richie. Everything is cool. Little Molly's had an accident, that's all. They have taken her to hospital and they will fix her up like they fixed my leg that time. Remember? Don't cry!' Even in my confusion, I was proud of him.

Poor Richie was not so easily consoled and grabbed hold of me, almost knocking me over. I put my arms out and drew both my boys into a circle of sorrow. We sobbed together, our mantras converging, making a sad, sad song and capturing our warmth, our smell, our being in a melancholy trio of despair, an island in a massive mess of sirens and strangers.

My young and raw boys are vulnerable and so very tender. How could I have considered leaving them? My thoughts spilled like carelessly thrown jigsaw pieces, some clearly remembered, some too painful to recall, the picture emerging but incomplete.

The ambulance man peered into my eyes, took my blood pressure, checked my pulse and concluded that despite the terrible situation, I did not need to go to hospital myself. Into this shemozzle descended my parents in a Garda car. Poor dears! Mam's coat was buttoned up in the wrong holes, her hair hadn't been combed since her shower that morning and she wore no make up. She looked concerned, old and tired. 'Holy Mary Mother of God, Jennifer, what's happened?'

Da couldn't help himself. 'Jennifer,' he said, putting his oar into the water, 'your mother has filled me in on what has been going on in this family behind my back and I'm not happy.'

'Hush, Seamus!' Mam interrupted. 'This is neither the time nor the place for that. Now tell me, lovie, what has happened and what would you like your Dada and I to do?'

'Mam, Molly's in hospital and I'm going to go to her in a minute,' I managed to blurt. 'Can you take Junior and Richie back with you and I will phone you when I get there and find out how Molly is?'

Richie ran to his grandma, the most solid thing in his life of late, and enveloped in the softness of her arms, began sobbing his little heart out. Junior stood with his grandfather in a manly embrace, the older man with his arms around the younger one's shoulder.

'And what about Stuart, where's he in all of this?' Mam asked.

'I don't know, Mam. I … I really don't know where he is. Just take the boys away from here. Look after them. I will call you.'

The Garda interrupted to tell me they would take me to Molly just as soon as reinforcements arrived, that Kevin had gone with Molly in the ambulance to the hospital and that Mr Hoare was in another ambulance on his way to Beaumont for observation.

'What! What happened to Stuart?' I asked incredulously.

'Passed out and hit his head, madam. He's okay though. Just a precaution.'

My God. That man is unbelievable. I thought no more of him as my parents reassured me that all would be fine and left the scene with the boys. It was beginning to get dark and it would be a while before they got home.

'What about Tom? Where is Tom?' I asked, suddenly remembering the reason for this trip. 'What happened to him? Did he catch the plane back to London?'

'Hardly,' said the officer.

'What do you mean, hardly?'

'We are talking about the Englishman who suffered the beating, aren't we?'

'Beating!'

'He has been shipped off to hospital in a bad way. Apparently that husband of yours packs a mean punch. It's all been attended to, so don't you worry.'

He ushered me towards another car. 'Are you ready to go now? Your Molly has been taken to the National Children's Hospital in Tallaght.'

I didn't know what to think. As he started the car, applied the flashing lights and slowly manoeuvred his way down the ramp, I sat in a daze, questions swelling and subsiding like the lava in a bubble lamp.

What had I done to bring all this on us?

Did I care about Tom any more?

Did I care that Stuart had punched him and put him in hospital?

I felt dead inside.

MOIRA, STUART'S MOTHER

I had gone to Stuart's place that morning because I didn't want to see him completely bulldozed by that O'Brien mob. I wanted him to know that I was there for him because I know Jennifer is strong-minded and can be brutal.

He was angry when Jennifer ambushed him like that - and he blamed me for being complicit! But I wasn't. I just didn't want him to be "O'Brien'd".

I explained to him that Jennifer had made up her mind to go to London with her lover and there was nought he could do about it. It was better to let her go without a fuss as she was going to go anyway. He was really upset about her taking Molly, as he didn't want the family to be broken up. The boys love her and she adores them. He loves her too.

I said, 'Give Jennifer her head, son! Let her go.' I quoted that old saying, 'If you really love her you must let her free and if she is really yours then she will come back to you.'

We left it at that, as I had to get home to my own dear Richard who couldn't be left by himself on account of his Alzheimer's. The council worker sitting with him was due to finish up for the day.

MARY, JENNIFER'S MOTHER

After the family had left for the airport in such a tense state, Moira and I had tidied up the living area and put away the shoes, wet-weather gear and drink bottles that the boys had left lying around when they had come in from golf. We made ourselves a strong cup of tea and sat down to mull over the happenings of the morning, both agreeing that the situation was far from ideal but that we would both help Stuart make the best of it.

Naturally Moira saw everything from her son's perspective and thought it was wrong of Jennifer to take Molly away from her family. However, I could see that Stuart would find it very difficult to fit Molly into his busy schedule. He left early in the morning for work and he often didn't get home until after she was in bed. Perhaps it was better that Jennifer took her for now.

I was a bit embarrassed to be told that the Hoares had a name for Jennifer's inclination to lean towards her birth family rather than going Stuart's way. I know we are a big, noisy mob and move about in a pack but I always thought we graciously included Stuart. They call it being "O'Brien'd!" That set me back a pace or two.

I went home and tiddled around in the kitchen a bit. I didn't want to tell Seamus what had happened, as he would not approve. And besides, he was happily busy between the form guide, the television in the front room and his mates at the betting shop.

Halfway through the afternoon I got the phone call from the boys. 'Mammy is unconscious and Molly is hurt and I don't know where Da and Uncle Kevin are,' Junior blurted out. 'Can you please come, Nanna, and help us?' It was such a shock, I could not quite grasp what it was all about other than there had been some terrible incident on the motorway.

I threw my overcoat over my housecoat, backed out the car and drove to Ladbrokes to pick up Seamus who was better dressed than me in his Saturday punter's outfit of grey trousers, blue checked shirt, sports jacket and nifty hat. He had been up and down the street all day putting his bets on the horses.

'Junior phoned and there has been an accident out near the airport,' I said. 'He and little Richard need us to go and get them. Molly is hurt and is going to hospital but Jen can't leave until we get there.'

That was the easy part. As we drove, I then had to 'fess up' to the story of the morning's events and the horrible background to it all. To say that Seamus was unhappy is a gross understatement. He was furious at both Jennifer for breaking up the family and me for not keeping him informed.

Poor Seamus is old school. To him, the man is the head of the house, what he says goes and the family unit is sacrosanct. To me, all of that went out with the ark. I've always done what I wanted; I just haven't told him about it. And I still haven't let on about me looking after Molly and picking up the boys from school all those times that Tom had come across to Dublin and Jenny had gone to see him.

Fortunately the Garda were on duty, directing traffic. I managed to convince them that we needed to go through, that we were the grandparents and had to go to the young boys, so a young officer went to his car, talked on the radio for a few moments and came back to where we waited. 'Put your car up on the embankment there for the time being,' he said. 'I will take you to the scene as soon as a relief car turns up. Won't be too long!'

The tailback on the southbound section must have been four or five kilometres long but the police had blocked and cleared the northbound section near the accident, so we flew past with sirens bleating and lights flashing. When we got to the bridge it was mayhem.

'The boys are on the flyover,' the Garda directed, 'this way'. Normally I would have complained about walking up that incline to the road above, but I just gritted my teeth and followed him, aware that Seamus' heart condition would slow him down. 'Take your time, lovie,' I instructed. 'I'll see you at the top.'

When I got there, my heart broke for the lads. They were clinging to their mother like two frightened little monkeys, teeth chattering with the cold and shock. I can't really remember what was said or the sequence of events but we left Jen to go to Molly in the hospital and made our way back to the Garda's car.

The only thing I clearly remember was a very hysterical lady clutching at me and screaming. 'You have to know this. It was not an accident. I saw it. The man in the grey coat threw that little girl over the top. I was sitting in my car. I saw it! He threw her over the bridge.'

Another member of the Garda extracted her from me and took her with him. When we got home I ran a nice warm bath for the boys, found pyjamas for them and made up my version of spaghetti bolognaise with a can of tomato soup. The boys love that. I threw their dirty clothes in the washing machine, switched it on, turned around, rested my back against it, and burst into tears. What an awful day!

STUART

When I finally came to, I was on the move. The bright lights, vaguely familiar equipment and rolling motion made me aware I was in the back of an ambulance. 'Welcome back to the land of the living, Mr Hoare,' said the warm voice of a young paramedic, barely out of graduation and keen to show her skills. 'We're taking you to hospital.'

'Can't I just go home?'

'Of course you can go home, but only after they have checked you out at Beaumont. Molly is off to the children's.'

'Molly,' I said slowly. 'Yes. My dear little Molly.'

She waited for me to say more. After a few seconds, she broke the silence.

'You do realise, Mr Hoare, that …'

'Yes, yes, I know, Molly is not well.'

'Well, more than that. They are getting her to the best treatment available as quickly as they can. But don't despair, children are resilient and often surprise us.'

I dropped my head back, stared at the white ceiling of the ambulance, and clenched both fists. A pain shot up my right arm.

I looked down to see my hand was swollen and two knuckles scraped. Each time I bunched it, the pain came on. That felt good.

PARAMEDIC

It's amazing how, whenever we arrive at an accident scene, everyone breathes a huge sigh of relief. It was mayhem underneath that flyover but we took charge, checked the scene and realised that it was a life and death with the little girl. Time was of the essence.

We stabilized her, quickly got her into the ambulance, and looked around for the mother. But when she could not be immediately located, we gave her uncle something to calm down and suggested that he ride with her. 'If she regains consciousness, it will be good for her to see a familiar face,' I told him. And besides, there would be forms to sign.

Having been in this game for seventeen years, I am no longer surprised at anything. I have seen people fall from two metres and die, and I have seen people hit the deck from ten metres and survive. For the moment, she is one of the latter. Her tough little body seems to have handled the impact well. My real concern is that bump on her temple.

We monitored her all the way and phoned ahead so that when we arrived an alert had gone out and the doctors were waiting to assess her and take her away to surgery.

THE DOCTOR ON DUTY

At 3.55 pm a call came through to Emergency that a five-year-old female patient had been injured in a road trauma and was on the way. We prepared for her arrival.

At 4.10 the ambulance docked with the victim and she was immediately taken to Operating Theatre Number 3.

The girl, Molly Hoare from Dalkey, was accompanied in the ambulance by her maternal uncle, Mr Kevin O'Brien. The girl's mother followed in a police car. Mr O'Brien was not certain how young Molly ended up on the motorway but he thought that her father had accidentally dropped her over the edge. He could not be absolutely sure. The father was not present.

Prognosis not good.

JENNIFER

The Garda ushered me through the hospital door and sat me on a straight chair while they went to speak to the staff, whispering something to the nurse on duty who listened intently and asked questions. She disappeared, but returned with an older nurse who came to where I was sitting and kindly put her arm around me.

My clothes were dirty and wet, my hair was dripping, I had a stranger's coat flung across my shoulders and whatever makeup I may have applied that morning for Tommy had either been washed away by the rain or smeared around my face with tears.

I responded by clinging to the nurse and saying, 'I've come to sit with Molly. A terrible thing has happened, and I have to see her!'

'Please,' I added as an afterthought, remembering my manners and not wanting to put the staff off side.

'Let's get you a cup of tea and dry you out first before we do anything else,' she replied tenderly. 'You look as if you have been through a car wash. Molly is in theatre at the moment so there is nothing you can do for her just yet. Come with me and we'll get you a nice warm shower. And then you can see her as soon as the doctors are through.'

I was touched by her caring and gentle attitude and could no longer hold back. I sobbed so hard that I shook like a Salvation Army tin on collection day. Shockwaves wracked my body.

The nurse gently took my hand and led me to a bathroom where she ran a hot shower. I let the warm water wash over my body, so consumed by my grief that I hardly noticed the staff drying and dressing me in blue hospital garb. 'We'll have to find you some shoes,' the nurse declared, leaving me sitting on a bath chair and coming back with a dressing gown and a pair of slippers. Probably some poor dead person had left them behind.

While they were helping me, staff came and went, looking at me with sympathy and speaking to each other in whispers. They brought me a cup of tea and a cheese sandwich, suggesting that I should eat up because I would need my strength for Molly. It tasted like cardboard but I did as I was asked and when I finished they took me to a room outside the operating theatre.

Zombie like, I walked through the waiting room, a grey, desolate but brightly lit place with grey linoleum on the floor and grey institutional chairs lined up in front of grey-blue walls. Hoisted high on the wall, out of harm's way, a television set flashed Ryan Tubrity sitting at his desk clapping his hands along to one of his guests singing a beautiful Gaelic aire that we learnt at school, 'Oro Se do Bheata Bhaile'. The audience was joining in with happiness and gusto, momentarily transporting me back to simpler days when I was a child and the world was good. Just twenty minutes drive away, the audience of Tubrity Tonight was in a warm studio, enjoying themselves, laughing and singing to the music of a dark-haired songster with bushy eyebrows, completely unaware of the hopeless darkness unfolding here in this hospital at Tallaght. So close and yet so far removed.

I shuffled in my ill-fitting slippers to a seat in the corner and sat down, pulling the dressing gown around me to try and ensure my modesty. Some time passed before it dawned on me that I had company. That the man sound asleep in a chair in front of the television was Kevin.

I was elated to see my brother and anxious to piece together the happenings of the afternoon so I went over, tapped him on the shoulder and waited for him to awake with a jolt and take a few seconds to acclimatize to his surroundings.

He stood up and put his arms around me, hugging me like he'd never let me go. 'Oh, Jen, we're in the middle of a nightmare,' he said. 'How did our family get to this place? I just don't understand. This is the worst thing that could happen to anybody. Jenny, I am so sorry. It's bloody awful!'

His voice faded as he became unable to control his distress.

Time was immaterial as I clung to him and we sobbed together, united in our grief. A nurse interrupted us, carrying a tray holding a teapot, two cups, milk and sugar.

NURSE SIMMONS

I have seen people in a distressed state in my time, but this was almost overwhelming. In total shock, the both of them.

'Come now, it's going to be a long night,' I said. 'Have a cup of tea and save your energy. You will need to be strong. The doctors will let you know as soon as they are finished. It's a dreadful thing but we are all praying for your family. So God bless you now.'

I put the tray down and was about to leave the room when I noticed the hospital gown on the poor woman was gaping and untidy.

'Dunne's will still be open over there at Tallaght Square,' I suggested. 'You might be able to buy some warm clothes before the shops close. Marks and Spencer shut at half five but Dunne's keep trading until ten on a Saturday night. On account of the groceries and all of that. Perhaps you could send your brother over there on a mission to buy you some clothes, Mrs Hoare. It's only across the road.'

My suggestion was greeted with silence. Fearing I might have overstepped the mark, I backed out of the room saying, 'Now be sure to drink that cup of tea, lovie. I shall collect the cups later.'

JENNIFER

'Why is everyone tiptoeing around me?' I asked, afraid of the answer.

Kevin avoided the issue by giving my gown a playful tug and suggesting that he best take the nurse's advice and get over to Dunne's before closing time. What was it I wanted him to buy?

'Get me anything that's warm and size ten. Don't worry about the shoes, I'll make do with these slippers until I get home.'

'I'll be off then,' he called as he almost ran out, relieved to escape the doom in the room.

Left by myself with the Tubrity show in the background, I sat down. The situation was hopeless. Nobody was telling me anything about Molly. The staff seemed to be either extra kind or avoiding me altogether, leaving it to the doctors. And they seemed to be permanently unavailable.

Twenty minutes later, when Kevin returned, the tea was getting cold in the pot and I had not moved. 'I asked the shop assistant and she suggested I get you this,' he said pulling an ugly navy blue tracksuit out of the familiar green plastic bag. 'She told me that you can't go wrong with something like this. It's warm and practical and if you are going to be at the hospital all night it's comfortable as well. I didn't argue. I just asked her to get me a good quality one in size ten. Is this all right then?'

He held it up for me to approve. It's something I would never have chosen, as I am usually a dress or skirt girl. I rarely wear trousers and never a tracksuit. But it was far better than what I was wearing so I took it gratefully and disappeared down the corridor to find a toilet cubicle in which to change. I emerged looking like a mixture of a nursing home resident and a gym junkie. It was however warm and modest.

When Kevin then took my hands so carefully the fear of God raced up my spine. Kevin is my brother, a special brother no doubt, but this display of kindness and consideration was completely out of character for the sporting, macho salesman. His words brought me down to reality with a jolt.

'Jennifer, things are really bad.'

'I know that Kevin. Why else would we be here! But the doctors, they are doing all they can. They are fixing Molly up.' I was desperate for his confirmation, as my mind was operating on autopilot and had ceased to accurately process what was going on around me, cushioning me from the truth.

'Jennifer, no, the reality is that Molly may not make it. I'm sure they are doing the best they can, but we have to be prepared for the worst.'

Up until that moment I was sure that Molly would be okay, that the staff would put her little shattered body back together and that life would go on as usual, just like it had in the past when bad things had happened but we got over them.

'Listen, she is going to be all right,' I said firmly. 'I know she will be. She has to be. She is a fighter.' Even as I said those words I knew that they rang hollow.

I could see that in Kevin's face too as he outlined how he came to be with Molly in the ambulance. 'There wasn't time to find you, Jen,' he said. He didn't know exactly what had happened up there on the flyover. He didn't see Stuart get out of the car. But he did hear me scream and when he saw that our little girl had gone over the side, he took off down the hill. 'In the madness of it all, I somehow thought I could catch her, that I would get there in time to stop her fall! Crazy, wasn't it? But my first instinct was to get to her.'

He stopped talking as his body convulsed into sobs. It was several minutes before he could pull himself together to continue. I was in a trance, holding his hands, clinging tight. I wanted him to stop, but I knew he had to go on.

'It was awful, Jen, bloody awful! It was like hell had descended, cars everywhere, rain, horns, smoke. And little Molly was lying on the ground where Stuart had dropped her, deathly quiet, our little Molly.'

'Don't tell me!' I said. 'Don't say any more. Don't!'

I covered his mouth with my hand.

KEVIN

To be perfectly honest with you, until Jen woke me up I hadn't really given too much thought about what I had witnessed on the flyover. I'd simply taken off after Molly and then there was the ambulance ride, the doctors and nurses milling, panic stations all around. I felt helpless and useless but signed all the papers for the surgery, kissed little Molly as she was wheeled off to go to the theatre and then waited. I sat in front of the television and went to sleep. It's a protective instinct I seem to have. When the going gets tough I go to sleep. It sort of blocks out stimulation and gives my brain time to process and make sense of things.

But can anyone make sense of this? How the feckin' hell did little Molly end up down there on that median strip in the first place? I am sure I saw Stu throw her over. Maybe I didn't. My intellect says he would never do that. He may be a prick but surely he's not a killer. He is usually so protective of the children; they are like his alter egos. Damn, I just keep having this image of him tossing her over the edge! Did I see that? Am I making that up? With Stuart, you can't tell. You can never tell with Stuart. Even though my brother-in-law has been in the family for more than fifteen years, I just don't get him. He's more English than Irish, speaks in that plummy accent and thinks he is better than the rest of us.

But I can't say anything. Right now, Jennifer believes - or at least wants to believe - that this was an accident. That no matter how much Stuart has hurt her in the past, he would not be capable of deliberately doing something as horrible as this.

So when the nurse suggested I go across to Dunne's to buy Jennifer some clothes I was grateful to get out into the fresh air. The walk across to the shops gave me time to think and to consider what I would say to her.

When I returned I sat down beside Jen, took her hands in mine so that I knew I had her attention and told her how bad things were for Molly, that she may not survive.

Clutching at straws, she begged, 'Miracles do happen.'

'Yes, miracles happen.'

LOVER, HUSBAND, FATHER, MONSTER

Part Two

STUART

They kept me on a trolley for a mandatory four hours observation at the hospital. After checking me over, the duty doctor cleared me to go home but advised that I should call a taxi as he didn't want me driving for a day or two.

'Your concussion is only slight and as to what caused the collapse, I am inclined to think that it was not your heart or anything sinister but simply a response to the most unusual situation.'

'You're right,' I said. 'I haven't had a cigarette for years. It tasted terrible and made me feel dizzy. I don't know what came over me and why I asked for one.'

The doctor was uncomprehending. 'I … I was thinking more of, you know, your daughter. It is a shocking thing that has happened to her. Very upsetting, indeed.'

'Oh, yes, yes, of course, a terrible thing.' I had put Molly right to the back of my mind. 'Where is she?'

'They have taken her to the Children's at Tallaght,' he added. 'There is no reason why you shouldn't go straight there.'

'I don't feel up to it,' I said. There was no way I was ready to face Jennifer with this raging headache. 'I'll go home and rest up. She'll wait. Jennifer will keep an eye on things. I'll see her tomorrow.'

He mumbled something about Molly maybe not seeing another tomorrow, which I thought was a bit unfair. It seemed to me that he was trying to saddle me with the guilts when I wasn't feeling the best. Without taking his eyes off me, he stepped back slowly out of the room and quietly closed the door.

I got a cab back to Dalkey and was surprised to find nobody home. There were two messages on the phone, one from the usual intrusive hopeful wanting to quote on double-glazing and the other one from damn Wendy. That woman! She is as much a cause of this as anybody with all her advice to Jennifer. She has been undermining me for years and now that Jennifer has threatened to leave me she is feeling very smug. This Molly thing should take the smile off her dial.

'Jen, Jen,' her familiar, grating voice was frantic. 'I've just heard the terrible news. Someone said it might be Molly that was on the motorway. Is that true? Is it her? Is everything okay? I'll try you on your mobile.'

I erased it and went upstairs to lie down in the marital chamber, a place from which I had been banned for many months. It is a better bed in there and Jennifer is at the hospital and will never know. Now is as good a time as any to wrest back control of my own household.

BEAUMONT DISCHARGE NOTES

Mr Hoare was admitted to casualty by ambulance at approximately 4.55 pm suffering from concussion and shock from a fall that occurred when he fainted and hit his head on the pavement. He put it down to his response to smoking a cigarette for the first time in many years. The further complicating factor is the accident involving his daughter.

At 9.10 pm he was discharged and put into a taxi, opting to go home to Dalkey rather than to make his way to his daughter's hospital bed in Tallaght. In my opinion he was affected by the shock, as he did not appear to fully comprehend the seriousness of her situation. I advised him not to drive for three days and made a note to phone his home tomorrow to check on his progress.

WENDY

I was watching the evening news and suddenly it had my complete attention. They had footage of an accident and tailback in the rain on the M50 and there, soaking wet and looking disoriented were my two darling boys, or to be specific Jennifer's boys. I stood up and walked to the television, peering hard, hoping to see what was going on. There was a bedraggled figure with a coat over her shoulder that could have been Jen; I couldn't tell. Then at the last second of the footage I spotted Mary and Seamus.

'My good God,' I thought, 'something terrible has happened. Jen is in trouble.'

I had been at her house for the tumultuous meeting that morning but had left before anyone else because what was happening was really none of my business and it made me feel very uncomfortable being there. I never thought I'd say this, but I even felt a bit bad for Stuart who had obviously been ambushed and had absolutely no inkling of what was about to happen. Some men truly do bury their heads in the sand.

Also I didn't want the boys to blame me in any way for what was happening to their family. I love those boys, and Molly.

I phoned the house but it went to message. I tried Jen on her cell phone but it also went to message.

I worried for the rest of the evening and prayed that they were all okay.

JENNIFER

I sat waiting. I had no idea where Stuart had gone or what had happened to him. Nor did I reflect on his part in all of this. Whatever happened up there, he is a victim too. Molly is our child and we have to put aside our grievances and see this through together. We love her and I need him to be with me at this time. Molly needs him to be with her, too.

My entire focus is on Molly and I am scared.

What if Molly dies?

How can I cope?

How will the family cope?

We love her, adore her. She is our daughter, their little sister. We can't do without her.

Kevin left the room to telephone his wife Amy, and shortly afterwards she arrived with a change of clothes for him to replace the ones he still wore that were wet, torn and stained with grit.

While Kevin was changing, Amy broke up a chocolate bar that she produced from her bag and gave me some, saying that I will need plenty of energy before the worst of this is over. She put the rest for me on the tray next to the cold tea and told me that Kevin would stay for as long as I wanted him to - and to ask him to do whatever I needed done. She said she would phone my folks to let them know what is going on. I love Amy and she understands me. We've been friends since school.

Before she could go, a tired looking doctor dressed in a blue gown emerged from the operating theatre.

'Mrs Hoare?' he enquired looking from one to the other.

'Yes, I am Mrs Hoare,' I said, jumping up and stepping forward.

His expression was weary, blank and unreadable.

'We are continuing to do our best,' he stated in a flat tone, 'but she has a big battle ahead, a long way to go. We are taking her to intensive care now and you can see her in a few minutes. Gather your things and make your way down there and they will let you know when you can go in.'

'You go Jennifer,' Amy said. 'I will wait and tell Kevin where you are and we will join you soon.'

'Sorry,' said the doctor overhearing this, 'but it's only parents at this stage.'

Kevin emerged in his clean clothes and could see from our expressions that things were not good. He offered to stay on. 'You go home and get some rest, Kevin,' I said. 'Go with Amy. I have my phone so I shall give you a call in the morning.' I said goodbye and went with the doctor.

The intensive care ward is an intimidating place to the uninitiated with machines attached to tubes attached to people, the silence broken only by the beeping of heart monitors. Angels dressed in white gowns moved quietly around; adjusting this, tweaking that, making sure that everything was as it should be.

In the midst of this was my little Molly in a huge bed, a tiny figure held together with bandages and attached to all manner of tubes and lines. My little girl who only this morning was full of expression and vitality was now a little rag doll, grey and lifeless. I stood at the foot of the bed and stared, unsure of what to do.

The doctor saw my hesitation and sensed my fear. He gently led me to the side of the bed where I could see Molly's cherub face. He pulled up a chair saying, 'Sit here and talk to her. At the moment the machines are all that is keeping your little girl alive. But children are amazingly resilient. We will give her forty-eight hours and see how she responds. She may surprise us.'

My heart sank as the truth slowly dawned. He was telling me that Molly may not survive, preparing me in case the worst happened. Numbly I sat down as he directed.

'Stay here with her in case she regains consciousness,' he suggested. 'You will be the person she wants when she wakes up. Talk to her because we know that even an unconscious person can hear and respond. It may give her that extra motivation to fight hard, to stay with us. I am going home now, but I will be back in the morning and we will know more and can talk then. The nurses will bring a beanbag for you so you might be able to get some shut eye.'

He introduced me to the night staff who were quietly going about their business in a professional and impressive manner.

'Doctor, can you please phone my husband?' I asked. 'He will want to know what's going on. I'll give you his number.'

Someone produced a piece of paper and a pen and I scribbled Stuart's cell phone number on it and added the home phone just in case.

He took it, nodded his head and left the ward, saying, 'I'm sorry the prognosis isn't any better, Mrs Hoare, but we can only hope and pray.'

I sat next to my little girl quietly singing the songs and lullabies I had sung to her since she was a babe in arms. This soothed me and I hope it soothed her as well. She didn't respond.

STUART

I shut my eyes and went into a blissfully deep sleep, the events of the day put behind me. I had forgotten how comfortable this bed was, one of those memory foam ones that fit your body shape; it was good to be back in it.

A couple of hours into the land of nod my cell phone catapulted me back to consciousness. It was the doctor from the children's hospital telling me that Molly was out of theatre and in the ICU. I should come if I wanted to see her.

'Is Jennifer there?' I asked.

'Mrs Hoare?' asked the doctor. 'Of course. She is sitting with Molly now.'

'Perhaps I had better not come then.'

'She expressly asked me to call you.'

'I don't want to cause a scene.'

'Why on earth would that happen?' asked the weary doctor. 'You're the girl's father. Your wife asked me to phone you. She wants you here.'

'She told me to go to hell and never come back. She was leaving for London with her fucking lover boy. They've been screwing themselves stupid behind my back for months now.'

'Oh. Oh!' He was taken aback; you could almost hear his mind whirring over the phone. But not wanting to get into our issues, he continued, 'Well, all I can say is, she specifically asked me to phone you.'

'Well,' I said calmly, 'you have done what she asked you to do, doctor, and I thank you.' And I put down the phone, confused. What's going on? The bitch has done a complete turn around. She wanted me out of her life and now suddenly, I've got to front up and hold her hand. You never know with Jennifer, one minute she can be swimming in innocent circles with the grace of a dolphin and the next, you let your guard down, and she turns into an attacking shark and is all over you. After a big slug of whiskey, I decided to risk it, pulled on my pants and shirt, collected my shoes and set out for the hospital where I found the nice Jennifer extremely pleased to see me, embracing me and sobbing against my chest.

Perhaps the bitch has learnt her lesson.

JENNIFER

At about three in the morning my head jerked forward, waking me from my fitful doze. Unable to sleep further because of the horrible memories of yesterday that flooded back to me, I began to question my motives and myself.

Is this all my fault?

Has my forcing the issue with Stuart brought this terrible fate upon Molly? Should I have stayed in the marriage and put up with it for the children's sake?

What about Tom?

Can I ever go with him now after this has happened?

How can I ever look at him again?

How can I ever live with myself after this?

Is there something evil in me? Maybe that is it. That I am a bad person and I deserve this.

A nurse interrupted my thoughts to tell me that Stuart was outside but was hesitant to come in as he thought he would be intruding. In the months leading up to this I could not bear to be in the same room as him and now I wanted him with me more than anything. He was, after all, Molly's father and we were in this together.

He came in, we embraced, I felt comforted. We knelt and prayed for our little girl. Despite all the crap that had gone on before, it was grand to have Stuart here to share my anxieties and my grief. We sat together beside the bed with our precious daughter until it was daylight.

THE NIGHT NURSE

Human nature is a funny thing. I went to go to the kitchen to get some ice and there was a man standing in the foyer outside the ward, hands in pockets, casually looking at one of the paintings on display. He struck up a conversation with me, nodding at the painting and saying that he had gone to school with the artist.

'He showed no artistic talent at all in his younger years,' he said. 'He was more of a sports jock with not an emotional or creative bone in his body.'

'Obviously not much has changed,' I replied. 'That painting leaves me cold.'

It is a landscape but it is dark and dank and unappealing, more like something that somebody in the depths of despair would paint. It depresses me to look at it.

We talked for a few minutes longer but I couldn't linger as it is a busy ward and the end of my shift was approaching, so I finished the conversation by asking him if there was anything I could do to help. He said his name was Stuart Hoare and that his daughter had been admitted earlier, but he was unsure if he should go in to see her as his wife was in there. That is not really unusual as we come across all sorts of funny things in this job. It is astounding how some couples operate and the acrimony that exists in marriages.

Only recently we had a difficult birth and the poor mother was suffering and I walked in to clear the room of visitors. There were two men there and I said, 'We can just have the father only, please.' And one of them said, 'That's me.' But the other indicated he was not leaving, so I said, 'Who are you?' And he said, 'I'm the husband …'

So, you just never know. I asked Mr Hoare to wait while I went and explained the situation to Mrs Hoare. Rather than being angry, she seemed relieved that he was here and asked me to send him in immediately, which I did. They hugged and appeared genuinely pleased to see each other, then sat together with their child for the rest of the night and were still there when I went off duty this morning.

It certainly does take all types.

STUART

We sat beside Molly's bedside and fervently prayed together, completely at one with each other, stroking our baby gently, talking to her, singing her favourite ditties.

The hospital staff is wonderful and I have full confidence that they will save our child and that Jennifer will see the error of her ways, forget the whole London thing, and stay home with her family.

JENNIFER

In the morning Molly had not regained consciousness so we agreed that Stuart should stay with her while I collect the boys and take them home to get them ready for school, then grab some clean clothes and a bite to eat and return. I phoned my dear friend Wendy and enlisted her help. She is totally devastated for us all and volunteered to move into our place with the boys.

'Jen, that will keep their routine as normal as possible while you are at the hospital,' she said. 'That is the most important thing we can do for them.'

This is a huge help and lifts an enormous burden from my shoulders. Now we can concentrate on Molly and getting her well. Stuart and I will play tag team to ensure at least one of us is by her bedside at all times so that when she awakes from her coma a loving, familiar face will be there for her.

The hospital has become my world where nothing matters except Molly's survival. I sleep in a beanbag by her bedside, while Stuart supports me. The rest of the world outside can continue on its merry way, unaware of the tragedy that is playing itself out in these four walls.

STUART

As daylight slipped in under the blinds, the texts and phone calls began. Jennifer and I hadn't talked a lot during the night but what we said was civil and devoid of rancour. It was mostly to do with the logistics of how we would navigate through the next few days although we did recall some of Molly's highlights and laughed at how, on the day after we brought her home from hospital, Junior came in and deposited a gift from the garden in her bassinet, a small green frog. He couldn't understand why we weren't as pleased with it as he was!

I believe that this devastating thing that has happened to a little girl we both love so much has brought Jen and I back together. Whenever we refer to the incident on the bridge we call it 'an accident' and have come to a peaceful truce where we will make sure Molly is never left alone. It reminds me of the early days of our marriage when we worked together for our common good.

However, I am mightily pissed off about the prospect of Wendy living in my home. Of all people to ask for help, Jennifer had to phone her. But what can I do, except leave her to it and try to ignore her presence? I can't afford to rock the boat and draw too much attention to myself. Anyway, I am only at home to sleep, and somebody has to see to the lads.

WENDY

Eventually Jen and I spoke. She phoned me this morning and told me what had happened. She was in a bind because she needs to be with Molly but the boys also need to be cared for. Fortunately, I am between relationships ... again ... so it is easy for me to simply change my abode and move in with the boys while Jen is busy at the hospital. It won't be forever.

Jen knows they will be okay with me. I love them. 'Tell you what,' I said. 'I will also keep an eye on Tom for you and do his washing, as he hasn't anybody else here in Ireland to give him a hand.' She didn't seem too concerned about poor old Tom! She is so focused on Molly, and I guess that is rightly so.

Still, I couldn't believe my ears when she then said that Stu was sitting right there with her at Molly's bedside! What the? Unbelievable. Jen is afraid of him; the last time we spoke, she said she never wanted to be in a room with him by herself ever again. That's why she asked me to be at Dalkey when she told him it was all over. As a sort of insurance. If I was there, he wouldn't hurt her.

Now, everything is hunky-dory and they are acting like a devoted old married couple, all lovey-dovey!

There are rumours beginning to circulate on social media asking whether Stuart deliberately did that thing to

Molly as payback to Jen for leaving him. Sounds awful, but I wouldn't put anything past him. I have seen him in unbelievable rages when he is totally out of control.

One thing stays the same though. Stuart still hates me. He totally ignores me if our paths cross.

TOM

I woke up in hospital with a raging headache and an immobile jaw. My eyes had disappeared, particularly my left, and I felt like shite warmed up. I didn't really know where I was and what I was doing here.

The nurse came into the room and told me that I had been in an induced coma for two days but that now I would be okay. 'I'll let the doctor know you're awake and he will speak to you when he is doing his rounds later in the day,' she said.

She hustled off saying that she would gather the things to give me a sponge bath and how that should make me feel better when Jennifer's friend Wendy popped her head in the door. I have only met her once before but she seems a cool chick. She was pretty brightly dressed and seemed a ball of energy.

'Hi Tom, you're awake at last,' she said. 'Jennifer is tied up at the other hospital with Molly so I have been keeping an eye on you. Is there anything I can get you now that you are in the land of the living?'

The mention of Molly triggered some vague memories of rain and cold and screaming. They were images that I didn't want to visit, so I pulled myself back into the present and thanked her as best I could, asking her to buy me some toiletries next time she came in. She said she would do that and left me to search my memory bank and wonder how on earth I got myself into this predicament.

JENNIFER

On the third day, despite our prayers and our love and our constant vigil, Molly's condition was showing no improvement. She just lay there, hooked up to the machines, her breathing even, her heart constant, her eyes closed.

Across the fourth, fifth and sixth days, the same thing. Then as we entered the second week, tired and brittle, the only change we noticed was in the atmosphere around us. Whereas there had been restrained optimism and vocal encouragement among the staff, now there was a sort of resignation combined with brisk efficiency.

So my heart sank when her primary physician, Doctor Greg, took us aside and said, 'Can I have a word please?' I could tell by the way he said it that we were about to enter a dark space.

'Yes,' I whispered. Stuart nodded.

'Stuart, Jennifer, all along we have been amazed at how little Molly survived that ordeal,' he said. 'Falls like that are unpredictable. You could get a big feller of a hundred and thirty kilos dying from a drop like that. But she is resilient, her tiny heart is strong, her lungs are clear and basically there is little wrong with her organs.'

'So, the prognosis is good then?' I said hopefully.

'Well, ah …'

'We were just saying when we gave her a wash last night that to look at her, there's nothing wrong with her. She's unmarked except for that ugly bruise on her temple. And that's coming down too.'

'Sadly, Mr and Mrs Hoare, that's what we are concerned about. You see, she struck her head on one of the concrete buttresses that forms the median strip. It may well have helped break her fall, which explains the minimal damage to the rest of her body. But …'

'Yes?' My bottom lip started to tremble.

'She has suffered a dreadful trauma to her skull, and …'

'Yes?'

'She is brain dead.'

'Dead? What do you mean?' I asked the question in desperation, even though I feared I already knew the answer. 'Her heart is beating, she is warm, she is alive. How can she be dead?'

'Sit down, both of you.'

Brain death, he explained, is the term used when all brain activity stops permanently. The total and irreversible loss of brain function. The patient is in a coma and can no longer breath without assistance.

'There is no likelihood of any change,' he added. 'Unfortunately, that is Molly's diagnosis.'

'But …'

'I'm afraid it is decision time,' he continued, not enjoying this task at all. 'If Molly was my daughter, and I appreciate that she's not, I'd take her off the ventilator, hold her in my arms and let her pass gently to God.'

'Well, you're right!' I screamed. 'She's not your daughter and I can't make that decision. If God wants her then he has to jolly well come and get her!'

'Mrs Hoare, I know this is extremely difficult for you and your husband to take on board, but I have had the best neuro talent available to examine Molly and our considered opinion is that the machine that is keeping her alive should be turned off. There is nothing more we can do.'

I put my head in my hands and sobbed. Doctor Greg had obviously been through this before with other parents because he bided his time, let me cry and when I had calmed down he continued, reiterating that Molly's condition would never improve and any treatment was now futile.

'I think it's best that we call a meeting with the members of your family and discuss the situation,' he said. 'I have arranged a social worker and the hospital chaplain to be here this afternoon at three. If you can make a list of the people you want to be with you, along with their phone numbers, I will contact them.'

I looked up and around. Suddenly it dawned on me that Stuart had been by my side throughout this entire conversation and had not uttered one word. 'Say something!' I fumed at him. 'Have an opinion for fuck's sake. You do on everything else! Support me, Stuart.'

He didn't budge. He just stared at me.

I pummelled his chest. 'Go on! You're her father! She's your daughter too! Speak up. Don't let them turn the machine off. She isn't dead!' My words reverberated around the hospital.

'Shhh, calm down Mrs Hoare,' shushed the doctor. 'I'm afraid it has to be. We will make it as easy as we can for you. You will have plenty of support.'

Stuart remained unmoved. A terrible immobilizing sadness welled in me. Until then I had taken every minute as it came and dealt with it, focusing on Molly and getting her well again. Now the truth was dawning that she would die. I felt very angry. Then, over the next couple of hours, that feeling somehow propelled me out of my depressed state as the adrenalin surged through my body, energizing me, preparing me for the life and death decision that lay ahead.

That afternoon Mam, Da, Kevin and I assembled in a meeting room at the hospital at two forty five. I considered having the boys involved but decided that this decision was too great a burden for young shoulders. It was for adults only. The boys were at school and Wendy promised to bring them in after she picked them up.

We hadn't been there long when Father Shane O'Neill came into the room, wearing his collar back to front and looking very serious. Da knew him from the golf club where he always played on a Monday, the priests' day off, and so he introduced him all around. He was a kindly man with a shock of white hair, no doubt earned from having to deal with situations like ours. He murmured his condolences and sat quietly with us, but after a few minutes had elapsed and the silence was still hanging heavily in the room, suggested we pray.

'Let us say a prayer for God's guidance in this matter,' he said, taking his rosary beads out of his coat pocket. I knew that it would comfort Da and Mam and even Kevin, and although it was years since I had recited this contemplative chant I lowered my eyes and joined in. That is why I didn't notice the two doctors, along with Stuart and his mother, slipping quietly into the room until Moira came up and put her arms around me and sobbed.

'Poor little Molly, poor, poor child,' she said. 'I love her. I can't bear that this is happening to her. How will we ever get through this?'

I hugged her back and we cried together. I had no argument with Moira; we were friends as well as in-laws and we both loved Molly.

'What is happening to our family?' she sobbed.

I looked up and there was Stuart again, saying nothing.

'Ask your son that question,' I surprised myself by saying. 'Ask Stuart why he did this horrible thing to Molly.'

STUART

The good doctor completely put the wind up me when he sat us down and told us that the right course of action was to turn Molly's machine off. It suddenly struck me that if she dies I will be right in the firing line because I was the last person to be seen with her.

It hadn't occurred to me that she might not recover - I had been praying for her with every ounce of my soul, willing her across the line - and now here he was telling us that this was never going to happen. This was bad news for me. I went all silent and that's when Jennifer turned on me and belted into me, washing away all the common ground and mutual support and trust we had enjoyed through Molly's illness. When I moved forward to finally say something, Dr Greg put his hand up in a 'stop' motion so I realised that it was not the time or the place.

I wasn't surprised when the good doctor took charge of the afternoon meeting right from the start. 'I know this is very stressful but let's try to keep this civil for little Molly's sake,' he warned. 'She's the reason that we are all together, so let's put everything else aside and try to focus on the here and now and decide what is best for her.'

He then got down to business, describing the horrific extent of Molly's injuries. Just as he was getting to the crucial point, we were interrupted. A woman rushed into the room like the grim reaper, a study in various shades of charcoal. She wore a black and grey checked skirt, black top, grey jacket, and a black and white silk scarf around her neck. Her legs were camouflaged by thick black stockings and grey leather boots. Her hair was dyed bright red except for a purple patch that flopped over her left eye.

We waited as she breathlessly mumbled a well-practiced apology for being late and got herself organized.

Glad of the diversion, I examined her and concluded that if her hair had been left untouched her natural prettiness would have shone through. Her skin glowed with a translucent flawlessness; her eyes were the classic Irish blue. She had the air about her of a person who had grown up attractive and knew it.

Doctor Greg gave her time to settle and then filled us in. 'I'd like you to meet Orla White. She is the social worker appointed for this case and she is here to help in any way possible. If you have any concerns please speak to her.'

One by one we were introduced and Orla distributed her card with her contact details. She pulled out a clipboard and pen and informed us she would be writing the minutes, which seemed to be a bit futile seeing as half the meeting was already over.

'As I was saying,' Dr Greg continued, 'the machine is the only thing that is keeping Molly alive. I understand how upsetting this is for everyone, but considering the patient's condition it would be wrong to keep her on life support when she's clearly not going to get any better.'

So far, so good. But then he concluded, 'Other people could be using that machine.'

We froze. What was this? Our little girl was being taken off life support because the machine was in demand! At that point we cared very little about other people. Our Molly was our concern.

'You want us to play God and turn off the very thing that is keeping her alive?' I protested loudly. 'Just so you can strap it to some other kid and play God there too?' Father O'Neill looked decidedly uncomfortable. Jennifer appeared bemused. I had finally said something.

'No one is asking anyone to play God,' continued the doctor. 'Nobody is God, but God himself. What we are proposing is turning off the equipment, thus allowing Molly's body to choose whether to live or die, so to speak.'

His voice trailed off.

KEVIN

I felt I had to ask the question that everybody in that meeting wanted answered. 'Are you sure of what you are telling us, Greg? Are you sure that Molly is not going to get better?'

The doctor was brutally honest.

'She should have died on the Saturday when the ambulance brought her in. We tried everything in our arsenal to bring her back to you, but to be perfectly honest, we have been keeping her alive artificially since then, hoping a miracle might happen. She has been brain dead for nearly two weeks. Sadly we can't do any more.'

Father O'Neill broke the ensuing silence with his wise counsel. 'Let Molly die in peace in the arms of people who love her instead of being surrounded by wires and other intrusive things. Allow her to go to her God and the angels. It's a dreadful thing, indeed, but it is for the best. May God bless you all.'

Unfortunately he then added, 'God said suffer little children to come unto me. And let's not forget that God sent his only son to be sacrificed for the sins of the world.'

That made me bloody angry. How dare he quote the Bible about looking after children when all the headlines were about the paedophilia in the church? I know I turned rude but couldn't help myself because I've become impatient with platitudes and religious talk. 'Molly never committed a sin in her short life,' I remarked. 'How you can sit there and think she has to suffer while maggots who prey on little kiddies walk free is beyond my comprehension!'

I countered with the quote that starts, 'Whatever you do to one of these, my little children,' but I had no idea what comes next. It was left hanging uncomfortably in the air, but the Reverend Father took the hint and said no more while an empty silence engulfed the table as we all sat deep in our thoughts.

JENNIFER

Words cannot describe how horrible it is to be told that you have to shut down the only thing that is keeping your baby alive. Part of me would surely die with her.

After Kevin said his bit there didn't seem to be much more to say and we were about to disperse when the doctor added, 'There's just one more thing. The matter of organ donation. Because Molly is on life support, and her little body has survived much of the ordeal, she is an ideal candidate to donate her organs. Have you ever considered it? Did you ever speak to Molly about it?'

'Oh, for God's sake, the child is only five years old,' Moira exclaimed in disbelief. 'We didn't know any of this would happen. How could we have talked to her about something like that? How could you talk to any five year old about organ donation?'

I hadn't had much to say all meeting but the thought of it appealed so I told Moira to keep out of this. It really had nothing to do with her and I felt we should seriously think about the idea that Molly's organs could help another child - or children - to live a healthy and productive life.

'Maybe something can be salvaged from this wreck,' I said quietly.

Stuart protested loudly, and in an effort to intimidate us stood up and thumped the table. 'You are not cutting my child up and distributing her organs willy-nilly to all and sundry!'

I looked at him with contempt, remembering why I had left him and thought, 'That's a funny opinion for a man who carelessly dropped his daughter over a bridge!'

I managed to answer him coldly and clinically, without giving eye contact, not even saying 'you are the one who brought us here' or anything like that. Instead I maintained my cool and reasoned with him. 'Stuart, this situation is awful but some good can come from it. Perhaps Molly can keep on living in some other child. Perhaps we can add meaning to her short life on earth. I think we should ask the boys what they think when they come in after school.'

STUART

That meeting was difficult. Doctor Greg outlined Molly's state of play. Our tough little girl had shown tremendous resilience. But now, despite her courageous efforts, even if she did survive, she would be in a permanent vegetative state, needing constant twenty-four hour care.

As I sat in that stuffy little room listening to the doctor talk, I began to realise that I could be very vulnerable. I know enough about the law to realise that if Molly dies my situation may be precarious. If they turn off the machine, that they may hold me responsible for her death. I could be charged with murder.

I began to argue with the doctor against making that decision. Surely they should give her a few more days; there must be alternative specialist treatments they haven't yet tried.

'I've read of people who have stayed attached to those machines for years,' I said.

'That's the point,' Dr Greg said. 'She might. But she will never walk, talk, be able to eat.'

'And then by some miracle, they wake up.'

'Miracle is the word, Mr Hoare. For every single, isolated incident of sudden recovery you hear of, once every twenty or thirty years, there are hundreds of thousands in the same situation as Molly. To all intents and purposes, Molly's life is over. So sadly, what we are asking you and Mrs Hoare to do is to make that decision official and turn off her machine. We can then see whether she can survive by herself.'

The social worker obviously had another meeting to be late for. There were things to do! This was clearly not the first time she had witnessed this sort of scenario and she remained business-like, forcing the issue. Packing up her folders and notes and pens, she instructed briskly, 'My heart goes out to you all, but it is a decision that has to be made, and we have to make it today.'

I made one last protest but Kevin suggested in no uncertain manner that we would not have been at that meeting 'except for you, Stuart, and don't you ever forget that.'

That was unfair and it hurt. The chaplain quoted from the Bible once more and put a weary hand on my shoulder saying, 'It's God's will, my son.'

The social worker and the doctor got their way and with much misgiving we decided to turn off the machines and let Molly go to God that evening at six.

But it wasn't quite over yet. There was the question of donation. 'How can you give our Molly's organs to some other kid?' I argued. 'They will cut her up into pieces. Butcher her like a piece of steak. I will not have it!'

The doctor turned towards Jennifer, seated in a lounge chair in the far corner, slumped forward and crying. 'Mrs Hoare will wait to discuss that with your boys before she makes that decision.'

He turned back and stared directly at me. I slowly nodded agreement, he acknowledged me and headed out into the corridor, following the social worker.

DOCTOR GREG

I was aware of the stirrings in social media regarding this little girl and her family so didn't really know what to expect in this meeting. It is always difficult to deal with cases like this even when the family is totally in tune with each other, so I was reluctant to begin until the social worker arrived. But she was late and flustered. Not her fault - too much to do and not enough staff to do it.

Still, I was pleasantly surprised when things started out well. Mrs Hoare was sad but listened. I explained that no person fulfilling the criterion for brain death has ever recovered. 'Molly's journey is over,' I said. After her initial sadness, Mrs Hoare became excited about organ donation but wished to speak to her sons to canvass their opinions first.

Mr Hoare on the other hand, was bullish and argumentative, wanting more time on the machine and being positively against organ donation. This caused the only acrimony in the meeting. Other than Kevin, the uncle, the other family members had little to say. They were simply there for support.

'Time is of the essence but you will have the opportunity to say goodbye to Molly,' I said. 'However, we must move on this in the evening.'

After the meeting concluded the family went to the ward and I began to make arrangements for the transplant teams as I had already begun preparing the legals. He is an explosive, unpredictable character, the husband, but I knew Mrs Hoare's opinion would prevail.

LOVER, HUSBAND, FATHER, MONSTER

Part Three

STUART

I always thought Molly would pull through, never imagining that they would make us turn off the machines after a period of time that to me lasted no more than a mere blink of an eye. Don't doctors have to take the Hippocratic oath? Aren't they supposed to preserve life, not take it?

If Molly couldn't survive on her own, if she died, then I was the person who was responsible. I dropped her. That could put me in a dubious position with the lawmakers. They might charge me with murder. Or manslaughter at least.

The boys were due at any minute so I waited by Molly's bedside trying to come to terms with the course of action being taken. I was overwhelmed with remorse and fear and started to cry.

Jennifer shot me a look and took me aside out of Molly's hearing. She pointed her finger at me in warning. 'Get a grip on it! If you cry in front of the boys I will personally throttle you. We have to be strong for them, so pull yourself together.'

I did my best. I held Molly's hand, told her that her Da loved her, talked about the boys and pre-school, all of those things, but the sadness overwhelmed me and I had to retreat to the corridor.

Mother followed me out. We aren't the most demonstrative of families, always keeping a tight lid on our emotions, stiff upper lip and all of that, but it was all too much. We hugged each other tight, our sobs wracking our bodies. She stroked my back and soothed me. This kind of thing hadn't happened since I got too big to sit on her knee, but I realized then that my mother was on my side and that she would stick with me no matter what happened.

'Come now, Stuey!' she said. 'Wipe the tears and be strong for our Molly. We can't be having the O'Briens thinking you are a sissy. Let's go in there and make the most of the time we have left.'

I wiped my tears, took a deep breath, pulled back my shoulders and taking my mother's hand like a small boy returned to Molly's bedside to wait for the lads.

JUNIOR

Wendy picked us up from school as usual and told us we'd have to miss hurling as Mammy wanted us at the hospital. Rich and I hate the hospital because nothing ever happens there. We have to sit beside Molly who is asleep all the time and does nothing. And there is nothing for us to do and Mammy gets cross if we play with each other and tells us to be quiet and it is awful.

When we got there both Nanna and Grandma were there, as well as Daideo and Uncle Kevin and Mam and Da, and they were all sad. Mam said she had something she wanted to ask us. Jesus, I hoped it wasn't going to be that we would have to go and live with that weaselly little Tommy Terrific who thinks he's great because he bangs drums.

But it wasn't that! Mammy told us that Molly is going to go to live with God tonight and that she wouldn't need her heart and other things that she needed on earth, so should we give them to some other sick kid?

We had talked about donating organs at school and I think it is a good idea and I reckon that if Molly woke up she would want to give all the things she's finished with to somebody else. She is like that. She sometimes gave her toys to the Travellers who lived near the forest. She is a kind girl.

RICHIE

I don't want Molly to go away but Mam says that she is too sick to stay here with us, so she has to go to be an angel in Heaven. If we can't have her here then it is good that her things will make some other child healthy. I just want to be normal again. I miss my little sister.

JENNIFER

I had to tell Stuart to stop the snivelling. It's no help and it's upsetting and not good for me or for Molly or for anybody, especially the boys.

'This may be the one last time we have Molly with us,' I told him. 'We need to keep the atmosphere peaceful and think happy thoughts. We must hold it together for her.'

It's the least he could do. I didn't want him crying when the boys came in. We will have plenty of time to cry when we get home. We'll have the rest of our lives to cry.

That evening the fragile threads holding Molly to life were severed when the support machine was turned off and our baby was unplugged and detached from the lines and tubes that kept her breathing. It was so unbearably sad saying goodbye to our cherished Molly but it will be a precious memory that I will hold in my heart until the day I see her again.

Stuart's mother, my Mam and Da and Kevin spent a brief time alone with her and then it was our family's turn to be by her bedside. The four of us gently held her and hugged her, talked to her and told her what she means to us. Such a short precious time! Gone so quickly. Even in my grief, my heart burst with pride as I witnessed my boys being so tender with their little sister. I could see in them the essence of wonderful men - stoic, solid, emotionally able. It broke my heart to realize that this would be the last occasion I would see my three children together. I wanted time to stand still forever but it went all too fast. Then came the moment for us to leave the room. Forever!

As we said goodbye, a transplant team stood at the ready. There are now four Irish children who are living happy and healthy lives because our Molly died. That knowledge is comforting but it doesn't really make it any easier to cope.

No parent should ever have to lose a child.

STUART

My heart almost broke when the transplant team arrived and took Molly from us in a cold professional sort of way, saying, 'Your little girl fought a most ferocious fight but now she is at peace. God bless you all.' And that was it.

I don't think I have ever been so overwhelmed with grief as I was at that moment. No matter what had happened on that flyover - who said what, who did what, whose fault it was, that was all going to be sorted out anyway - the simple fact is that my little daughter is now dead. I dropped my head and began to cry, and through my tears, whispered something that I felt any father would request, no matter what the circumstances. 'You can't have her. You can't chop her up in pieces. She belongs to me!' I blubbered.

Jen took one boy by each hand and hurriedly shuffled them out of the room, hissing, 'You are disgusting, Stu. Control yourself, the boys don't want to hear that. Pig!'

I was left alone and isolated. A minute or so later my thoughts were interrupted by a voice. 'Mr Hoare, I've just dropped by to see how you are coping.' It was Orla White, the social worker. 'Let's find a quiet spot where we can talk.'

She led me to a meeting room and sat down opposite me. I put my head in my hands and cried and cried. She let me go, not saying anything until I was through, made me a cup of tea, phoned a cab and saw me safely into it. She was very kind.

ORLA WHITE

I don't think this family can survive this. The two camps are at each other's throats already and we haven't had the funeral yet. Everybody is upset. It was not easy for anyone.

Often it is the person who has the most regrets that is the most upset in these matters, so maybe Mr Hoare believes he is responsible. I must say I felt sorry for him when the wife and boys left him high and dry in the ward and went home without him. He was like a lost soul. So sad! I was at the end of my shift so I gave him time to compose himself and sent him home in a taxi.

I don't know what to make of the tweets that are going around about the accident possibly being a deliberate act. Mr Hoare seems genuinely cut up, but who knows? Maybe he is conscious of the potential murder charge. I meet some strange types in my job.

JENNIFER

When I emerged from my hospital cocoon to resume my life after Molly's death it suddenly dawned on me that the Irish public was sharing in our most private suffering. There was mayhem outside as the cameras flashed and journalists tried to persuade me to say something as Kevin and I battled our way through to the car.

'Look straight ahead, don't acknowledge them and keep moving,' said Kevin. 'This circus has been going on for ages. Don't these bastards have any respect?'

The home I returned to was so different from the one I had left. Molly didn't live here any more; she was in heaven. In the days since this horrible nightmare had begun, I had pretty much spent all my time in the hospital, occasionally coming home for a shower and a few minutes in my own bed but not really at home at all. Stuart was splitting his time between home and work. 'I have to keep the business up and running,' he kept telling me.

I looked around at the place - familiar, but somehow so different. I picked up one of Molly's dolls that was lying on the couch, sat down and hugged it to myself, smelling her smell, missing her. How had it come to this?

We were all exhausted, emotionally drained, incapacitated by grief and fatigue. Nobody had the stomach to eat the dinner Wendy had left for us. We just wanted to go to bed early to grieve, each of us in our own way.

I was just dropping off to a fretful sleep when the pitter-patter of bare feet signalled I had a visitor. Richie had come to get into bed with me. Before long Junior was in on the other side. We shared our thoughts about what had happened that afternoon, about Molly and about the forthcoming funeral.

'Mam, can I say a poem for Molly at the funeral?' Junior asked.

'That will be lovely if you think you can do it without becoming upset, Junior.'

'I want to do it Mam. I found one on the internet that is just perfect. I read it and it makes me feel better.'

'Okay, we'll have a look at it in the morning, son. You can read it to me and we'll see how you go,' I suggested, thinking that it would be a difficult task for him to accomplish.

'I can say it for you now,' he volunteered. 'It keeps going around and around in my head. I know it off by heart.'

'All right! Say it for us,' I encouraged.

Solemnly he recited the poem that he had committed to memory, making me feel that my boy had more of a handle on the situation than I have. 'It goes like this,' he said.

Do not stand at my grave and weep;
I am not there. I do not sleep.
I am a thousand winds that blow.
I am the diamond glints on snow.
I am the sunlight on ripened grain,
I am the gentle autumn rain.
When you awaken in the morning's hush,
I am the swift uplifting rush
Of quiet birds in circled flight.
I am the soft stars that shine at night.
Do not stand at my grave and cry;
I am not there, I did not die.

'That is beautiful Junior,' I congratulated him with tears in my eyes. 'Who wrote it? Is it Irish?'

67

'Her name is Mary Frye and I think she's American,' Junior answered. 'I can't get it out of my head.'

'Do you really think you can say that on the day? It will be marvellous if you can.'

'Yes, I can do it,' Junior resolved. 'I want to say about the donor organs that live on because of Molly as well.'

I asked him to repeat the poem again. It was so beautiful. Our warmth soothed us and we drifted into an exhausted sleep. We were emotionally drained. I didn't hear Stuart coming in.

STUART

It was all too much, I had gone to the golf club for a drink and got home at about 11.30, to find the lights were out and everybody was asleep, in my bed! That made me angry because after all, Jennifer had left me and my home. She didn't live here any more. She had made her bed and now she was sleeping in mine.

I thought about waking her up and telling her to sleep somewhere else but I didn't have the energy for a fight. Besides, the boys were with her and they had had a torrid day. Instead I made for the spare room, from where I had been earlier banished when all this crap with lover boy started. Bugger me if that obnoxious Wendy didn't have her pyjamas tucked under my pillow and her makeup all over the dressing table. I chucked her clothes on the floor, fell onto the bed, pulled the covers over my head and went to sleep with the smell of her perfume up my nostrils. I hate that woman.

Tomorrow I will make it quite clear that Jennifer will not be sleeping upstairs in the main suite by herself. That is my room and the only way she returns to it is to be with me as her sleeping partner. Either she shares it with me or she can sleep in the spare room.

WENDY

I did as Jen asked and dropped the boys at the hospital after school. I took them to the ward, spoke briefly to Jen who told me the sad news and I kissed little Molly on the forehead. As soon as I was out of sight I sat on the nearest chair, put my head in my hands and bawled my heart out. It is so unfair.

Instead of going home I went to see Tom at the hospital. I have been taking his washing for him every couple of days and it is encouraging to see him slowly coming good. He has been moved to the brain injury recovery section and they are taking it very gently with him. He has his rehab routines, physio, and each day they ask him twelve questions. Sometimes he gets cross when he answers the first eight correctly. 'I told you that yesterday,' he will say. But then he will stumble on a couple of the questions and the nice nurse says to him that they are only doing their best to make sure he is mentally one hundred per cent before he flies back home.

I took his hand and told him what was going on at the other hospital and we just sat together in silence. He couldn't bring himself to talk and I could not find words to express my sadness. But it was comforting being with somebody else who cared.

I stayed with him and helped him with his dinner of soup and custard. That is all he can eat at the moment. Poor chap. I feel sorry for him being caught up in all of this. I phoned Mary to find out what was happening. She said that Jen had gone home with the boys, so I decided to catch up with friends from our meditation group to pray for Molly's safe passage into the spirit world. I didn't get back to Dalkey until after midnight.

I tiptoed in very quietly so as not to wake the family but when I turned the light on in my room, I woke up Stuart who had been snoring and dribbling onto my pillow. He was not happy as I am not exactly his favourite person. And he certainly isn't mine! While I had been helping out with the boys, we had adopted a truce and pretty much stayed out of each other's way. But now, the ceasefire had obviously been called off. My stuff was strewn all over the floor. 'Get out of my house and my life,' he sneered.

I got in the car and drove home to my flat. God knows how it will work with him and Jen under the same roof again.

TOM

Jennifer's friend Wendy popped her head in the door. She is a cool chick.

She was really upset about little Molly who was being taken off life support and she told me that she will probably die tonight. I can only imagine how sad Jennifer is. She adores her daughter. It is devastating news.

We sat silently together for a long time just holding hands, the human contact comforting us both. How I wished it was Jen's hand I was holding, but I understand that she can't be in two places at once.

The funeral is to be on Friday. Jennifer must be beyond distraught. I asked if I could go but the treating doctor shook his head. 'You'll frighten the children the way you look at the moment,' he said. He has a point. All the bruises are out but the swelling is still up and I have this contraption on my face like robot man. I suspect, though, he does not believe I could physically and mentally cope with such an event.

I keep having this awful nightmare and in it that husband of Jennifer's is throwing little children over a bridge into a river below, one after the other, like bags of spuds. I always wake up at the point when he chucks Molly over. He is throwing her over the same bridge where we were on that Saturday.

I lie there sweating. It haunts me.

Press report

Little Molly Taken Off Support

Molly Hoare, the five-year-old girl who fell from the bridge on Flyover 3 on the M50, has been taken from life support and has died at the National Children's Hospital at Tallaght. It is believed that her organs have been donated and will sustain other sick children nation-wide.

'It is with much sadness that we announce the death of our little Molly at 6.45 pm this evening,' Mr Kevin O'Brien said on behalf of Molly's parents who were too distressed to talk. 'She died surrounded by her loving family and her organs have been taken to provide life to other Irish children. We will announce the funeral arrangements as soon as we have the details.'

The people who live on the quiet, tree-lined street where the Hoare home is situated in Dalkey describe the family as an ordinary one where the children are polite and the parents,

Stuart and Jennifer, are hardworking and successful. The large white gabled house has alternating red and white roses lining the fence that faces onto the road. Out the back there is a vegetable garden from which many of them have received excess produce each autumn.

Shocked neighbours stood outside the once ordinary house and held each other, laid flowers and cried for the little girl they loved and who tonight lost her fight for her life.

'It's terrible that this has happened,' said one neighbour. 'She was such a lovely and happy little girl.'

Another said, 'I can't get this accident out of my mind. One can only imagine how they must feel, particularly Stuart, because unfortunately he was the one who dropped her.'

When the child fell onto the median strip of the M50 a month ago, a mother's anguished screams could be heard as Jennifer Hoare realised that her child had fallen. Veteran police and ambulance drivers who have witnessed many tragic and gruesome accidents and who were called to the scene could scarcely hold back their tears.

'It is one of the saddest accidents that we have ever had to attend,' Head of Disaster, Tom Donovan said. 'Many of our men have young children and found this to be a highly emotion-charged event. They are receiving counselling.'

Funeral notice

A funeral service and High Mass for Molly Claire Hoare will be held at St Patrick's Anglican Church, Dalkey, Friday, at 11 am. Only cut flowers from personal gardens are requested and in lieu, please be generous and make donations to Organ Donation and Transplant Ireland (ODTI).

Newspaper column

Flyover girl notice

A man who fatally dropped his five-year-old daughter to her death on the M50 has penned a death notice for his 'Irish Colleen'.

It reads, *'In loving memory of my little Molly who was born, lived and died on Irish soil. Forever with your loving father and precious brothers as we live our lives, not without you, but with you constantly by our sides. You can never leave us again. Rest in peace in a better place, my Irish Colleen, my darling daughter.'*

Meanwhile, police are continuing their call for witnesses to the accident and urge anybody with information to call Crime Stoppers on 1800crimestop.

WENDY

That message Stuart wrote in the Times was sick. It made out that he and the boys were alone in their grieving for Molly, as if they were the only victims. If he was going to write a notice for the newspaper you would think that he would acknowledge Molly's mother whose heart is broken.

Also why didn't he write a proper notice acknowledging all the people who were important in Molly's life? And what's that rubbish about being born, lived and died on Irish soil? Is that a dig at Jen for wanting to take her to London?

MARY

That notice gave us goose bumps of the most horrible kind. If we had known that he was putting something in the paper we would have contributed and acknowledged all the people who loved Molly and who were important in her short life.

It is almost as if Stuart is claiming that Molly belonged to him alone and is telling the world that he is the only aggrieved and bereaved person. No mention of poor Jennifer, her mother.

This put-down has hurt the family like you wouldn't believe. It's a huge kick in the pants to all of us who loved her. It's disgusting, sick!

MOIRA

That was a strange kind of thing for Stuart to be putting in the paper. He is usually such a private person and I wouldn't have expected him to wear his heart on his sleeve like that.

My heart breaks for him, poor darling, his whole world is crumbling and he doesn't know what to do about it. It's difficult for a mother to see that happening to her son.

JENNIFER

The two days between Molly's death and the funeral went very, very quickly, but we felt it best to lay our little pet to rest before the weekend.

No parent expects to have to organise a funeral for a child, but this is what we faced. However, as this was our last physical act of caring for Molly it gave us purpose to get through those awful days. As a family we just wanted to do it right. We decided to bring her home one last time, on the night before, with drinks and nibbles and an open casket for friends and family for a couple of hours. We are Irish and this is a very special and important time. 'It is the way we do it,' I explained to Wendy. 'The laying to rest of the dead.'

I chose Molly's favourite white party dress, with little red rosebuds along the bodice, and teamed it with pretty little socks with lace at the ankle and I had a garland made for her hair. She looked beautiful in her all-pink coffin lined with pink satin. We adorned it with white and yellow daisies that she had planted in our garden from seeds last spring. The boys put drawings and notes of love as well as her favourite soft toy, a bear named Max, into the coffin with her so she would be comforted on her journey. Then they kissed her and said goodbye.

Family and friends came with flowers and food and the children came to look at her in her tiny casket. They are so matter-of-fact about death. I felt overwhelmed but at the same time, I don't regret that decision to bring her home, as it was a wonderful thing to do.

Because I practice Buddhism, I would have liked a cremation but the majority of the family, spearheaded by Stu, insisted on a burial from St Patrick's. I gave in, as I didn't want more conflict at this time. The priest knows us well because Stu is his organist and right hand man so we were able to plan the service the way we wanted. I made sure that the boys had a chance to pay a tribute to their little sister, as I believe it is a very important part of the grieving process.

We talked everything over with the boys and agreed that Junior could do the poem, as long as he practised it. He wanted to add something just about Molly, so we tossed ideas around and came up with two new lines before the last stanza.

'I am the child who plays because of Molly's giving
Whose soul soars high but whose organs go on living.'

He read it, with apologies to Mary Frye, at Molly's ceremony and I was proud of him.

The children released balloons, which made them feel that they were an equally important part of the ceremony, but their release proved to be just as meaningful for the adults. The only flowers were cut ones from our garden and we made it known that we preferred donations to the transplant team at the Children's Hospital. I busied myself making a photo book of Molly's short life that could be distributed at the church along with the order of service.

The country cemetery in the beautiful hills overlooking Dublin is near where we live so we can visit our baby frequently. There is running water and a lovely forest nearby where Molly can run and play.

The thing the boys found hardest was when Molly's coffin was lowered into the ground. They hadn't expected that and I had overlooked it and failed to explain it beforehand. They broke their little hearts.

As my last gift to my daughter I was determined to give a eulogy, which told the congregation who she was and what she meant to her family. I laboured over the words, rewriting and rehearsing, determined that this last thing I was doing for Molly would be done as well as I could possibly do it; that she would be proud of me as I was of her. 'Molly was not just a five-year-old who has met with tragedy, but a fully functioning, beautiful human being who had her whole life before her,' I said. 'A complete person with a personality of her own on the way to becoming a wonderful adult. I am proud of my daughter and I want you to know that.'

In the writing, I shed many tears, but I remember standing in the church looking at the little pink coffin that held the broken body of my baby girl, willing myself not to break down, to be strong for her. I suppose I was naive. The media and other people did not see this stoicism as brave and noble. They saw it as a heartless abomination.

The public don't like the way I behave. 'This is not the way a mother should grieve,' is a common statement. The internet is full of vitriol against me while the talkback radio jocks blame me and encourage hatred towards me. Public opinion is leaning towards Stuart, who declined the opportunity to speak saying he was too upset and instead opted to play the organ for the service.

Unbelievable!

STUART

The funeral was a wonderful occasion. We barely had time to make the arrangements but Jennifer didn't wish to prolong the pain over the weekend and that was probably a good idea. I spent much of the two preceding days with the vicar organizing readings and music. I wanted people to know that we are a good, solid Christian family.

Jennifer seemed determined to make the whole thing a bit of a circus and I kept trying to temper her ideas somewhat. She was adamant that we have Molly's body at home for a wake so that family members could stay with her all night to make sure that evil spirits didn't claim her. This was all part of Jennifer's embedded pagan Irishness and I had no hope in the world of deterring her from that plan.

I will admit, having Molly at home with us on the night preceding the funeral turned out to be grand, almost like a party with family, friends and my business associates and fellow golf club members coming to the house to pay their respects. Those who had not been to our place before could see how well we live and realise that I am a man of substance.

We are once again a family unit and I have great hopes that Jennifer will see sense and abandon that drummer boy of hers. She hasn't spoken of him all week. I'm glad I clouted him, the little bastard. How dare he break up my family!

I was happy about the wake, but then Jennifer wanted to turn the funeral into a feel-good gathering of her Buddhist mates. I was adamant that our daughter would have a Christian burial and fortunately the O'Briens supported me on this and sense prevailed. Molly was buried from our parish church, St Patrick's Anglican Church, Dalkey, on the Friday following her death.

Against my better judgment, Jennifer insisted that she and the boys do an oral tribute. She knows that I think women have no place in the ceremonies and rituals of the church. As far as I am concerned Jesus and the disciples were men, and women played no role in the liturgy. However, at the end of the day, I have to admit, it was very moving that my lads had the gumption to get up and say something about their sister to all those people. 'I am very proud of them,' I whispered to Mum later.

Even the voodoo touches that Jennifer insisted on adding turned out to be effective. Initially she wanted the cousins to sing and dance to Molly's favourite party trick, the Macarena, but I hit that on the head! Then she wanted all of the kids to accompany Molly's coffin out of the church and I thought that was a recipe for disaster. What they say about dogs and children on the stage is true but Jennifer got her way in the end and the parade of young ones wasn't as bad as I thought it would be. When they let the balloons go it was impressive. The cousins behaved well and despite some tears, everyone in the church that day felt great pride and hope for the next generation.

I would have preferred a florist's flowers for the coffin as those home-grown ones made us look lousy. As I said to Mum, 'It's as if we are too poor to pay for the real thing.'

By playing the organ I hoped that the Irish public, who are so interested in this tragedy, would realise that I am not just a casual churchgoer but an essential and important part of my congregation. I organized a video camera inside the church and took photographs both outside and at the graveside, as I wanted memories to keep and to use them on my recently launched website. It will add humanity to my business profile and give my colleagues something to relate to, and that can't be bad.

I don't know why we went to the expense of printing photo books, but that was Jennifer's project and it kept her busy and off my back.

The church was full - family, friends, neighbours, business associates and a lot of sticky-beaks. But really, our sorrow is nobody's business and I am getting sick of all the talk about Molly's situation on the airwaves and the crap they are writing in the papers. I deliberately took the morning paper with me when I went to golf today as I didn't want Jennifer and the boys to see the funeral details splattered all over the front page.

THE REPORTER

The editor pulled me in and gave me this story. 'There's been a few rumours on the net,' he said. 'May amount to nothing but take Maeve with her camera and get some photos of the little girl's service. The readers love a good funeral. They're glad it's not them in the coffin.'

He laughed at his own sick joke. I didn't join in because I have a girl the same age as Molly Hoare and I think the whole thing is tragic. Especially if the old man did what people are saying he did.

Maeve and I went along. The church was packed. Always is for a young person and there were some lovely touches; her brother reading the verse with a bit of his own words at the end, that would have taken courage; the cousins accompanying the coffin out of the church, that was sweet; the father playing the organ, well, that was different! Apparently he is the organist at the church so it was him or nothing. It was a little weird though when he took photos of the coffin and the kids releasing the balloons afterwards. I'd be too cut up to do that.

MARY

As a grandmother I was only too aware of the pain my family was going through but I didn't really agree with them bringing Molly home the night before the funeral. However, as a mother I knew Jen deserved the right to do what she wanted, as this was her last time to do something for her child. My daughter wanted to make this a celebration of Molly's life. She wanted everybody to know that her little girl was loved and cherished, that she had a beautiful home and a personality all of her own.

Jennifer also wanted our little Molly cremated and she knows that this goes beyond the beliefs of the Catholic Church and how we brought her up. Luckily Stuart was of the same opinion as we were and the boys certainly didn't want her burnt, so a Christian burial it was. Molly deserved that much.

I feel for Stuart, as he seems to be bearing the brunt of the blame for what has happened. Seamus says that it 'takes two to tangle,' as he likes to put it. 'Had Jennifer been true to her marriage vows then none of this would have happened,' he keeps saying.

He may be right but that is all water under the bridge now. I am totally supportive of whatever Jennifer wishes, even if I don't agree. That annoys Seamus!

WENDY

If you could say such a thing about a child's funeral, yesterday was a real tribute to dear little Molly. The church was full, the ceremony was beautiful. It certainly helps in a situation like this when the vicar knows the family well and it was apparent that he was fond of them.

Stuart insisted on playing the organ for the service and a lot of people found that strange but I suppose when you know the real story about him and Jen it made sense to keep them apart. More comfortable for everyone!

Jen preferred to sit with her Mam and Kevin. Richie sat next to Jen and Junior sat next to Moira. Old Richard didn't really know whether he was coming or going but he was very sad; he cried all the way through, poor man.

Despite Jen's urging that we were 'family' and to come up the front, Karina and I sat together down the back with the hoi polloi. Didn't want to upset Stuart. He hates me. Blames me for the whole situation.

Little Molly is in a beautiful place on the hill just beyond Johnny Fox's pub. But I tell you what was weird though! Stuart taking photos outside the church like it was a wedding or something. He's a strange one.

STUART

After my golf game today I was having a few drinks in the bar when Declan O'Farrell, a man that everybody loves to hate because he is so loud and inappropriate and delights in seeing his fellow clubmen squirm, came in, spotted me and loudly announced that there were two chaps in the foyer dressed in cheap suits wanting a word with me. 'They look like detectives to me, Stuart, old boy,' he said loudly.

The whole members' bar came to a halt, with everyone looking quizzically at me. Just a momentary pause, but enough to notice before the buzz started up again.

I put down my whiskey and stood up feeling sick in the stomach and went to head out there, when Declan starts laughing his head off, saying that there was nobody there at all and he just wanted to put the wind up me. His idea of a joke!

I sat down again and finished my drink, making it clear I did not enjoy his attempts at humour and left shortly after. But it has made me think. I know my own motivation but people from outside the family may not see it my way. My story needs to be watertight.

I sat in the car outside the club with my head between my hands and reviewed my story, making sure I considered all aspects. The best thing all round is to say that I dropped Molly accidentally; that I didn't mean to do it. 'Keep it simple and as close to the truth as possible, Stuart,' I thought. 'There are a lot of jealous bastards out there who will want to trip you up.'

I had already used the Catch Molly game as an explanation to the old biddy on the motorway and I clearly remember that when I got out of the car to escape Jennifer's nagging, we began to play the game because Molly had begged me to. 'Please, daddy, can we play Catch Molly in the rain and you can stop me from falling into a puddle.'

So that's what I did a couple of times and that is the absolute truth. I held her over the water and pretended to drop her, catching her at the last moment. She laughed and thought it was grand craic. We were enjoying it.

However, when I saw Jennifer heading my way I snapped. I don't know what got into me. Almost instinctively I headed for the balustrade and threw Molly over the side. If I had stopped to think I don't believe I would have done it but I just wanted to show that bitch that she can't mess with me.

Of course, I won't admit to any of that. I will simply say it was a game of Catch Molly that went horribly wrong. And, to all intents and purposes, it was! In that context, I have come across the perfect solution. I saw in the Ryan Report about the paedophile clergy preying on little children that when some priests are asked an awkward question that could elicit an incriminating answer they use a technique called "mental reservation." What they do is verbally give the part of the answer that does not do them any damage, but hold back on the incriminating part and say it mentally to themselves. So, in their mind, they have "answered" the question without lying!

One Archbishop used it to avoid admitting that he knew all about the heinous activities of some of the priests in his diocese but did nothing about it. Dear me, only the Catholics could come up with a devious technique like that! However, staunch Anglican that I am, in my situation I am not too proud to cross the aisle and use it …

That evening at dinner I tried my story out to see how it would wash. First, I related to the boys and Jennifer the incident at the golf club and then asked them to listen to me while I told them what had happened with Molly just in case they came across the same thing at school or while they were out and about.

'There are always going to be mean-spirited people out there who want to make you feel uncomfortable,' I said. 'So if they have a go at you regarding Molly's death, I am telling you about it now, exactly as I remember it.'

I then went through each detail, sequence by sequence, omitting the final act. I explained the reason I was in the car, why I got out, the game, the accident. They bought it hook, line and sinker. Not one query or raised eyebrow! It looks like I have my story, but hopefully I won't have to use it again. Things will die down, life will go on and we can put it all behind us.

Part Four

JENNIFER

And then there was nothing. After such an onrushing series of overwhelming events, everything suddenly stopped. On the day after Molly's funeral I awoke to a house full of gloom. The boys didn't go to their weekend sport and I didn't get out of the Dunne's tracksuit that I had taken to wearing to bed because it reminded me of the last time I had hope for Molly.

Fortunately Stuart opted to go to golf. I suppose he reckons that the club is infinitely better than being at home with me, although he came home a bit upset as apparently there was a nasty undercurrent flowing.

To give him his due though, Stuart brought the subject up over dinner. He explained in full about Molly's accident, apologized sincerely to the three of us for his lack of judgment and said that if he could change things he would. 'I just want you to know the facts in case anybody implies evil intent to you,' he said. That cleared the air and in some ways made me feel better. I know what Stuart can be like when he gets angry - Lord knows, that was one of the reasons I was leaving him - but I am sure he would never have deliberately hurt Molly, he just wouldn't go that far. Wendy tells me that there have been some vicious rumours flying about the internet, but I have been on social media enough to know that it is a haven of nasty knockers who will say the most spiteful, negative things without knowing anything of the story at all.

Mam came by with some rashers, eggs, butter, bread, a few things like that, and we talked about the funeral and the happenings of the previous day. She still has some house guests down from Kerry so she tidied up a bit and made a pot of chicken soup and then went off home to make lunch for the hoards. The boys and I moped around.

Later Wendy arrived with coffee and cakes for me, and fish and chips from down the road for the boys. That cheered things up. She is great, just knows what is needed.

'Jennifer, I think it would be good to visit the grave and make sure that Molly is okay,' she suggested as we sipped our coffee.

'I can't, Wen. I can't move today. It's too much to get dressed and go out. I don't want to leave the boys and besides, look at the weather.' I gestured to the typical Irish rain that was pattering against the windowpane.

'Well, what about tomorrow? Karina thinks that we should do something as a group to make Molly's passage into her new world easier.'

'Oh, Wen …'

'Well, Jen, she is your spiritual advisor; she has been very good for you.'

'I know, I know. I've spoken with her a couple of times in the past week. But …'

'I won't take no for an answer. I'll get everyone together, you won't have to worry about a thing! I know it's difficult but it has to be done.'

I reluctantly agreed.

On Sunday Karina, Wendy, the boys and I visited Molly in her grave. I invited Stuart as I didn't want him to feel left out, but he didn't want to come and made it very clear why. 'I am not going anywhere where that Wendy woman is,' he said darkly. 'That witch has a bad influence on you, Jennifer. She puts ugly thoughts in your head. I wish she would get out of my life and go back home to New Zealand, as far away on the planet as possible.' Instead he opted to catch up on some of the work he had neglected. All along, I had known that he wouldn't want to come and privately was pleased when he didn't.

As it turned out it was a wonderful way to soothe our new, raw grief. We collected flowers and autumn leaves from the garden. Da had made a little white cross with Molly's name painted on it, so we took it to the spot where the fresh earth formed a lonely mound on the hill overlooking the bay. We pushed it into the ground to mark the spot until we get a proper headstone in place, and scattered the leaves and flowers over the earth like the story of the babes in the wood.

My boys each brought one of Molly's favourite storybooks, which they took turns in reading to her. We sang the songs of Celtic Woman, a group that had been formed the year Molly was born and which was her favourite music in the car, and when we could sing no more we played their CD, 'The Greatest Journey'. It seemed so appropriate.

Karina lit five candles - one for each year Molly had lived - and we sat in a circle on rugs on the cold earth and spoke, sometimes about Molly and sometimes to her, until they all burned down to the wick.

'Molly is our own special angel now,' Karina told us. 'She will help us live our lives so that when we die we are as pure and as good as she is.'

When the darkness and dew came down upon us we went home.

JUNIOR

Mum and Aunty Wendy took us into the hills where our Molly is now and we spent some time with her in case she was lonely up there all by herself. I read her 'A Million Chameleons'. She always likes that one and I said my poem for her again. We put a little cross in the ground to show everybody where she is until the big one comes. We could see all of Dublin from up there.

Karina said some prayers and told us that Molly is our special angel now and will help us forever. We have to go back to school tomorrow and I might find that hard after all that has happened. The hurling championships are in a fortnight so I hope that they haven't dropped me from the team because I wasn't there. I would hate that!

RICHARD

We made that pile of dirt look really pretty with all the red and yellow leaves we scattered. There is that fairy tale and a song about the two children who kept themselves warm by making a blanket of leaves so I hope that Molly stays warm and cosy. I know that she is my special angel now and that she will be there to help me all the time, but I want her to come back home with me. I miss her. It is cold up there in the hills, but it was warm in the pub and the hot chocolate was pretty good.

KARINA

It's so sad for Jennifer and the boys and they are quite lost at the moment. I think our ceremony on the hill by the graveside began the long journey towards healing. Jennifer realises that we can't change what has already happened; that we can only learn from the past and move onwards. She knows that nothing is permanent except change and I am sure that her faith will pull her through. 'She is one strong woman!' I said quietly to Wendy.

The young boys are like two birds with broken wings. They are so confused and injured at the moment but youth is resilient and I believe that if they can talk and rationalise about what has happened to Molly then they will come through okay and survive.

Wendy was a bit naughty taking them into Johnny Fox's pub on the way home but the pint of stout did Jennifer good and the boys liked the hot chocolate and chips. It warmed them up.

WENDY

We are doing what we can to help Jennifer and the boys get through this but it is difficult, especially when I am grieving for Molly myself. I loved that little girl.

I have been visiting Tom in hospital, as he has nobody here in Ireland to take his pyjamas to wash and things like that. He is all wired up and can't speak much, can only eat pureed food and is still feeling pretty sore and sorry for himself. He is gradually improving but as he has an acquired brain injury they are not letting him go until they are sure he has fully recovered and got all his marbles back. They are confident he will be fine, but don't want to take any risks.

They are saying that he can go home perhaps on Monday or Tuesday of the week after next. His jaw will still be lightly wired but the doctors can attend to that in London.

I know this sounds weird, almost outrageous, but Jennifer hasn't visited him yet! She says she has been so busy she hasn't had the time, but will see him once the boys are back at school. I think that deep down she is reluctant. That she feels partly guilty for what has happened to him, and unsure about where their relationship will go from here, if it has anywhere to go. And so she is uneasy about meeting him face-to-face and keeps putting it off. I don't think she knows what she is going to say to him.

'Hard and all as it might be, Jen, it is something you simply have to make the time to do,' I say to her. 'You can't avoid him altogether.' But she just stares into the distance.

It's awkward for me being 'little Sally in between' trying to keep everything going.

JENNIFER

On the Monday morning following the funeral I couldn't get out of bed. My legs simply would not hold me up. I phoned Stuart who was sleeping upstairs in our bedroom and asked him to wake the boys and get them ready for school. Even though it may seem harsh, I know that there is no point in them staying home with me amid all the sadness that is in our house. They are better off with their mates, distracted by schoolwork and sport.

Before Stuart left for work with the boys he brought me a cup of tea and said he would phone to check on me later. The turnaround in him is astonishing.

I was grateful and thanked him and went back to a fitful sleep until I was jolted out of my trance-like state when Mam called from the bottom of the stairs, 'Are you home Jenny, love? I've brought you some soup.'

I replied from where I was, in the spare room, and following my voice she walked over and peeked in the door. Seeing her was too much and I could not stop myself from bursting into tears. She came and lay on the bed with me, both of us clinging together, united in our sorrow, not needing to say anything for we both knew how the other felt. I cried and I cried until I could cry no more. This opening of the pent up floodgate cleansed my spirit and made me realise that I had to get up and keep going.

When Mam left, I showered and brushed my hair but was so spent by the effort that I sat at the kitchen table, inert, with my head in my hands unable to make a decision or do a thing.

Wendy found me this way when she dropped in after lunch. She brewed a cup of tea and we talked. And talked! We talked about Molly, the boys, the situation, the funeral. At times we even laughed when we recalled a happy time, a funny turn of phrase, a precious moment. This debriefing was good.

In the end, Wendy gently took my hands in hers and looked me in the eye.

'Jen, I know this is probably not the time nor the place, and I know that it will be an effort for you, but I think you should go and visit Tom. He is lying there at St James's, sucking his food through a straw, with a very sore head and a whole lot of regrets. You haven't seen him Jen, and that is completely understandable because Molly was your first priority, but you should go while you can.

Come today because, if you don't, he will be back in London before you know it.'

'Wendy,' I blubbered, 'After what's happened, I can't look Tommy in the eye.'

'You can, Jen, and you must. You owe him that at least. You dragged him into this and he's in hospital because your Stuart put him there. You have to visit him and see how he is. That is the least you can do. No more putting it off. I will take you in today.'

'If I hadn't brought Tom here then Molly would still be alive,' I sobbed. 'It is Tom's fault that Molly's dead.'

'For fuck's sake, don't start thinking like that! Jen, listen, Molly's dead because Stuart dropped her and made her dead. Christ almighty, it has nothing to do with Tom. He just got caught up in the whole sorry saga.'

'At least Tom is alive. Molly is dead.'

'Ahhh, damn, damn, damn. Jennifer, stop it! I'm telling you, you must go to him. I'll come with you if you want, but you have to make the effort. Right now, I'm off to work, but I can drop you in your car on my way and then I will get a cab from there.'

I went.

What choice did I have?

WENDY

I don't think I have ever been so cross with Jen before in all our time as friends. Or ever raised my voice to her like that!

But it had to been done.

JENNIFER

Matters were not made any better when outside the hospital I was recognised by a journalist hanging around trying to rake up some muck. He began to ply me with questions, following me all the way to the main door where security stepped in and asked him to desist. It was awful. 'Mrs Hoare, Mrs Hoare, is there someone special in the hospital you have come to see? Would that be Mr Knight? Is that his name, Mrs Hoare?'

I was directed to Tom's room, and found him dozing, incapacitated, neck brace on, jaw wired up and one leg on a pulley. Apparently he had dropped so instantly and awkwardly he had wrecked his knee and shredded ligaments in an ankle. My heart jumped a little at the sight of him and I immediately empathized, wanting to be near him. The old magic was still there.

I quietly pulled a chair up next to his bed, sat down and took his hand. An amazing feeling of tenderness and peace overtook me. After a few moments, Tom opened his eyes, slowly focused on me and then smiled just a glimmer of the sparkly smile that is his calling card.

'Jennifer,' he whispered. 'Jennifer, oh Jennifer!' He began to weep. I put my head on the pillow next to his and wept with him. There was so much to cry about. Not to talk about. Not to make decisions about. Not to lay blame about. Just simply to be together and shed tears about. Wendy was right. I had to see him. I stayed until it was time to fetch the boys from school.

That night, the news services had pictures of Tommy and me in our private grief, heads together on the pillow. Somehow the parasite journalist had taken photographs through the hospital window.

Stuart went crazy, standing over me menacingly, spewing forth vitriol and hate, his sentences laced with vile obscenities. 'How fucking dare you go flaunting yourself like that with that adulterer, you sleazy little cunt! And our fucking daughter still warm in her fucking grave! Was it all for nothing, you fucking bitch? Have you not learnt anything, cunt?'

Once I would have copped it. But he will not intimidate me any more. He has done the worst possible thing he could have done to any family so I gave it to him back, hitting where it hurts most. 'I wasn't the one who dropped Molly,' I sneered. 'Who dropped Molly over the edge, hey? Wasn't me. It must have been, oh, wait a minute, wasn't it Stuart who was the last person seen holding her ..?'

He reacted to my backchat by pushing me back against the wall, careful not to strike me, but shoving my head back and doing something to my neck that made me freeze rigid with pain.

Junior and Richie begged him to stop. 'Da please don't! Mammy didn't mean it. Please Da, don't hurt Mammy!'

That only made him angrier and he told them to get upstairs as he increased the pressure until my feet slid from under me and he stormed out of the room. If the boys had not been there I am sure I would have ended up in hospital with Tom.

My life has fallen apart and my family is shattered. His pathetic behaviour has reminded me that his vicious anger is why I left him the first place. There is no going back.

Press column

Molly's mother visits lover in hospital

Jennifer Hoare, the mother of little Molly who lost her life on the M50 Motorway was out and about yesterday visiting her lover at St James's Hospital.

Thomas Knight, an English national, has been hospitalised since the accident after an altercation with Molly's father. Mr Knight suffered a fractured eye socket plus skull and other injuries including a badly dislocated knee when he fell and hit his head on the tarmac.

The lovers sat together, holding hands, consoling each other after a torrid fortnight. It remains to be seen whether the pair will set up house in London or in Dublin and who will gain custody of the Hoare's two other children. When asked her intentions regarding Mr Knight, an angry Mrs Hoare was tight lipped.

Earlier this morning, her husband Stuart, a well regarded Dublin financier, returned to his workplace after his daughter's funeral last Friday, spoke to our journalist and released a statement saying, 'My daughter Molly died in tragic circumstances but we, as a family, have clung together and are restarting our lives knowing that we have an angel in heaven to look after us. My main aim now is to return to normal so that our other two children can enjoy their lives, drawing on happy memories of their little sister to sustain them.'

JUNIOR

Mum was on the news tonight with that bastard Tom who is in hospital. I hope none of the kids at school saw it.

Da was furious and said things about Molly not being cold yet and how shameful it is for Mam to be seen

95

with the mongrel and how Tom is responsible for all the bad things that have happened to Molly and us.

Mam stood up to him and ended the argument by telling him that he was the one who had dropped Molly over the bridge, which was unfair because Da feels awful about it. Richie and I got out of the way and came upstairs to my bedroom. I had to cuddle Richie because he was crying.

STUART

When I left for work on Monday morning Jennifer was in bed, unable to get out, or so she said. But as soon as I turned my back she was over there to lover boy making a spectacle of herself and my family.

I was bloody angry when I saw my wife and that low life on the television news and in the morning newspapers sharing their 'grief', as they called it. Grief. I'll give them feckin' grief, all right. Airing our dirty linen all over the media, that's what I call it. How bloody humiliating for the boys and me. I'm glad father has Alzheimer's because if he was aware of what is going on in our household he'd be over here to shoot the two of them. My only regret is that I should have finished off the job when I had the chance and killed that bastard.

When I bawled Jennifer out about her behaviour she had the cheek to tell me I was the one who dropped Molly over the feckin' bridge. That may have been the case, but she and that scumbag effectively did the deed. If they hadn't been running off together to London then none of this would have ever happened. They are to blame. They made me do it.

TOM

My heart skipped a beat when Jennifer came into the room.

I was completely overwhelmed with the wave of emotion that she engendered in me. I love that woman and I can't wait to live with her and share her life.

We must be together, especially after all that has happened. The nurses tell me I should be out of here in a few days so I am hoping that Jen will come home to England with me. That is my first preference but I realise that I may have to wait and in that case, I will live here in Dublin with her. It's as simple as that.

JENNIFER

Now that I have seen Tom I know that I need him and that he is the only person in the world who can help me get through this. All of Ireland has an opinion about Molly's accident and by and large, they have come down on Stuart's side. They are loudly proclaiming that I am the scarlet woman. I simply don't get it.

If you want my opinion, Molly's accident is a wonderful distraction to the recently released Ryan Report on paedophilia in which our Irish patriarchal society - the government, the church and judiciary - are being confronted by the evil that has been perpetuated and condoned by all three institutions for generations. The men in the pulpits are conveniently ignoring their own sins and deflecting the spotlight onto mine. I am the perfect scapegoat and decoy, and the compliant press is their loyal servant, keeping our story alive and in top spot on the media listings. The way this nation is controlled never ceases to amaze me.

Bereft and empty in my zombie state I move around the house doing the things I need to do, seeing to the boys, speaking to visitors who call. Stuart occupies the top half of the house and I sleep downstairs in the spare room, only venturing up if I need to grab some clothes from the closet and even then, only when he is at work. I live out of my suitcase, the one I had packed to go with Tom that day.

Stuart goes to the office before I get out of bed and isn't home until late. The boys and I eat together and I leave his dinner in the fridge to be heated up and if he doesn't come home in time, I give it to the dog in the morning. On the weekends he goes to golf. I don't question. I don't care!

Things drag on. I try to run the family as normal and do things for the boys as I have always done - dress well, cook, shop, garden, meditate and keep social niceties in place. Sometimes I even smile. But then, when nobody else is around I get into the shower and scream my heart out for Molly.

I type long, calm emails to my friends and extended family in the middle of the interminable nights, desperately trying to keep my social networks in place. Sometimes in the daytime, I cannot bear to see people or take their calls. I know I am shutting out those who may speak up and support me but I don't want their sympathy or their lasagnes.

Stuart has pretty well blocked my family from coming here. He asked Kevin to leave and makes Mam feel uncomfortable. He has forbidden Wendy to set foot in the doorway but of course that doesn't stop her. She says she's not afraid of him and what he doesn't know doesn't hurt him so she comes when he is at work, which is all the time these days. I don't know what I'd do without her.

98

STUART

Jennifer seems to be obeying my rules and keeping her head down, looking after the house and the boys. I have told her to curtail her contact with Wendy as she unsettles her and makes her question my authority. 'She is not allowed to come anywhere near the place,' I said. 'Understand? You can meet her at your meditation group on Tuesday nights but I don't want her here or near me, or to have any influence on my children.'

As well, I have set about getting rid of all the hangers-on from my house. I am sick of the O'Briens wandering around like lost puppies all the time. Jennifer has to pick up the threads and get on with her life and having Mary here looking sad is no help whatsoever. She disrupts the calm and pokes her nose into everything.

Last time Big Kev parked his arse on my sofa I gave him short shrift, telling him that he and I have absolutely nothing in common and that I didn't want to see his ugly mug in my home again. One of the other brothers, Paddy, has returned from the west - all screwed up and minus his marriage - to live with the oldies. I have also made it clear to him that my home is not a gathering place for mediation and endeavours to solve his problems, whatever they are.

I could also do without the idiots in the street who shout invective, spit or try to remonstrate with me, suggesting that somehow I am responsible for Molly's accident. That includes 'the look' that some people give me. It's a sort of shake-of-the-head tut-tut display, a mixture of astonishment, puzzlement, disbelief and confusion, overlayed with a tiny veneer of fear, a hint of high moral dudgeon and a serving of distaste. I see it on all sorts of faces, male and female, old and young, family and strangers.

Others get agitated, and then there are the spooky few who half-smile in a knowing way, giving the impression that they admire me for what I have done and that they would like to attempt something similar if they could muster the stomach. It unsettles me but I can't do anything about it except to try to ignore them.

Newspaper Opinion

Who are these people and why are we so interested in them?

Stuart and Jennifer Hoare are a well off, well-educated couple who live in an exclusive part of Dublin.

Jennifer is the only daughter of the well-known and liked O'Brien sporting family. At one time three of her four brothers played for Dublin County football team, have excelled in other sports such as rugby and golf, and she herself was a good tennis player. She is a qualified lawyer although she hasn't worked in the field for the past twelve years while she has been raising her family of two boys and a girl. She is pretty, petite and well liked, helps out at the school, fundraises for the local chapter of the Red Cross and is well known in the Dublin social scene.

Jennifer was brought up as a Catholic but is now a practising Buddhist. Her father and mother, Mary and Seamus O'Brien, once owned a huge British Leyland car dealership in central Dublin, part of a colourful and varying entrepreneurial career over the years. They also owned and ran several Group 1 racehorses that did well on tracks in Ireland, Britain, Europe and even as far away as the Melbourne Cup in Australia. They are highly regarded in church and philanthropic circles.

Stuart Hoare is a well-dressed, well-educated professional financier and developer, a successful businessman who was the only child in a well-respected military family. He is a board member of his local church, a member of several influential clubs and the father of three. In fact Stuart Hoare is a person we would all like to be. The couple have two older sons who attend a well-known private school.

To all outward appearances these are two 'normal' parents and the family is a 'normal' family. The tragic incident involving little Molly happened on a 'normal' Saturday afternoon in a seemingly 'normal' place. People from all over Ireland are asking how can something like this happen? If it can happen to the Hoares, then could it possibly happen to anybody!

Perhaps this is why the general public regard this family's personal tragedy as a form of reality television.

WENDY

The way I look at it is that at the moment Jen has two choices. One is to return to the past and to continue the life of hell she was living before the split with Stuart.

The other is to accept what has happened, continue to move forward and change her life as she had planned to do before the accident. It's not easy I know, but she has to grasp the future and go with Tom.

'That will take courage, Jen,' I said, 'but the process will empower you.'

That's why I have suggested that a weekend away in a retreat house in the Wicklow Hills will help her to draw a line in the sand, accept what has happened and move forward. I think she may do as I ask.

JENNIFER

After a bit of thought, I took Wendy's advice and went to the retreat in the hills.

I was back home after the first day!

'My brain will not stay still, and I cannot find peace,' I told her as I unpacked my bag. 'All that silence is not helpful, rather it's counter productive. It makes me dwell on what has happened until I think I am going insane. It is just too early.'

Tom's broken jaw and eye socket are healing and he is being discharged from hospital soon, and a big decision has to be made. He needs outpatient treatment for a couple of weeks and the doctors would prefer him to stay in Dublin for that. They do not want him to risk a flight at the moment.

Once again my true and loyal friend Wendy has stepped in to help, this time offering to take Tom in at her place. When I told my family about this arrangement the criticism was immediate and cruel. Da was angry, Ma was cross, and even Kevin asked me what was I doing. 'Do you not care about public opinion?' he said.

'No, I don't,' I replied, 'because it's no business of the public.'

There is no way Tom can stay at my house as Stuart would never allow it and I can't say I blame him. At Wendy's I can look after him in the daytime and take him to his medical appointments and things like that and then she can be there at night for him. So that's what is going to happen, whether they like it or not!

WENDY

There is no way Jen can have him at her place because Stuart will finish off his dastardly deed and kill him in his sleep.

So when Jen suggested that he stay at my place I agreed, although I made sure I did not go too over the top in my response. 'It's only a small apartment, Jen,' I said. 'But I will be at work all day so that shouldn't be a problem.'

What I didn't add was that Tom is charming and funny and has a sort of energy about him that is both soothing and invigorating at the same time. I am actually looking forward to it.

TOM

I have to stay in Ireland for a while after my discharge from hospital but Jen can't have me at her place. She tells me it's because she doesn't want to attract adverse media coverage, but I know that the real reason is Stuart. He will kill me, and I don't want that!

When Wendy suggested that I stay with her I accepted because she is a fantastically cool chick. She's great fun to be with and does everything with such enthusiasm and charm. We are kindred spirits!

Jen comes over every day while Wendy is at work and we hang out together listening to music, talking and watching a bit of daytime television. She takes me to all my appointments but that is the only time we go anywhere, as she doesn't want to be seen with me.

You never know what is going to happen. Sometimes she completely closes down and I just don't know what she is thinking. Other times she is her old self, fun to be with. 'She runs hot and cold,' I tell Wendy. 'It's hard to predict which version you are going to get.' I know she has many things to cope with so I don't push the point.

Because Wendy is no cook and rarely makes a meal, we go out most nights to listen to a bit of music, or enjoy a stand-up comic, or Wendy will conduct one of her meditation group talks. On those nights, I man the table in the corner and sell copies of her self-help books to the punters. She has a good little business going there.

It is good to get out and about, makes me feel human again. But there is something that worries me. One night, after we had come home and were in the kitchen having a nightcap, we were laughing about something or other and I swung her around in a dance move and we ended up face to face. We almost kissed. Fortunately we both had the sense to pull back.

JENNIFER

Each morning I drop the boys at school and then head over to Wendy's to spend the time with Tom. It is private there and I enjoy our time hanging out, cuddling and talking. We go to his medical appointments and watch television or rent videos or just listen to music. But he is developing cabin fever. As a free-spirited muso, he is not used to being restricted in his movements so as soon as the final medical consultation is completed and he is given the all clear to fly, I think he should leave and go home. 'It will give us time to sort things out,' I tell him.

It will be hard to say goodbye, but I have to accept that perhaps it may never work out with Tom and me and that I have to tell him to get on with his life, go back to doing the things he normally does and try and forget this nightmare. Most of all he has to be patient and give me time. I have to think of the boys first. Poor mites have been through enough and need gentle, loving care. We have to put ourselves to one side and wait until everything dies down.

One thing for sure. I will never go back to Stuart's bed and I have told him so, although I think he believes it is just a matter of time before I will continue on as if nothing has happened between us. Return to being the perfect little housewife? No way!

WENDY

It's great having Tom as a house guest. I love coming home of a night to find him curled up on the sofa ready for a chat. We watch the news together and talk about what is happening in the world.

I said to him, 'You are extremely well informed … for a drummer!' He gave me a playful punch and said, 'You ought to talk, Miss La-La Self-Help Living In Crazy Place Fairy Land.'

I absolutely get what Jennifer sees in him and love bundling him in the car and taking him into Temple Bar for dinner. Well, to watch me eat dinner, really. He still can't eat properly, so he usually settles for a soft dessert with extra ice cream on the side. Jen makes him fresh homemade soup for lunch so he probably gets a balanced meal over the twenty-four hours. We go to live music pubs and just hang out. He likes that because he says that he feels very confined being at home all day. I shall miss him when he heads back to London town. I have grown very fond of the little Pommy bastard.

TOM

The doctor has finally cleared me to fly out and I am glad to be going home, not the least because I am afraid that I am getting a little bit too fond of Wendy.

Having said that, I'm not giving up on Jennifer Mary O'Brien and we will be in contact every day and will work things out. I said to her, 'I am only going home because I have to make a living and London is where my work is. Otherwise I would stay here with you.'

But to be perfectly honest, life is a misery for me here in Ireland, living in a bubble with the media always ready to pounce.

JENNIFER

It occurred to me one day that I should shave my head in mourning. But instead I went to a parlour named Inkspot in town. People can now see a tattoo on my ankle reading 'Molly' and know that I have been changed forever. What they can't see is the angel on my shoulder who guides me through this mess.

My grief is raw and ugly and messy. I am envious of people who seem happy, and I display an irrational resentment towards them because they are not suffering like I am. Why did this happen to her? To me? To us! I cry when I see families enjoying each other because that can never be us again. I am not a nice person. I am angry, resentful, envious, and my hatred colours my world.

I sometimes blame Stuart although I never verbalize this and do my best to shield this thought from my children because I have to respect that he is still their father. At other times I blame Tom. Either way, I always blame myself.

I hate going outside the house because I feel that everywhere I go people point at me, stare and talk. So I fill my time visiting her grave, and when I come home I draw on the film footage I took in happier times to create a Molly tribute video. My little girl comes alive on the screen and I can lose myself in the fantasy. As well, I am constructing a gratitude journal and that also distracts me.

Now that he is back in London, at night I sit up talking to Tom on the internet until the wee hours. He keeps asking me to come over and although I long to be with him I am afraid of leaving my home and the boys and most of all, little Molly who is lying up there, dead, on the hill.

STUART

As my father says, sometimes you have to lose the odd battle to win the war. I think I might be slowly winning the war.

JENNIFER

A couple of times I have braced myself and purchased a plane ticket to London only to pull out at the last moment because I just can't cope with the packing and all that's involved - mainly, the explosive response from Stuart that I will no doubt have to endure. I realise that sounds weak, but he has killed one of my children already, so who knows what he might do to me or the boys - or anyone else within striking distance for that matter - if he hears that I am off to see the man he loathes so much. The man he blames 'for breaking up the family and everything we have built.' It's all too horrible to contemplate.

I know it's a cop-out but I send sweet Wendy over there instead to jolly him along a bit. She is free to come and go as she pleases and always has things to do in London for her business.

My boyfriend and my best friend hang out and I feel lucky that they are friends.

WENDY

There is a mutual attraction between Tom and me that developed fairly early in the piece. He is eccentric, interesting, sexy and fun, but Jennifer seems to push him away and keeps reneging on opportunities to meet up in London. She sends me and I feel I am being dragged into a whirlpool.

I want this situation resolved because things are getting pretty steamy between Tom and me. Four times Jen has pulled out and stayed home when she has promised to go to London.

The first three times she gave the ticket to me. I always have things I can do over there so I used it, but on the fourth occasion I knocked her back. Tom and I have spent far too much time together and the electricity between us is sparking hot. Jen is my best friend and Tom's lover, so it's a dicey situation. We both love her too much to betray her. Fortunately, so far we have resisted the urge to do anything, but there is no denying it, he is one great hunk of spunk and I know he likes me.

To calm things down, I came up with a plan. I suggested to Jen that she take a trip away with Tom - somewhere, anywhere, away from Dublin and London - so they can regroup and make sense of the horrible mess they find themselves in. I will look in on Junior and

Richie while she is away. I regard them as the children that I left too late to have; they are my boys.

'What about Stuart?' Jen said. 'He will go mad if I thinks I am going off with Tom.'

'Don't worry,' I replied, 'I know exactly how to handle Stuart.'

Part Five

JENNIFER

It is early November and a melancholy cowl has descended over our little island as we come to terms with the realization that winter still has to be endured. The rains have started and Dublin shelters under umbrellas while up north floods have brought everything to a halt. Christmas will be a very low-key event this year.

Wendy is afraid that if I don't do something about Tom he will get sick of waiting. He has been very patient and given me time but no doubt he is tiring of our dreary relationship. Sometimes he must wonder what his life has become. So she has come up with a scheme. At the foundation of it all was this conversation I had with Stuart in the kitchen one morning:

'Stuart, I need to get out of Dublin for a while. The weather, the media, the memories, it's all closing in on me. I need a break.'

'Ha! Don't take me for a sucker. You just want to go to London! I'm telling you right now, I forbid you to go over there to see that fucking home-wrecker.'

'No, no, no,' I replied, biting my tongue and deliberately avoiding the issue of his assumed control of me. 'I'm not going to London. I'm going to New Zealand.'

'New Zealand?'

'Wendy has to go home for a while and see her ageing mother, and …'

'You're going to New Zealand with that little Kiwi slut?'

'Yes,' I said, once again ignoring his nasty approach.

'I couldn't think of a better place to ditch the bitch! Do me a favour and leave her over there when you come back, will you?'

And that pretty much was it. He was vaguely interested when I added that an equally important reason for the trip was that Buddhism is very popular in New Zealand and that there is an internationally renowned meditation centre near Wellington. 'A retreat there would do me the world of good,' I added. 'I can visit a guru, meditate and get my spiritual life back on track.'

'Yeah, yeah,' he said, 'whatever.'

However, he started to warm to the idea when he began to realise that the two women in the whole wide world who annoyed him most would be out of his hair for three entire weeks and he could wander around the house in his underpants drinking whiskey to his heart's content if he liked.

Two days later he handed me an envelope and inside were not one, but two Emirates Airlines return business class tickets from Dublin to Auckland! 'Boy,' I thought, 'he really does want to see the back of Wendy.'

JUNIOR

Mam needs some time away and is going on a holiday to New Zealand. Cool! That is where they made 'Lord of the Rings' but she says she is going because it has lots of Buddhists and she will be able to do spiritual things that will help her to get over Molly's death. I think it is a good thing because she has been really sad and I want my old Mam back.

The week after next I am going away on a hurling camp to Galway for a week so Richie will be home with Da by himself. Suffer!

RICHIE

Mam is going on a holiday and is not taking us with her. She says that Molly will be okay up on the hill by herself but Nanna Mary said she will take me up there to see her while Mam is away, so it will be okay, Molly won't be lonely. I might go and stay with Nan while Junior is away at camp.

WENDY

Faaarrrr out! I knew Big Stewie wanted me out of the country, but I didn't think he would send me off in such style! Can't wait for the 'welcome aboard' glass of bubbly from a nice handsome cabin steward, some signature chef's food and a big sleep on a flat bed all the way home to the Land of the Long White Cloud. Whoo-hooo!

JENNIFER

I don't like lying but it is the only way that I can survive until I gather the strength to make a clean break from this marriage. 'Suffer, Stuart!' I chuckle secretly to myself. 'I can still beat you. I am in charge of my own life now!' I will admit that tricking him was probably made easier because he is more than a little distracted with business lately; it has become his life.

As the time approaches doubts are creeping in and I am experiencing my own form of Irish superstition.

Perhaps God will punish me again. He has already done that twice before. Should I pull out now and let Tom go live his own life? When I voiced these concerns to my spiritual advisor she dismissed it as an unenlightened way of thinking.

'In the Buddha's teachings, the Four Noble Truths are like a doctor who diagnoses an illness and then prescribes the treatment,' Karina explained. 'He must know what the illness is, what causes it, what might cure it, and find the method that will finish it forever. Jennifer, you have come to the curing stage. You know you are sad and melancholy and you know why that is. It may be that Tom is your cure and if he is, you will find peace. You cannot dismiss that without testing it.'

'What about my committing adultery with Tom?' I asked. 'That is against Buddhist Law. That might be the illness.'

'No, no, no, we have no such law, Jen. Buddhism is not about believing things. It's simply a spiritual map. If what you are doing is wrong, you will know it doesn't feel right. Hold your ideals in your palm, keep an open mind and meditate.'

My wise and neutral Karina is not interested in gossip and hearsay, only my spiritual well being, so I am taking her advice and have gone into overdrive organizing clothes and food for the boys and ensuring things will operate smoothly on the home front while I am away. I owe Stuart that much. I told the lads that I am going on holiday to New Zealand with Aunty Wen because I needed a rest and spiritual nourishment. They are considerate and caring, agreeing that I should go, that things have been tough.

But our real plan of action is to fly from Dublin to Dubai where I will meet up with Tom, who will have flown in earlier. He and I will go on from there to Thailand, while Wendy continues on to Auckland.

My excitement overrides my apprehension. My only request to the cabbie was that he take me to the airport via any road other than the M50.

Tom must still love me. He pawned a prize set of African djembe drums to join me in business class.

STUART

Jennifer is off to New Zealand. She came to me and said that after all we have been through she needed some headspace and the opportunity to do Buddhisty things to settle her thoughts spiritually. I don't see any harm in that and I am happy to help her. It will make her see sense and realise that this impasse is not doing anybody any good; it is better that we pick up the pieces and salvage our marriage.

Down the track I might even go to counselling with her, like she wanted me to a couple of years ago. That might convince her to leave the spare room and come and sleep upstairs with me where a wife should be.

I think initially she was worried that I wouldn't agree to the trip but I don't care where she goes as long as she stays away from that drummer boy. That's why I made sure the ticket has no transit stop in London.

I hesitated briefly on buying a ticket for that blasted Wendy. But then I thought, 'No, just do it. It will show that I am not the monster she believes I am. And it will be worth every precious moment of not having her skulking around the place and putting crazy ideas in the boys' heads.' If necessary, I would have paid first-class to get that incorrigible woman out of Ireland. Bought the whole fucking plane, if need be!

The boys will be safer in the hands of their grandmothers, who will take it in turns to help me out. Hopefully, dearest Wendy will become besotted with an amorous New Zealand sheep farmer and stay there forever.

Orla, our social worker, believes this trip is a good thing for Jennifer to do. She told me so, last night. Over dinner.

DETECTIVE BRYAN KELLY

It has taken a very long time tracking down and interviewing people who were either up on the flyover or down on the motorway that day and whose names were in the officers' notebooks as witnesses. I listened patiently and took a lot of notes, but as it was such an emotion-charged event, I decided to let it settle for a while.

There was a lot of confusion over what actually caused the pile-up. After all, the little girl did not fall directly onto the road itself, rather into the median strip. We eventually found the driver who was at the 'lead' of the pack when it happened, and he explained all.

'Just prior to going under the flyover, I swerved when a black and white object suddenly appeared from out of the sky and hit my windscreen,' he explained. 'I got such a shock my automatic reaction was to swerve. You know, you think you are going to avoid it, but it's already too late.

'I lost control in the greasy conditions, the car went sideways and veered into the next lane and the vehicle behind had no choice but to cannon into me. All hell broke loose from there.'

The positive side, if there is one, is that while the pile-up was spectacular, and an insurer's nightmare, most drivers got out relatively unscathed. One man spent several weeks in hospital with spinal injuries, but there were no deaths. There were a couple of cases of whiplash, a few broken limbs and plenty of minor cuts and bruises, but otherwise most were back to work within a few days.

The downside was that it took us a long time to find out what the black-and-white object was and I can tell you that even the most hardened officer on this case was moved to tears when we discovered it in the thicket on the slope of the motorway. It was the little girl's favourite soft toy, a panda, which she had been carrying when her father got her out of the car. It had apparently slipped out of her arms when she went over the edge and fell into the traffic.

The sad point was after we found it, we were about to get it down to the Children's, hoping it might help things along when the news came that her life support was being turned off. It's a tough game, this.

JENNIFER

I sat in business class, awaiting take off, feeling like an errant school kid who has evaded an ever-vigilant head teacher. I looked across to the plush seat beside me and there was Wendy, eliciting a third round of champagne from the handsome steward while checking out whether he was available, married or gay.

She turned and passed a glass to me, held hers aloft with a big smile and said, 'To Stuart.'

'To Stuart?'

'I always knew deep down he loved me!'

And for the first time in such a long time, I roared laughing.

A little over seven hours later we landed and when I saw the size of Dubai airport I panicked as it occurred to me that finding Tom in this crowd would be like finding a needle in a haystack. But I was wrong!

Waiting at the gate as I emerged was my hero, looking every bit as cool and desirable as he had always been. After all he had been through, his Euro-Asian looks had not faded, his figure was as trim as ever, and he was still a snazzy dresser. He looked great and my heart skipped at the sight of him.

I dropped my hand luggage and ran to his embrace. It felt so good and right. We hugged and stepped back to look at one another, giggled and embraced again. It was wonderful. The tension completely evaporated and I knew that this was completely the right thing to do.

We had a five-hour wait at Dubai before our onward flight for Bangkok. We set up camp in the business class lounge and Wendy discreetly said she had 'things to do' and evaporated. But, after a few minutes feeling a bit cloistered in the tranquil atmosphere, we went out and wandered around the airport hand in hand. While looking at all the duty free shops and taking in the exotic costumes of the locals we talked non-stop, just enjoying our closeness. Every now and then Tom would take me in his arms, dance me around and kiss me. Nobody took much notice. This is a busy international airport where people of every race and culture mingle and move. A meeting ground for the whole world and a couple of crazy Anglo-Saxons is par for the course.

Then somehow we discovered the sleep cubes, a new innovation being trialled at Dubai. For a fee you can hire a cubby just big enough to hold a bed, for however many hours you needed. The attendant wakes you up in time for you to board your onward flight.

'Do you see that?' Tom excitedly pointed to the sign. 'A bed! Imagine what we can do with a bed? Let's hire one!'

After negotiating a time the attendant led us through a narrow passageway to a door numbered 26 that he opened as he flicked on the light.

'There are blankets there and the buzzer will sound when your time is up,' he advised. 'The cubes are soundproof so you shouldn't hear anything. Sleep tight,' he added as he closed the door behind us, leaving us blissfully alone.

I unzipped my black leather boots, put them together in the corner and peeled off my stockings, a little apprehensive but excited. 'Whoa!' Tom exclaimed at the sight of my bare legs. 'I can't believe this is really happening.'

He kicked off his shoes and we fell into an eager embrace, kissing each other all over. Light, fluffy kisses. We held each other tightly, pressing one body against the other as though we were desperate to meld together. Our tongues explored and probed, our kisses were deep and longing. Eventually our pent up desire overtook us and with a flurry of discarded clothing we united and made passionate love in the tiny room, deliciously consummating our reunion. As our bodies cascaded towards orgasm, we grasped the moment, stopped, and became still, letting it come, trusting it would happen, waiting, delaying the ultimate reward. Warm glorious emotion flooded our every ounce.

At the end, surprised by the extent of our passion, we collapsed into each other's arms, delighted at what we had achieved, feeling wonderful as the endorphins did their feel-good work. We lay face-to-face, relaxed, kissing, exploring, caressing, unable in our excitement to sleep. Tom and me alone in our world!

Too soon, the buzzer sounded, the light in the cube came on and it was time to board our onward flight.

When we got back to the business lounge to get our things, Wendy was reading a magazine. She looked up at me, then at Tom, then back at me. A big smile split her face. She looked back at her magazine. She didn't have to say a thing.

TOM

I have never felt so in love before. Never. That is all I can say. All those weeks of pent-up emotion, released. I love Jen and will never leave her now.

When I went to give a farewell kiss to Wendy, who had to wait another hour before getting her flight to Auckland, she pulled me in really close and whispered in my ear, 'Aren't you glad we behaved ourselves?'

'Oh, my God yes,' I whispered. 'Yes, yes, thank you, Wen, yes.'

JENNIFER

On to Bangkok, this time together, side by side, so many things to talk about, enjoying being close.

Then suddenly, we were at the console waiting to collect our bags before heading into the oven-like warmth of the city where we were staying overnight before heading north to Thaton, in the province of Chiang Mai, Tom's mother's village. In the back seat of the taxi we watched in awe as the driver blended into the frantic flow of this city that never sleeps, its constant noise, movement and amazing infrastructure taking our breath away. Tuk-tuks, bicycles, scooters, buses, cars all swirled round, miraculously merging without incident while high above on an orbit of its own, the Skytrain avoided the chaos.

'It's amazing, ' I commented to Tom as we sat in our humid bubble, 'how quiet it is in all this traffic. The people seem so calm, just waiting their turn.'

'That's Buddhism for you,' Tom surmised, as we passed another of the city's many colourful wats.

TOM

My exile in London without Jennifer has been unbearable, so it is awesome being together at last. My patience is being rewarded and I am overjoyed that I am reunited with her. I have no doubts at all, just butterflies from excitement. We have wasted too many years and I yearn for her with my very being. She will be enough.

Bangkok is a long way from the dingy doggedness of Dublin or the grimy grandeur of London. The street markets and food courts are frantic with people of many races and creeds exuding a bustling energy of intoxicating textures, smell and colours.

In this place where Buddhism is a major religion I feel right at home; perhaps this is where I belong. Maybe I am more Thai than I am British. Perhaps the only British thing about me is my accent!

We booked into our hotel, Siam on Siam, made afternoon love and slept till evening, waking up excited and hungry. Outside, the city buzzed with lights and activity. We put our trust in a tuk-tuk driver who roared us out into the traffic and delivered us to a huge night market where the food was laid out in smorgasbord style, with so many choices that it blew the mind. I took Jen by the hand and led her to a stall that had large tanks filled with languid fish and lobster. 'Let me do the ordering,' I said, as she looked on in awe.

I chose a large lobster to be netted and, kicking and protesting, taken to the kitchen to be prepared. We sat in the sultry night air at an outside table watching the world go by, happy to be in each other's company in this exotic place. The meal delivered to us was a taste treat beyond anything I had ever imagined - chilli hot, citrus sour, honey sweet with a salty undertone, the freshest of fresh seafood.

I was in my spiritual home with my love by my side. There we sat, the juices of the lobster running down our chins and through our fingers, eating as if we were starving, relishing every morsel and sucking every leg and claw until there was no meat left, just empty shells. That night we made love the same way.

Next day we flew north to Chiang Mai, in mist-covered mountains near rolling rivers, and from there we travelled to my ancestral village. Could it be, that the evil spirits have been appeased and my world is beginning to look marvellous again?

Mother met us at the bus depot and took us to the family commune, a collection of bamboo houses where the entire clan was there to welcome us warmly. Food kept coming all night, music played, people danced and talked. Everybody was happy. Although many years have passed since I have been to this village, I slotted seamlessly back in. These are my blood relatives who look like me and think like me and embrace me with joy and love. This is where I belong, not in cold drab England.

'Tom, I have never seen you so centred,' Mum said. 'With Jennifer you are calm and living in the moment, not impatient with life.'

She begged me not to let Jen go this time. And I won't.

JENNIFER

I love the gentleness of this country. Yes the people are poor, by our standards, but seem content and happy. Here, I am the different one, red headed and Irish. My fair skin has to be kept out of the sun, I can barely make myself understood, and even though I am not a big person, I am bigger than all the women in the village.

It is blissful to be away from Ireland and all that is happening there. It is thrilling to be anonymous and away from the hell of the past year. In this country, nobody knows me and I can go anywhere and do anything, just another face in the crowd that nobody judges. I am free.

Tom's mother, Leah, and I have connected as if we had known each other all our lives. I recalled that Christmas we first met and how it snowed when we were on our way home from the park and she held her arms out and made noises like an aeroplane as she ran down the hill. My mother would never have done that. Leah seemed so young in comparison.

Leah never knew what had happened between me and Tom all those years ago, but had remained disappointed because she thought we were perfect for each other.

When I explained we came to a road we couldn't go down together, she said that Tom never loved anybody else and has been unsettled since then. She thinks that with me, he is fulfilled.

That night I snuggled next to Tom and went to sleep almost immediately, the sounds of the jungle far away but close enough to hear.

This trip to Thailand is shaping into a spiritually healing journey and I believe I am achieving inner peace in these beautiful mountains. We walk through the hills to another world and pause to sit silently and contemplate, at one with each other. When I speak of Molly's death I recall a dreadful accident but I am not angry any more, I know she is in a better place. The spirits have sent me here to be healed.

At a hilltop temple we offered sacrifice, lit candles, meditated and spoke with the master who freely gave of his time and wisdom. 'You are right leaving a man you no longer respect,' he told me. 'Men and women must have the liberty to separate if they cannot agree with each other.' Then he nodded towards Tom. 'But you and this man?' he continued. 'Do not rush. You two people must deny yourselves until you find inner peace and your children are happy.'

This was not what I wanted to hear. We have denied ourselves for far too long.

WENDY

Golly, New Zealand, hey? It's great to be back, but I am not sure it is my home anymore. All the rellies have welcomed me with open arms, but my dear old Mum is not well. I don't think I will have much time to spend with her.

I sent Jen an email to say I have arrived okay, but of course she is up in the Thai hills somewhere and I have not got a reply. That's either because they have no Wi-Fi or they are too busy screwing their brains out.

So while she is out of contact, I have kept up another important part of our devious plan. Jen gave me the password to her email and I have been replying to the boys as if I am her, saying how much 'she' is enjoying New Zealand, so no one will tumble to our plot. I even sent a reply to Stuart's curt note asking her if she had made it safely.

Of course the boys write to their mother all innocent and love-dovey, telling her how they are getting along just fine and doing their homework and behaving themselves. But Junior sent me a separate email, telling his Aunty Wen the real truth. 'Da is always at work and never comes home until after we go to bed,' he wrote. 'And while the two Grans come and make meals for us they don't hang around for very long 'cos Grandpa Seamus is always grumbling that no one is looking after him and Old Richard has lost his marbles and thinks he is fighting the war all over again. So for most of the time we are home alone. Well, not entirely alone, Aunty Wen … we have a party every night! Girls and boys from school come over and watch videos, play computer games and generally have a really cool time.'

I suspect they are also getting into Stuart's stash of grog. But that's his problem. The selfish prig has obviously made no allowance for the fact the boys' mother is away. No wonder Jennifer felt she had to take Molly to London with her. He would not have coped with a little five-year-old as well as the boys and she would have really suffered.

Next week Junior is going away on camp and Richie is going to his grandparents place. I do worry about him as the poor kid is still so sad about Molly and is very vulnerable at the moment.

TOM

The last ten days have flown past, a mixture of the spiritual, the physical and the emotional. The closer we get to returning home the more morose I become lest our carefully built-up holiday happiness slips from our grasp. I suggested that Jennifer return to London with me, but she replied that that was just not possible.

'It would destroy the family,' she said.

'God almighty, the family has already been destroyed!' I protested. 'By Stuart!'

The tears welled in her eyes.

'Look, Jen,' I continued, calming down, 'I am not asking you to do something you weren't willing to do before Molly's accident. I am not asking you to abandon your boys. Not so long ago you were happy to leave them in Dublin with their father and come with me. So what has changed?'

'Everything has changed,' she sobbed. 'I have lost a daughter; the boys have lost a sister. Now I am frightened that Stuart will harm them if I leave. He hates me but thinks the boys and I belong to him, to do as he pleases. I'm scared, Tom!'

'All right! Then we will go about it the other way. I will come back to Dublin with you and be by your side.'

This shocked her even more.

'That's worse,' she said. 'Stuart will kill you if he gets his hands on you, Da will ostracise us, Mammy will be upset and the media will camp outside the place and write horrible things in the newspapers.'

'Forget everybody else!' I pleaded. 'We can't let them run our lives, Jen. You don't belong to Stuart, he doesn't scare me, your mother has lived the life she wanted and the television and the press will soon get sick of seeing a happy couple going about everyday living. Happiness is not newsworthy. Misery is!'

JENNIFER

To be perfectly honest, the thought of Tom coming back to Dublin fills me with horror. There is no way I can see our relationship working in Ireland. Has he not taken on board anything that the master said to us? That it is better to be patient and wait until the time is right, when old wounds are fully healed?

The old impetuous imp of a Tom is back and, love him as I do and try as I might, there is nothing I can say to convince him that now is not the right time. But he says he is coming home whether I like it or not. I have tried to put him off by pointing out that he doesn't have a ticket from London to Dublin. But he has made a game of it. 'If a ticket is available when we get to Dubai, I'll come and live with you in Dublin,' he says. 'But if they are sold out, then you have to come and live with me in London. Deal?'

As far as I'm concerned neither of the above will happen. I will go to my place and he to his, end of story.

As we set off for Bangkok airport, I was excited but apprehensive, nervous but exhilarated. What are we doing? What will happen to us?

LOVER, HUSBAND, FATHER, MONSTER

Part Six

M A R Y

O n the morning that Jennifer was due home I called around to put some milk and bread in the fridge. There was a loud knock at the door, and because I was the only one there, I answered it, only to be confronted by two members of the Garda. Young they were, wet behind the ears, but their appearance still gave me a fright because I thought something had happened to Junior who was due back from camp that day.

However, they said they wanted to speak to Mr Hoare and take him down to the station. When I explained that Stuart had already left for work long ago, they said they would catch up with him there.

They left without saying anything else. I wonder what it is about?

D E T E C T I V E   B R Y A N   K E L L Y

This has been such a sad, sad investigation and I was looking forward to going to see Mr Hoare, getting his statement, putting the file away and letting all those involved get on with their lives. But my interest was suddenly stirred after a few people came forward and said that they did not think it was an accident; that the man

Stuart Hoare had deliberately flung his child over the bridge.

My initial response to that was one of disbelief. This man is a fine upstanding person, a businessman of considerable merit, a pillar of his church, a leader in his community and although he showed stupidity by putting his little girl in such a dangerous situation, I doubted that there was malice behind his act.

Mr Hoare claims he was merely playing a game called Drop Molly, which they had been doing since she was a baby. I can understand that. We all have fun with our little ones in our own different ways. But, then you have to ask, why was he doing something like that up there? Overhanging a dangerous motorway? When everyone was obviously in a state of emotional turmoil and at one another's throats? There are only two possibilities, either he was being stupid or it was a deliberate act. I need to discount the latter.

I have three people raising doubts about the whole thing, but their veracity worries me. One is convinced she saw 'something odd' and a second says she watched the whole sorry episode from her car while she was doing her knitting. Can you knit and watch at the same time? I am not an expert in the art. The third witness - who was there with her husband - was distracted by the accident they were involved in, so her evidence might not stand up in court, either.

I want to finally close the case and tidy up the paperwork, and so I think it might be best if we bring Mr Hoare in for questioning.

STUART

The two officers did not look much older than Stuart Junior, who still has a good four years of schooling ahead of him, so at first it was difficult to take them seriously. They ambushed me at the business but fortunately as it was just 7.30 in the morning, only Buchanan was with me in the building. The effrontery, coming into my place of work when they have nothing on me! It was absolutely breathtaking and I told them so in no uncertain terms. I have a full day today, no time to waste with these two.

I was surprised because I thought that if the Garda were going to do anything they would have done it weeks ago, straight after Molly died. I had begun to feel confident that it had all died down and gone away. Even then, I always thought that if they did come to see me, it would be at home, on my turf and on my terms, and I could speak to them rationally, man to man, and explain cogently what actually had happened, make them see reason, persuade them that any action against me was completely unnecessary as I am a law abiding citizen.

Now, just when everything is getting back to normal, the business is flying despite all the challenges this country faces, the boys are settling back into school and Jennifer will be back from New Zealand tomorrow, they are asking questions. Damn.

I could see there was no point in refusing to go to the station, so after having a word to Buchanan and filling him in on my diary, I went quietly as I figured it was better to play their game by their rules. I've done nothing wrong. It's that fucking English marriage breaker they should be talking to. Besides, I didn't want the staff coming into work and stumbling across the Garda talking to their boss. It would not be a good look.

When we got to the cop shop the two striplings stood quietly behind me while a rather careworn detective sat me down and started asking me questions about the day of Molly's accident. I seemed to be fielding them rather well and getting my story across until an older, decidedly unpleasant officer, a sergeant, came into the interview room. The mood of formal accord changed considerably. He made some rude comment about 'bastards in fancy clothes and shiny cars in the finance industry who have brought the country to its knees.' I didn't like his sarcasm, but knew I had to mind my manners, keep my head held high and remain calm. He took this the wrong way.

'See, boys,' he said. 'At least with your Limerick bank robber or pickpocket at The Curragh you know who you're dealing with. They know the rules. That sometimes things don't turn out the way they planned and they have to be prepared to cop it. But people like this feller here, they go through life believing that they never have to answer to anyone. That they are above the rest of us.'

This made me bloody angry. It was entirely irrelevant so I stood up and I told him so rather forcibly. 'I demand that I be allowed to go back to work,' I said. He shoved me back down into my chair and started to go on about Molly's accident. 'You deliberately threw her over the feckin' edge,' he screamed. 'Admit it!'

Using the mental reservation technique, I had my story rock-solid and was not going to be bullied by some two bob cop into deviating even though my emotions were inflamed and I was finding it hard to control myself. It was humiliating to be treated like a common criminal and I told him so in no uncertain manner. I explained that I didn't throw Molly over, that it was our game, our special little game, which went haywire when I was distracted.

'Mother of Mercy, your own flesh and blood,' he hissed, moving in closer, his face so close to mine I could smell the morning whiskey on his breath. Not to be intimidated I stood up to demonstrate how we played the game. I spread my legs wide and held my arms out pretending to drop her and then catch her at the last second.

'Jennifer's scream put me off,' I explained. 'Suddenly Molly, she was gone!'

'Like this,' he said, mirroring me, taking on a similar pose. 'Now I get it.'

I relaxed, thinking he was taking on board what I was saying. But then, when I least expected it, he whirled his arms in a complete circle like a helicopter's blade and connected, with a swinging punch to the gut, sending me reeling, winded, stumbling back into my chair.

'Bullshit! Just tell us the truth, sonny,' he screamed, his face hard up against mine again.

I'm afraid I lost it. I forget what I said exactly but through the tears and excruciating pain, I just blurted things out, anything, to get him away from me and stop hurting me. Something about it being all Jennifer's fault, that she set a trap for me when I came home from golf, that she was leaving me for that English drummer and that she nagged me all the way in the car in that bitchy whiny voice of hers until Molly and I couldn't stand it any more. She broke up our home, she screamed at me and she was going to take Molly away from me and I didn't let her. 'If I couldn't have Molly then neither could she!' I gushed, clutching my stomach. 'What happened serves her right! The bitch can meditate on that for the rest of her fucking life!'

DETECTIVE BRYAN KELLY

Unbelievable! I couldn't comprehend what I was hearing. I had come into this interview expecting it to be the final chapter in putting this thing to bed. And it would have been had it not been for the old Sarge who made Hoare so angry that he lost control. Surely a smart businessman like him would have had enough sense to make sure that a lawyer was in the room when he was being questioned. But he didn't! He opened the door into his fractured mind and now I think we have enough to throw the book at him. Perhaps we won't get him for murder but we will get him for something. You can't go playing around with a child's life like that just because your wife chooses to leave you.

I intervened after Sarge whacked him with the skill of a goalkeeper punching the ball downfield at Croke Park. His fist came to rest right into the pit of Hoare's stomach, bending him over in such agony he started to blabber. I didn't want to get done for unprofessional conduct - although I'm sure the O'Brien family would have been mightily pleased if we had fixed him up for good there and then - and so I eased Sarge away from his quarry before he did any more damage.

Right or wrong, you have to admire the old style of policing that we had just witnessed. 'There you go,' said the veteran copper as he wandered off. 'Immobilized, contrite and ready for processing with not a mark on his mealy-mouthed face. All that remains is to complete the paperwork.'

I followed, adding one piece of advice to our stricken man. 'You are going to need a lawyer, Mr Hoare.'

JENNIFER

We got to Dubai and had a couple of hours to fill. I was whiling away my time in the duty free section when my cell phone rang and my world was turned upside down in an instant. It was from the Garda at Blackrock telling me that they had Stuart at the station and that he was to appear before a magistrate at half-four in the afternoon to be charged with Molly's murder.

Murder? Murder! This was an enormous shock. Gut-wrenching. Soul-destroying! I know the dark side of Stuart only too well, I have felt the sting of his hand across my face many times, but I have always genuinely believed that what happened to Molly was an accident. A foolish unforgivable lapse of judgement, but nevertheless an accident.

Only a couple of nights ago, in the heat of northern Thailand, Tom woke screaming and drenched in sweat, coming out of a horrible nightmare. In it Stuart was throwing little children off the flyover bridge and Tom was down the bottom running back and forth, trying to catch them, but they kept slipping through his outstretched hands and every time he glimpsed a face, it was Molly's. When he awoke he was sobbing uncontrollably and after he calmed down, we actually canvassed the possibility that Stuart may have killed Molly deliberately. I discounted it as highly improbable because I honestly didn't believe that Stuart could do that to his own beautiful daughter! And now it seems that he may have.

Tom reappeared from behind the French perfume counter and looked quizzically at me.

'What's the matter?' he said anxiously. 'Jen, you've turned all pale.'

'It's Stuart. The police have charged him with Molly's murder.'

'Murder? Fucking hell.' He began looking around, his eyes settling on the customer service desk nearby.

'Well, that settles it,' he said, moving off. 'I'm going to get that ticket and I'm coming back to Ireland with you, no matter what.'

STUART

There was nowhere to sit but the cold concrete bench in the dank cell. The pain still seared through my solar plexus, like a knife had been driven into it. All sense had been knocked out of me. I had heard stories of police brutality on current affairs shows but I never thought that I'd be a victim. I resolved to report the matter to the ombudsman as soon as I got out of there. 'My God,' I thought, 'that was no calm, explanatory encounter in the leafy, seaside surroundings of Dalkey. I am now in a very dangerous scenario.'

Funny, though, how one's mind works. Even in my own moment of agony, I wondered if the king hit I had laid on that disgusting little Tommy character up on the flyover had hurt as much. I certainly hoped so!

The afternoon light was starting to dim when four officers came to escort me to court, where the formal indictment was solemnly read. Mercifully the session was brief, lasting not much longer than three or four minutes but I was so disoriented and humiliated that it all washed over me and I can't remember a word of it. This was my first time in front of a judge, or in any court for that matter, so I sat mesmerized as the charges were read and my counsel requested bail.

Instead of immediately making a decision on that, the judge declared he would need time to determine what risk I might be to my family and to society in general. And that he would carefully consider all submissions and announce his decision after the weekend.

Monday? How ridiculous! I need to be at Sunday service because it is my turn to read the lesson; the boys need me to drive them to their sport; Jennifer is coming home from her sabbatical. I need bail now, not then.

Handcuffed and wedged between two burly Garda, I was pushed and shoved along with two petty thieves towards a waiting van, where after a short drive we were delivered to the remand centre in Cloverhill prison.

I caught a glimpse of myself as we approached the automatic glass doors that swung open before us. My bespoke suit was looking decidedly bespooked, shirt tails hanging below the jacket and my tie askew, my shiny loafers dirty and dusty, and my hair in disarray. Was the person in the reflection really me?

'This is totally humiliating,' I thought. 'How quickly we descend to the low standards of those with whom we mix.' I determined I would use the washroom at the first opportunity to tidy myself up. But that was not going to happen. Instead they took my phone, my belt, my tie and my shoelaces, leaving me with no money or a pencil to write with or even a book to read. 'What will people think?' I mused as the camera took my mug shot and I looked around, 'I am not one of them!'

I soon learned I had been flung into an alien world of seedy characters ready to bum a cigarette, offer advice, ask anxiously for any tit-bit of information regarding their case, enjoy a simple chat or offer the inevitable opening gambit, 'What are you in here for, mate?' I didn't really want to answer. Even though I felt scruffy, my tailored suit, silk shirt and Italian leather loafers stood out amongst the tracksuit pants, hoodies and bomber jackets.

The younger ones were surprised to see me in their midst, wondering how a fellow of my calibre could possibly have fallen so low, dreaming that one day they will be wealthy enough to dress like I do. A snigger and a sly smile creased the lips of the more world-weary incumbents, experienced lags who eyed me off knowingly. They made snide comments, referring to me as a stooge, questioning my manhood, doubting my ability to do time and laughing at my vulnerability. It took me back to boarding school, an extremely uncomfortable place, but at least I had learned things there that put me in good stead for this place. I flashed a sort of know-it-all grin designed to show that I appreciated their black humour but was in no mood to become engaged.

I was careful not to give eye contact and when I spotted a space on a bench in the far corner I headed for it, moving through the crowd and sitting unobtrusively, making myself as small and insignificant as possible. My fellow prisoners soon tired of taunting and returned to their conversation or continued to stare at the blank walls.

But one bloke came over, as he was to face the same judge as I had faced earlier and he enquired as to his mood. When I answered that he was 'sombre', he looked bemused, considering carefully what a 'sombre' judge might do to a man who had nicked his neighbour's ride-on lawn mower.

'Why are you here?' he then asked.

As I considered my answer, another fellow lurking nearby and eyeing me off suddenly screamed for all and sundry to hear. 'That's the bastard who threw his kid onto the motorway!' he yelled. 'I thought it was you. I saw you coming into court as they led me away. Fellers, this prick killed his own daughter!'

He rushed towards me, gesticulating and shouting obscenities, and before long others surged forward

138

enjoying the divergence from the monotony, baying for blood. Helplessly I held my arms up over my head to protect myself, only to feel my jacket and shirt being ripped from my back. I turned to face my accusers and kicked up my legs in an effective judo move that kept some of them at bay. But I knew I couldn't hold them off for long. There was too many of them and they were having too good a time.

My skin was saved by the almighty blast of a whistle. A rescuer grabbed me by the arm, pulled me away from the milling crowd, and got me out into the corridor. Flinging me in to the safe haven of a small empty cell, he threw me a blanket and clanged the door shut. 'If I had my way, I'd have left you in there to be torn apart,' he said. 'Because that's all pricks like you deserve, so you can thank me for getting you out of there. Now cover yourself up until we get you a shirt.'

FINBAR MCMAHON

I had heard about Stuart Hoare around the traps. He is not the biggest developer in town by any means, but he is up there or thereabouts. Like many others, he had taken a big financial hit during the GFC but because he was not solely into property, having an insurance company and other avenues, he had clawed his way back. If you ask me it is fellows like him that caused the whole shemozzle and took us all down.

Mr Hoare was surprised when I walked into the freezing interview room. I don't think he had ever met a criminal lawyer before in his life - certainly not a relatively young one like me with minimal court experience. I had specialised in intellectual property up until then but had to rethink my career when the big players pulled out of Ireland.

When the phone call had come through to chambers, we were all in a festive mood as the staff Christmas party was about to begin. Nobody else wanted the job but I instinctively felt that this could turn into a high-profile case and might be very good for my career. So I took the punt and accepted the brief from the clerk who was waving it around offering, 'Anyone? Anyone?' He wanted to begin celebrations and so did everyone else.

I was over at the court in a matter of minutes as the bail hearing was due almost immediately. Apparently the defendant had not considered getting a lawyer, believing he could manage it himself. The classic mistake made by all first-timers. We got off to rocky start when I said the charge sheet mentioned the word 'charges' with an 's'.

'What do you mean charges?' my new defendant demanded. 'I am only aware of one charge and that is a complete fabrication. I did not murder my daughter!'

'There is also the matter of common assault of a Mr Thomas Knight, professional musician, of London,' I said, reading from the document.

Hoare became quite racist and abusive calling Knight 'a little half-Asian drummer boy' and remarking that he didn't actually assault him, he simply gave him something he thoroughly deserved!

'I was the cuckolded husband, claiming my territory back and giving my wife's lover one to go on with,' he said indignantly. 'Just to let him know that he has no right to steal her! That's not assault. That's a man's right, his privilege. It would have been remiss of me not to have clouted him.'

I pointed out that for quite some time the hospital staff had feared for Mr Knight's life and had him in an induced coma for days and that it took him many weeks to recover. This only escalated things into an even more violent and abusive rant, lamenting that 'the little prick is the main fucking problem.'

'He is the one who should have the book thrown at him,' Mr Hoare yelled. 'I should have completed the job and finished him off. He seduced my wife, wrecked my family, made himself out to be some sort of hero for the kids and set in place the series of events that has led me here!'

He stood up in a threatening manner, leaning into me, repeatedly banging his fists on the table. What a vile tempered man. The first thing we need to do is to coach him to control that temper of his. If a jury sees that on full display, they'll send him down for sure.

We finally headed into court and he was remanded until Monday when bail will be determined. It will do him good to have a taste of what is to come if he doesn't make himself nicer. I returned to the party, which was by then in full swing.

MOIRA

It was early evening when I heard about Stuart on the news. You would have thought those O'Briens would have warned me, as hearing it that way was a huge shock. They say he is being charged with killing our Molly on purpose. We are all staggered; I think the whole of Dublin is shocked. Nobody can believe it.

As soon as I heard, I got on the telephone to arrange a minder for my Richard for tomorrow afternoon. I will catch the bus in to Cloverhill and find out from Stuart what it is all about. I am sure there has been some dreadful mistake.

JENNIFER

I'd forgotten how awful the media circus is! We flew in from Dubai and almost as soon as we touched down were confronted by cameras, microphones and flashing lights. Kevin met us and used his bulk to shield me from the mob and his tongue to give them a verbal lashing, but left poor Tom to cop it sweet, like a lamb to slaughter. I tried to stay near him but we got separated in the mêlée and he found it very hard to keep up with us as we made our way to the car park.

Although I appreciate Kevin's support, I do wish he would be mindful of his language as the way he abuses the press doesn't do any good and only makes the O'Brien family look like a pack of hillbillies.

Eventually we got home to Dalkey where Mam, Da and Patrick were waiting. It was grand to see them as I really miss my family when I am away. Mam had hot vegetable soup on the hob and she'd made some of her delicious soda bread to go with it. It made me cringe when Kevin rudely pointed to Tom and said, 'What are you doing here?' I interrupted and said that he was here because I needed him here and for Kev to keep his nose out of my business and to speak civilly.

Then the entrepreneur and merchandiser in Da came to the fore. He took one look at my floral shoulder bag and at Tom's colourful silk shirt, put two and two together, and exploded in anger. 'You haven't been in New Zealand,' he yelled. 'You lied! You've been in Thailand together.'

'Da, I needed to get away, and Stuart wouldn't have let me go if ...'

He waved me away and moved towards Tom. 'Bloody marriage breaker!' he thundered at him. 'You're one of those types that causes trouble wherever you go.'

Mam stepped in and calmed him down but he was joined by Kevin in castigating us for tricking everybody with 'some elaborate fucking scheme to sneak off to Asia just so you can go and shag each other senseless.' Poor Tom. I bet he wished he had got off the plane in London.

After their rants the pair of them totally ignored Tom from then onwards. Paddy is sweet and tried to calm the waters but Kevin and Da are on the same side when it comes to Tom. They still see him as the initial cause of everything.

During the afternoon Finbar McMahon, Stuart's lawyer, turned up, mainly to see if we would contribute to Stuart's bail money! He was sporting a navy blue suit that had two-for-the-price-of-one written all over it, most unimpressive and down market. I wondered where Stuart had found him. Probably a contra deal or a job at mates rates. So typical. We made it quite clear that there was no way any member of the O'Brien family would give a cent to the 'get Stuart out of jail' cause.

The boys came in from school, it was so good to see them and to begin with, it was hugs and tears all round. They are very confused about the whole scenario and had copped a teasing at school. Children can be cruel and some pounce on any opportunity to make themselves feel superior.

Then Junior turned dreadful. Standing squarely in front of Tom and as rudely as you like, he asked him if he was here 'to fuck my mother.' Turning back to me he added, 'I don't want him here. He killed our sister.'

My heart sank, I felt sick in the stomach. He is taller than me now and has learnt the art of intimidation from his father. But I stood my ground and looked directly at him. 'That is a wicked thing to say,' I said. 'Tom had nothing to do with it. Apologize at once please, Junior.'

'He did so too,' Richie piped in, supporting his brother. 'Da said if he didn't try to take Molly away to London, then Molly wouldn't have been on that bridge to fall over the side. So there!'

'She didn't fall,' I muttered. 'She was pushed!'

'Well, he can't come to live here. This is our house. He didn't pay for it. Da did!' Junior spat it out with all the venom of a teenage rebel. He was not going to back down.

'Tom is here whether you like it or not,' I said, blushing with embarrassment at the behaviour of my sons.

Junior turned to me. 'If he stays, I go.'

I was so angry, I told him to go. 'Get out!' I screamed. 'Go on! And don't come back until you learn a few manners.'

He went straight up to his room, grabbed his footy gear and stormed out, right into the media melee that had followed us all the way from the airport and was now camped outside the front gate. Not for him the decision to ignore them. He'd been thrown out of home, he declared, and had to go and live with his grandmother because that 'mother fucker' from England was here. They loved it and it was all over the news for the next bulletin. What a disaster.

Richie sat next to me and stroked my hand and at least had the manners to make polite conversation with Tom. He has missed me, poor darling.

TOM

It was heavy stuff, with Junior all over the news bulletins.

Perhaps I was wrong to insist I come back with Jen. One minute we were enjoying the tranquillity of a far-off

144

Asian land and the next we were being hassled by a mad media mob in Dublin. I had no idea that it was so crazy here. But I'm here now and I'm not going anywhere until we sort this out and we know where we stand with each other.

I feel really sorry for Jen and all she is going through, and I'm not going to make her choose between the boys and me. But she walked out of my life once before and now we have found each other, I am damned if I am going to let her go again just because her son is a rude little prick. 'We are a couple,' I said, 'and we need to support each other.' I will stay with her until all is resolved. The good thing is that Stuart can't do me any harm while he is in jail.

Kevin was there at the airport to meet us, more than a little annoyed when he saw me, quite rude really, feeding me to the sharks. But I was not the only recipient of his ire; he wasn't happy with gentlemen of the media either. He lost his temper and grabbed somebody's camera, nearly shoving it in the photographer's face, and his language was pretty rough.

After a fair bit of jostling we made it home where Mary, Seamus and Patrick were waiting. Mary is lovely but those other two are positively hostile. The old boy spat something out about me being the cause of all the family's troubles. The O'Briens don't like me at all, but then they didn't like Stuart either so perhaps they don't like anybody who isn't an O'Brien.

The lawyer came in, Wendy arrived, the family left and then the boys came from school very happy to see their mother home, but not so thrilled to see me. Junior has learnt his manners from Uncle Kevin but Richie was sweet and asked me about my music and what we had been doing.

Stuart's lawyer came seeking alms; had the gall to imagine that the family might put up bail to get Stuart out of jail until his trial starts. Not likely! They didn't leave him wondering, either. They gave it to him straight.

After everybody left and the boys were in bed, Jen and I canvassed the notion of whether Stuart deliberately threw Molly to her death. Jen is still firmly in denial. She can't believe that Stuart would ever do such a thing to Molly. I'm of the opposite opinion mainly because of my recurring dream where the bastard tosses kids over the bridge like rugby passes. Perhaps I did see him do it?

JUNIOR

Mammy is home and that's really cool. Da is in the fuckin' slammer and that fuckin' sucks. I hate it when Tom comes to stay at our place. He thinks he's cool but he's really just an old dude. When I came home from school he was sitting at the breakfast bar as if he owned the fuckin' place. He has this really annoying habit of drumming with his fingers on the table when he is supposed to be listening and paying attention. Mammy goes all gooey when he's around; it sort of makes me spew.

If it weren't for him Molly wouldn't have been on the bridge that day when she fell over. I'm glad Da hit him. He fuckin' deserved it. Tom doesn't care about us. He just wants to sleep with my mother. I refuse to talk to him, so I left them and went and kicked the ball with the lads down the park, hoping he wouldn't still be there when I got back. He was!

RICHIE

I hate what is happening to my family, but I'm glad Mam is back from her holiday. I asked her what Tom was

146

doing here and she got into her lecture mode and told me that he is here because she asked him to come and she needs him to be with her because he makes her happy and she is going through a stressful time at the moment.

She said she was the grown up one and she will make the decisions about who comes to our house and who doesn't. 'When you grow up, Richie,' she said, 'you can be in charge of your own home.'

Just because she says it, doesn't mean I have to like it. So there!

Junior is always bagging Tommy but I think that sometimes he can be cool, although I would never say that to Junior. He hates him and doesn't want him here.

MOIRA

It was a cold damp day and when I got there they directed me to sit and wait for Stuart at a stainless steel table in a sparse interview room that was even colder than it was outside.

When he finally entered, my poor boy didn't know where to look or what to do. The first thing I noticed was the handcuffs that they insisted he wear whenever he left his cell. So humiliating! I find it hard to believe that they would shackle a responsible, upright citizen like Stuart.

At first he gave that lovely little half smile he gives when he is pleased with something but does not want to be seen to be over-enthusiastic. But then he noticed how sad and confused I was and his bottom lip trembled and a tear came to his eyes. He was doing his best to be strong and controlled in order to convince me that this is a farce and that he has done nothing wrong. It was as much as I could bear and I shed a tear in sympathy but forced myself to be bright and upbeat for his sake so I quickly pulled myself together.

Stuart told me that he understood his situation, but I don't know that he is fully cognisant of the crime they say he has committed. Of course I don't believe that Stu would ever do a thing like that, but mud sticks, so I looked him in the eye and asked him straight out. 'Did you deliberately throw our Molly over that bridge?'

'Ma, Ma! I didn't *throw* her,' he spluttered. 'It was all a mistake. It was Jennifer. Everything that bitch did that day made me do it. That's the truth. The honest-to-God truth, for fuck's sake.'

'Language, please, Stuart …' He knows I hate that word. And putting it in the same sentence as God, well, that was just too much!

'Sorry, Ma. But I didn't do it deliberately! I was calm. I knew what I was doing. Don't you understand?'

He stood up and banged the table with both hands, the sound of the cuffs on the steel resounding through the interview room. One of the guards moved forward to restrain him.

'Look at you! Just take a look at yourself, Stuart,' I said. 'Pull yourself together. This behaviour will get you nowhere.'

That seemed to snap him back into reality. He glanced down at the handcuffs, looked around at the room, rocked back and forward on his heels for a moment and sat down. For a moment I witnessed something in Stuart that has been there since childhood. If he is to get through this, he must learn to control that temper of his.

STUART

When the Garda first brought me in for questioning it never occurred to me that I might need a lawyer. Surely they would understand who I was, where I came from and what I stood for, and that I had no case to answer. But after just a few hours of total hell in the remand centre I determined I was not going to spend Christmas with that pack of dangerous bastards.

On a cold dank Dublin afternoon in December, legal eagles were rather thin on the ground and when I phoned the nearest chambers and explained my plight I could hear from the background noise that the Christmas party had begun and they were not really all that keen to hear me out. It was only after much begging and pleading that a junior counsel was dispatched to attend to my case.

Our association may not have begun well, but when it came to stepping up to the mark, Finbar McMahon belied his status as a lowly, underpaid new boy to the firm, presenting a sublimely eloquent, exquisitely researched and beautifully compelling proposition that I be granted bail.

He argued it would be several months before a case for the defence could be prepared and as I was yet to be proven guilty of anything, and I came from a good military family, was an upstanding citizen without the slightest stain on my character, a pillar of my local church and a well educated business man with an impeccably clean record of running my business with a high standard of professionalism, it was most unlikely that I would reoffend or pose any danger to the public at large.

The public prosecutor opposed bail, stating that I was up on the most serious of charges and therefore a potential danger to society. 'It would be foolhardy to consider letting a person of such obvious irrational tendencies go free while the case was being prepared,' he pleaded. Well, it's his job to put the opposite view so I took no offence.

Fortunately the magistrate came down on Finbar's side and bail was set with the restrictions that I have to surrender my passport, observe an evening curfew of 10 pm and not make contact with Jennifer or the boys unless duly authorized and under official scrutiny. I was also warned not to communicate with any witnesses. But the worst part is that I cannot live at home. It was directed that instead I must reside with my parents. That stinks. Dalkey is my home and I should be there for Christmas.

Nevertheless, at least I will be free. Then the amount of bail was set. Two hundred grand! That took the wind out of my sails. It will take some time to raise that amount and in the meantime I am stuck in this hellhole.

Mother came and 'tut-tutted' all over the shop. It was so humiliating for us both as neither of us could have imagined me in jail, even in our wildest dreams. Fortunately Father is non-compos and thinks I'm on holiday. Some vacation this is!

Our Rector and leader of the flock at Dalkey, the Reverend Iain Brown, took the time to call and see me, and that soothed me. I was embarrassed for him to see me in this place, but he is a man of sublime intellect and pastoral compassion, who has been my friend for many years so he listened carefully to what I said, nodding sagely and showed all the compassion of Jesus. His coming took a lot of the sting out of my situation and no doubt made the warders sit up and take notice.

We prayed together for God's guidance and he told me that the congregation said prayers for me at both Sunday services. I am confused about that, as I don't really want my situation common knowledge around Dalkey. However, I was comforted by his soothing non-judgmental tone, telling me that he felt confident that I was entirely innocent and it is all a horrible mistake. 'You are the rock of Saint Patrick's and a man of extremely high calibre,' he said.

I found his fulsome praise a little embarrassing, but he blessed me, telling me to trust in God and left, having given me affirmation, credibility and confidence.

His visit led me to recognise that my religion, which has been an all-important rudder to me throughout my life, is being tested by this horrible saga. The ultimate challenge is to hold my head high and let this thing pass.

I don't blame the Garda who are the upholders of the law and simply doing their job. For that I praise them and it was noticeable that I received better treatment after Iain came to see me.

REVEREND IAIN BROWN

When I arrived to take up my post in Dalkey, Stuart Hoare was one of the first people to come to me and offer his services and he has been a loyal and hardworking servant of the Lord ever since. I would go as far as to say that he is been my right hand man, my greatest support in my work. It was very sad when the family buried their youngest child and I must say that I admired the way they handled it, particularly Stuart who reined in his grief to stoically play the organ for the ceremony. My heart bled for him; it was so difficult.

Therefore, in this situation it is my duty as a friend and fellow foot soldier of Jesus to actively show him my support and loyalty. 'I take him for his word and absolutely give the man the benefit of the doubt,' I said to my wife when I got home. 'If Stuart says he didn't drop Molly on purpose then I believe him.'

In a more selfish vein I do hope they resolve this issue before Christmas because I am relying on Stuart for all the music that makes the season so special in our congregation. Even this weekend much of what he does without fuss has fallen back on me. I spent three hours on Friday evening erecting the Christmas crib. Stuart usually does that.

JENNIFER

A huge body of evidence must be accumulated in order to make the case against a person, so I found it unbelievable that they had enough to charge Stuart. 'I thought that he loved Molly,' I said to Ma. 'That he wouldn't do anything to hurt her.'

I know he has a terrible temper and I know he hates me, but since Molly's accident he has virtually left me alone and been almost kind to me. Well, by his standards, anyway. We managed to get through the funeral with little or no acrimony, and we have shared the same house albeit not the same bed. And when I left for overseas he willingly took over the care of the boys, although I would rate his performance as a carer at about a three out of ten.

But yesterday the investigators took me back to the scene to re-enact the situation and I began to doubt Stuart for the first time. I realize now that for Molly to fall the way she did, she would have had to have been held up and out over the motorway. There must be some other explanation; surely he wouldn't do that!

Part Seven

STUART

When the magistrate intoned, 'Bail is set at 200,000 euro,' my heart sank. It is an astonishing amount to find in these straitened economic times, and I'm certain that he set it at that because he reckoned I would find it impossible to cover.

He was not counting on my dear old mother! I am her only child and she was not going to let a mere couple of hundred grand get in the way of the freedom of her 'beautiful little boy', as she embarrassingly still calls me. Without blinking she went down to the bank and re-mortgaged the family home - a two bedroomed semi on the north-western outskirts of Dublin - to the absolute hilt.

'Why can't I do this to bail my son out?' she said to the incredulous Bank Of Ireland branch manager. 'When you lot drove this bank into the ground, the government bailed you out, didn't it ..?'

He drew up the documents without another word.

She laid out the papers and the cheque for ninety thousand euro in front of me with a little smile, pleased with her efforts and telling me not to mention it to Father. 'Imagine that. A mere woman running your father's financial affairs! He'd blow up in a red rage if he only knew.'

Ninety thousand was good but we were still less than half way there.

Where to go for that? Well, I can recount that never, ever have I been so glad to see the bright blue eyes of my good friend and business partner, Buchanan, staring at me across the remand centre table the very next day. He and I have always made an excellent team, with me supplying the vision and management to get a project up and running and him providing the muscle and vigour to get it across the line. I calmly broker away, while he vigorously 'busts their balls', as he likes to put it.

'Stuart,' he said haltingly, 'I can't for the life of me fathom what you did up there on that motorway and why you did it, and I don't think anyone on the whole feckin' planet can. Any other man would probably refuse to come and see you, much less go out of his way to help you. But you and I, we've been through a lot of things in our time, if you know what I mean …'

I knew what he meant. Over the years, I have accumulated plenty of Brownie points by pulling him back from the brink of devastation by creating an alibi, falsifying a diary or conjuring a ghostly appointment to cover for his playboy ways and keeping him and Aisling out of the divorce court. One thing about him is he is loyal.

In a good business there is not much lazy money hanging around as every penny is accounted for but Buchanan always made sure we had sixty grand or so fortuitously hidden away in case of emergency. But that left another fifty to find.

'Easy,' he said, dropping several neat envelopes on the table. 'They love you down at that parish of yours.

When I mentioned our challenge to the Rector, he quietly scribbled down some very heavyweight names on a sheet of paper, and bingo, all I had to do was knock on doors, explain the story and they came good with the readies. Businessmen mainly, a couple of MPs and a very, very, heavy heavyweight in the Masons. They trust you not to skip bail.'

Buchanan lodged the cash, McMahon finalised formalities, and we walked down the corridor and through the double doors and out into the real world again. And there they were. Cameras pointing, notebooks raised, the media immediately zeroed in on me, a noisy, swirling throng of photographers, TV cameras, reporters and commentators with microphones, anxious to get their juicy scoop or go live to air with any salacious angle to entertain their gullible readers and viewers. Christmas is almost here and they need something to fill the void in the holiday season.

A further posse of public revenge seekers declared their distaste for me by chanting and wielding signs that said things like 'Letterkenny Mothers for Abused Children' and 'Children are people' and 'Your kids are not possessions'. One of these, a woman with a red scarf and glasses to match, took on the line of guards, breaking through and getting close enough to whack me over the head with her sign before being restrained and hurled back into the throng. I'm willing to bet that they deliberately allowed her free passage.

Fancy me thinking that we could keep this episode quiet! It was like trying to negotiate through a pitch invasion after a Tipperary hurling final. McMahon stoically led me to his battered Peugeot, opened the door, told me to get in the back, lie down and put my coat over my head. I point blank refused and jumped into the passenger seat next to him, facing my enemy head on.

The noise and banging on the panels subsided as we took off up Cloverhill Road and home to Mother's place. The Christmas lights twinkling brightly in happy windows reminded me that Friday would be Christmas Day. But the headline on a newspaper poster outside a shop brought me back to reality. Below a big picture of me was the simple expression, 'Why?'

'Welcome to your new world,' said McMahon.

JENNIFER

Stuart has gone to his parents' and disappeared out of the house and out of my consciousness. At least Tom can stay with me. He is here by my side and is patiently navigating his way through difficult circumstances. I can't allow myself to think about Stuart as I become consumed with anxiety and hate, giving him space in my head that he does not deserve. Most nights I toss and turn, allowing many variations of 'what if' and 'if only' outcomes to swirl endlessly around in my head. I get up and make a cup of tea and talk to Molly. I keep a journal and perhaps one day I might write a book.

My family has rallied, overcome their disapproval of my dear Tom, and started to become supportive once more. Patrick is back living with Ma and Da. That's a turn up as I thought he would never leave Galway but he has had some sort of a breakdown and needs a place to stay before he resettles in Dublin. Christmas is next week and we are having it at the family home in Blackrock. I can't do it this year. It is beyond me.

My biggest challenge is that Stuart is trying for access to the boys. I am filling in forms and getting orders in place to keep him away, and it is taking a lot of time and effort.

Yes, he is their father, but as it continues to dawn on me that Molly's death may not be an accident, I am opposing him. 'I must make sure that I protect my boys,' I said to Ma. 'I can't risk him hurting them. I know it's harsh but he is not coming near them until his name is cleared. They have been through a lot and are really vulnerable.'

ORLA WHITE

I raised my hand for the Hoare access case when it came to the table as I feel I know something of the family dynamic. Mrs Hoare opposed access to the other children, but Mr Hoare insisted on taking the case to court and it was granted with him being allowed fortnightly, supervised visitation rights to his two lads.

Mrs Hoare Senior will pick them up from their home, take them to church and then to her place for a Sunday roast with their father, returning them to their mother at 4 pm. The judge has also granted a Christmas Day visit as the grandfather is not well and may not see another. 'I have no intention of supervising that event,' I said to my superior. In this game we all know how the supposed happy Yuletide family day can blow out into the worst of scenarios.

In court Mr Hoare looked very cool and handsome in quality clothes, repeating to the judge that he hadn't meant to drop Molly that day. He is a fine cut of a man.

JENNIFER

Damn it. I spent all week getting my case prepared and so I was not happy when the judge granted access. It is limited and with provisions but nevertheless it means

Stuart is allowed to see the boys and poison them with his strange view on life and on me. I have spoken to the lads and they seem happy enough to take part in this ritual.

I am pleased that Stuart is not to be left alone with them. The social worker will be there so that sets my mind at rest.

MOIRA

In a strange way I am looking forward to having Stuart home for Christmas. I cleaned all the ironing paraphernalia out of the spare room and made up his old bed for him and I have stocked the fridge with all of his favourite foods, including plenty of tomato ketchup and baked beans. I want him to be comfortable here.

It will be just like old times except that poor Richard is not quite sure whether he is coming or going. Every now and then he clicks back into our vibe and makes sense of the situation. Perhaps now that Stuart is here he will see what goes on with his father and me and realize how difficult it is and how I really do need help and support from him. He is always so busy.

I have presents for our boys and I am hoping that Jennifer will see the way clear to allowing them to spend some time with us as it may be Richard's last Christmas.

STUART

While I have been extricated from one prison, I have discovered after a few days that to all intents and purposes I have been re-located to another, albeit with invisible bars. I am back at home again, like a teenager, going through the same rituals of meals, conversation, getting my clothes washed and being quizzed on whether I have had a nice night's sleep, am enjoying my breakfast porridge and have cleaned my teeth.

'To make matters worse,' I told Buchanan, 'Dad wanders around the house regularly asking mum who is that "strange sandy-haired chap who has set up camp in the spare bedroom?"

'Occasionally it dawns on him that I am his son, and so then he asks how my night-school studies are going, an image from thirty years ago. It is driving me nuts.'

I have been set a curfew hour of 10 pm and the media have secured the address and set up operations in the street outside, to make sure I stick to it. There they are, cameras poised to catch any compromising shot, tape recorders at the ready to snare any exclusive quote. This temporary press village varies in size from day to day, depending on what else is in the headlines, and occasionally, at the request of the neighbours, the Garda drift by in a car to shift them. These interventions usually end up in a happy chat, a coffee and a cigarette before a couple of cars are moved into different locations and the officers drive off and normal transmission is resumed.

Getting in and out of the house is not an experience I wish to endure very often but I have to exit in order to work and to report to the local Garda station three times a week, as part of the conditions of my bail. It is all very trying.

My access application has been successful and I am going to be allowed to visit my boys once a fortnight - but only if I am accompanied by a social worker. That's ridiculous. I am not one of those welfare losers, so I don't know why some hired hand will be needed to monitor our personal get-togethers. 'It is an affront to me and a complete and unnecessary drain on the public purse,' I told Buchanan.

However, given that I have to have an overseer, I am glad it is that woman Orla who was at the hospital the day we turned off Molly's machine and who has called in once or twice to make sure everything is okay. We have enjoyed a few meals together out on the town and I feel comfortable with her so I have agreed to the terms.

MARY

When Seamus asked me to drive him around to Moira and Richard's, I agreed, thinking that he was going to discuss things civilly with Stuart.

I can't even contemplate that Stuart is guilty and I thought that if the two men sat down and chewed the fat together they might reach a truce. After all, Seamus is on Stuart's side regarding the problems in the marriage; he believes that Jennifer is entirely in the wrong and shouldn't have gone off and had an affair.

STUART

I had only been home a few days when I answered a knock at the door to find Seamus O'Brien, my father-in-law and the grandfather of my children, standing uneasily at the entrance.

We have never liked each other. From the day we first met the devil-may-care Catholic Kerry entrepreneur and the conservative Protestant Dublin businessman were never going to get on. He tolerated me through gritted teeth as I became part of the family and our married life unfolded. For my part, I avoided him whenever possible. As soon as he opened his mouth, I realized that nothing had changed.

'You feckin' bastard,' he shouted. 'You came into our family with the sole feckin' intention of wrecking it, and now you have, and I rue the day you turned up.'

'Shhhh! Shhh, Seamus!' I said, taken aback and frightened that the neighbours would hear.

160

'Don't feckin' shoosh me,' he roared. 'I never understood what Jennifer saw in you! You were the last resort!'

'Seamus!'

'She was afraid of being left on the shelf and you were the only excuse of a man available. The worst feckin' decision she ever made, and believe me, that's saying something!'

Red from the neck up from anger and exasperation, he hustled toward me, a caricature of a man. I stood my ground and when he went to throw a punch, I simply grabbed his hand. It was ridiculously easy to stop him.

'Don't Seamus! Please stop it, Seamus!' Poor Mary, her cheeks wet with tears, appeared behind him. 'Things are difficult enough without you getting involved.'

His cheeks were florid, there was spittle coming from his mouth and his eyes were popping. 'It's all about you, Stuart, isn't it? It's always all about you.'

I calmly stood and watched with disdain as he begrudgingly backed away and she took him off the property and sat him in the front passenger seat of the car. How has the woman put up with this rogue for all those years? She is an absolute saint.

But before she went around to the driver's side, her face hardened and she came back to me and hissed, 'You're a wicked man Stuart Hoare! You have ruined my family. I hope you burn in hell for all eternity!'

Perhaps she is not such a saint after all?

'Who was that, dear?' Mother called from the kitchen where she was tending the roast pork.

'Nobody Mam. Just one of those nutters with not enough to do and all day to do it,' I replied as I shut the front door, breathed deeply and returned to the front room where I had been reading the financial pages.

WENDY

Guess who's back in town? I sneaked in quietly last night. Mum finally succumbed to illness and old age, and it was a sad day when we buried her. But at least she lived out a full life. Not like little Molly. Or, for that matter, Jen, whose life seems to be snap-frozen in time due to her grief.

Personally, I am glad to be out of New Zealand and back to my Dublin home and business, but all I sense from the media and everything is sadness and anger. Don't think I will put my head above the trench just yet.

JUNIOR

Mam said that we were fuckin' cancelling Christmas this year but that she is giving Richie and me a hundred euro each to spend in the gaming section of Littlewoods online. I can't decide between Battlefield 2 and Titanfall. I'm trying to persuade Richie to buy one of them so we can have both, but he wants to buy some lame fuckin' music production program for his Nintendo.

We are going to wait until after Boxing Day to spend our money so that we can take advantage of the sales. Da won't be at Christmas dinner but that fuckin' bastard of a Tom will be. He's not my father and I'm not going to be nice to him. I hope he rots in hell after what he has done to our family. Fuckin' prick!

MARY

The whole family came down to Dublin this year for Christmas, as Seamus is not really well enough to make the trip to Kerry. The girls each brought something for the table so it was not too much work for me, and the boys organized a keg out in the garage. We had a grand feast laid out.

It is very sad without Molly and we all feel it. She was at the forefront of our minds. But nobody broached the subject of Stuart, as there's not much love for him in this family. 'He isn't here but he is certainly the elephant in the room,' I whispered to Kevin.

'Even if he was the size of an elephant, I'd still knock his feckin' head off,' replied Kevin.

It was very awkward having Tom come along with Jen and although everybody was polite, nobody embraced him or made an effort to make him feel at home. I felt quite sorry for the poor fellow. This can be a hard house to play at the best of times, much less in this situation.

When he tried to get a bit of African drumming going using the kitchen equipment, the adult response was lukewarm and uncooperative. However the kids got right into it and eventually the grown ups had to grudgingly agree that it was fun.

He left with Jen and the boys at three o'clock when they had to go to see their father. She was more than a little apprehensive but told me later she spoke to Moira and mercifully Stuart kept out of her way.

We all partied on into the wee hours. The day took a lot out of Seamus. He wasn't well on Boxing Day.

JENNIFER

Junior was sullen when I picked him up from his father's and grunted in response to my attempts to make small talk all the way home, where he disappeared into his room. Next morning he gave me the ultimatum. 'Mam, I am not staying in this house while your boyfriend is here. Either he goes or I go.'

Fruit doesn't fall far from the tree and I detected the tone of Stuart's resolve in his young voice.

'Where would you go?' I asked, thinking that he wouldn't have an answer. He was defiant and determined. 'With Da at Gran's place.'

I tried to reason with him and make him see that it just wasn't possible because the restraining order says that until the court case is over he and Richie can only see their father once a fortnight. I didn't want to dwell too much on that as I don't want him to resent the restrictions so I also pointed out that the Hoares live a long way from his school, that their small house is full up now that Stuart is there and that poor Gran is tied up doing for Grandfather. 'Living there would be like living in an old people's home, Junior,' I said.

His response was a mouthful of cheek liberally sprinkled with the 'f' word. 'I'd rather be over there with Gran and Da than in the same house as you while you are fucking that murderer in the other room. I hate you and I hate Tom.'

I was shocked. He had never spoken like that to me before. I instinctively leaned across the table and slapped his face. It's something I have never even thought about doing before in my life. He pushed his chair roughly back from the table, deliberately knocking it over and tipping it on its side. 'It's against the law to hit your kid,' he declared, bravely holding back his tears as he stormed off without eating his breakfast. 'If I want to, I can report you!'

I put my head in my hands and sobbed. How could I be provoked into doing that? I am becoming as bad a Stuart! I never thought things could get any worse but they just had.

Richie, quietly witnessing the entire incident, came and put his arms around me. Our tears mingled to form a warm, salty pool on the breakfast placemat. His little world was falling apart. Although he was disgusted at the way Junior spoke to me, he was equally shocked when had I slapped his brother. But mostly he was a sad and lost little boy whose life had been turned upside down through no fault of his own.

RICHIE

Christmas at Blackrock was fun. Daideo got his old ukulele out and we had a grand sing along. He sang some of the revolution songs. Nan sat next to him and they sang together and when they were finished they kissed a real smoocher. That was gross for old people to do that!

Tom got some saucepan lids out of the cupboard that made drums and kept time and eventually all of us kids had something from the kitchen drawer to make a noise with and it sounded grand. Uncle Kev played his harmonica. Mammy did some Irish jigs and showed us kids how to move our legs while keeping our arms still by our sides. She said another way to keep time was to beat our shoes loudly on the floor. The place was rocking. It was grand fun.

We had to leave early because we went to see Da. It was pretty quiet over there at Gran's but Da was pleased to see us and even cuddled us. Awkward! We had 'mello' slice and a can of Coca Cola for afternoon tea.

I was hoping that Mammy would come inside and talk to Da but when she came to pick us up, she stayed in the car and beeped the horn.

At breakfast this morning Junior said he was going to leave home and Mam hit him across the face. It was awful and it made me scared.

Molly has gone away, Da will probably go to jail and if Junior leaves there will just be Mammy and me and she likes Tom better than she likes me and that is not fair.

JENNIFER

Junior stormed off with his soccer ball and Richie and I set about our pre-arranged meeting with the country cousins who are in town for the season's festivities. Before we left, I went upstairs and spoke to Tom who had missed the morning's drama because he was showering.

'The press are outside,' I warned. 'They are waiting like ghouls for something to happen, so keep a low profile until I get back.' He agreed and turned the television on and went back to bed, but not before putting the hard word on me. 'C'mon Jen, a quickie before you go.'

Imagine that, wanting me to get back into bed with him when all this shit was happening and Richie was downstairs waiting? Of course there was no way I could do that! He doesn't seem to understand. I collected my things and Richie and I ran the gauntlet through the assembled media throng as we reversed out of the garage and headed up the road.

The mayhem was still there when we got back from the city. They descended upon the car with cameras poised and microphones at the ready, coming so close that I was fearful that I would run them over. Perhaps I should have. I opened the automatic door on the garage, rolling it down behind me entrapping one of my pursuers, who had slipped in behind me.

'Get out!' I yelled hysterically. 'Get out!' I pushed past him, determined not to speak to him, and rushed inside. I was about to lock the door, when a blur of colourful caftan, accompanied by a jangle of jewellery and a familiar waft of aromatic perfume, rocketed past me.

'Didn't you hear what the lady said?' said Wendy as she grabbed him by the scruff of the neck, opened the back door and frog-marched him down the yard and out the back gate. He didn't know what struck him. Then she returned to the kitchen, locked the back door, and sat down as if that was a perfectly ordinary thing to do.

When Tom came downstairs we were all still laughing hysterically.

'Wendy!' he said happily. 'You're back!'

WENDY

Poor pressman didn't know what struck him. I may be small but I pack a mean punch. Jen has been through the washer and the wringer with that mob bothering her and not allowing her to do normal things like taking her son to the city.

She didn't know that I had finally surfaced and gone around to her place to say hello, and finding it empty - or at least it looked empty me - let myself in with the key I had kept from my time looking after the boys. Bit cheeky of me I guess, but I just wanted to surprise her. Didn't know at the time that Tom was upstairs asleep. Maybe that was a good thing.

That press man coming into the house was the last straw, so I got rid of him good and proper.

It's tough on Jen. She can't move without cameras in her face, Junior has upset her and Tom is wandering around like a caged lion. Even in my short time back I can see they are squabbling like two children.

I understand both sides of the story and know it will take time to sort out. 'Calm down, Jennifer,' I said. 'Talk to the boys. They are good kids but they've been to hell and back.'

My work done, I said goodbye and left by the back gate before the media could get to me.

TOM

I'm not going to make her choose between the boys and me but she walked out of my life once before and now that we have found each other again, I am damned if I am going to let her go a second time. She says she didn't walk; that she was pushed. But that's not how I see it. I say she took off. Now she is the one who is doing the pushing. I can't win!

The media has a morbid fascination with this family and I feel really sorry for Jen and all she has gone through. They camp outside the house lying in wait and swarm all over me, even when I just go out to collect the morning paper. She told me I couldn't stay but I told her to chill, that the media would tire sooner or later. 'They won't sit around out in the cold forever, Jen,' I said. 'They will eventually go away.'

Apparently it isn't the media that is her prime worry. It is the boys. They do not want me here, especially Junior. I told her to loosen up and not to let two teenagers dictate how she is going to run her life. 'Sure, they've been through a lot, but what about me?' I said. 'I had my face punched in and my life ruined and we can't even be together without being told it's wrong by your pubescent son.'

I had never said anything like that to Jen before.

This morning she came upstairs after a blue with Junior and burst into tears and cried uncontrollably so I took her into my arms and when she calmed down suggested we release the tension and make the best of a bad situation. She went rigid and said that Richie was downstairs and she had other commitments, and stormed off to meet up with her cousins. The curtains in the bedroom were still drawn from the night before and the bed was unmade so I hopped back in. I can't go outside with that mob baying for blood.

At least I was blissfully more comfortable than the men and women in the street below who were waiting in the cold and smoking cigarettes, impatient for a story. The phone rang constantly but I ignored it.

I awoke from my dozing when I heard a racket downstairs, lots of banging and hysterical laughing. Wendy had turned up and unceremoniously evicted some poor scribbler who got caught up on the wrong side of the automatic garage door. I joined in the laughter and that eased tensions.

It is great to see Wendy back again.

JENNIFER

I am sorry for what I have put Tom through but if he forces me to make a choice, then I know who I will have to select. These are not just two teenage boys, they are my sons and they have been through a lot. I can't abandon them now.

When Mammy visited later that day microphones were thrust under her nose and a huge foot found its way into the hallway and held the door open. As she had her arms full of shopping when I opened the door for her, three other bully boys got in as well. I angrily screamed at them, 'Get out! Get out of my house!'

They would not budge so Tom weighed in and used a couple of expletives and manhandled them out the front door. Unfortunately, the whole sorry saga was caught on tape for the evening news services. Again!

The three of us retreated to the kitchen flabbergasted at what had just happened, with Tom beginning to realise that his being here only served to inflame an already sorry situation. 'They are on Stuart's side because they can't believe that a church-going businessman would do what he did,' he said.

Mam thinks it is simply that they want to make a story that sells papers and they don't care how they get it or who they hurt. She gently asked me what had happened this morning with Junior. He had turned up at her place saying that I had belted him and that he was never going home. I outlined the story and suggested it might better if Tom went back to London.

Immediately Mammy disagreed and said that if Tom was sent away with his tail between his legs then Junior would win and would never allow us to be a couple.

'Jen, you and Tom must stick together on this,' she said. 'Make a stand and tell the boys what you want from them. Make them realize that in a real family people make compromises and that even a mother has a right to happiness. Have a family conference where they can have their say and you can have yours and everyone listens to each other's viewpoint. Clear the air so to speak. You can't have Junior dictating the terms. Young minds are pliable and untended sores fester. The boys must listen and be part of the solution.'

Wise words. We decided that she will have a little chat with Junior and bring him back home and then this evening we will sit together as a family and talk out our differences.

Is there a future for us? Where will our relationship go? We really don't know.

TOM

I told Mary that the family can't live like this. 'The boys hate me,' I said. 'Junior says he won't even stay in the same house as me. And the press will not leave Jen alone while I am here. We'll have to find another way. I

170

will go to the airport and get a ticket and be gone before the boys get home. After all, that was what we were going to do before I decided to come to Dublin before Christmas.

'It is no good grasping for what we want. We will just have to allow this thing to unfold rather than try to force the issue. If we give the boys enough time they will come around. Initially, Junior will probably refuse to budge and we might have to wait until he is at university and doing his own thing.

'Richie is different. He is younger, softer and more emotional, and likely to see reason quicker. The greatest virtue is patience. I will wait until Jen can come to me.'

I said all of this but I don't really believe it and Mary enunciated exactly what I was feeling this morning when I lay brooding in bed. If we let Junior dictate terms to us now he will always have the upper hand and get his way. Jennifer and I must stand united. We must talk about it and hear each other out.

JENNIFER

When Mammy brought Junior back he was fully expecting that I would have succumbed to his wishes and sent Tom away. That's the way it usually played out. He would bully me, I would relent, and he would get his way. Just like I would give in to his father.

So he was one unhappy cookie when he saw Tom sitting comfortably in the lounge, cup of coffee in hand, looking quite at home.

'Why's he still here?' he asked accusingly, pointing to Tom.

'It's not "he", Junior,' I said. 'His name is Tom and he's here because I want him to be here.'

'I thought I told you to get rid of him,' he roared, standing over me, encroaching on my personal space.

Somehow I managed to remain calm. 'Are you trying to intimidate me, Junior?' I asked the question very clearly and waited for an answer.

'No, I just don't want him here, that's all.'

'Okay, let's talk it out then, shall we?'

He was uncomfortable at being challenged, so I knew now was time to confront his distorted thinking directly.

'Listen, I know that you don't like having Tom here. You have told me. However, your friends come and hang out here all the time. Think about it. What makes you think that you have more rights than I do?'

Tom sat quietly listening, allowing me to deal with my son in the way I thought best. I could feel his support there in the room with me. That was something I had never experienced with Stuart and it certainly made things easier.

Having given Junior something to think about I informed him of our planned family meeting to clear the air, and asked him to come down after Richie came home from his play date. He nodded his head meekly. 'Then I'll call you when Richie is here and we can talk about this,' I added.

Junior had one last attempt at intimidation, this time by questioning my love for him. He knew that was a very soft spot. 'You won't feckin' listen to me. Nobody takes any notice of what I think. You don't love me.'

I stood up and walked over to him, putting both hands on his shoulders and looking directly at him. He squirmed.

'Don't try and turn the discussion around,' I said. 'This is not about whether I love you or not. You know that I do, more than life itself. I have never given you reason to question that, so please don't.'

Amazingly I remained calm and gave him no excuse to storm off like he usually does when he is lost for a strategy.

JUNIOR

I decided to go home and see how things were. Tom was still there, sitting up in the lounge room! I was spitting! Mam was in her lawyer mode and wasn't going to listen to anything I fuckin' said. She tried to tell me that having Tom there was like me having my mates around. It's not! I don't fuck them.

She said she would listen to me and Richie tonight when we would all be able to give an opinion at a family meeting. Family? Tom's not fuckin' family; he's not even Irish! When I saw Richie walk up the path I tried to call out from the front window to warn him but he walked straight into their trap.

JENNIFER

The boys sat uncomfortably forward in the easy chairs and Tom and I sat on the sofa. I broke the silence asking them if they knew why we were here. There were nods of affirmation all around. The boys sat fiddling with their hands, heads down, not wanting to say anything. I could see that they wouldn't open up easily so it was probably best that I start.

I affirmed them by telling them that they were my precious sons and that I loved them both, that I wanted them to love me, but most of all I wanted them to respect me. I told them I would never ever stop loving them and I expected no more or no less from them.

'This meeting,' I told them, 'has very little to do with Tom and whether you like him or not, but it does have a lot to do with whether you respect me and the decisions I make.'

I went on explaining, 'I know it is difficult for you lads because you have never seen much respect shown to me in this house by your father. Or by my brothers or any of the men in my family for that matter! They all believe that women are second-rate citizens and I am afraid that that idea may have been passed onto the two of you. I may be a woman but I have just as much right to respect as any man.'

I asked them what was worrying them and was not prepared for the flood of answers, which made me feel terrible. My poor boys suffer from an intense sense of abandonment that began when I decided to leave them to go and live with Tom in London without telling them first. They felt helpless because I never explained why I was going or what they could do to make me stay. It made them feel as if it was their fault, particularly when I chose to have Molly with me. 'You preferred one girl to two boys,' Junior said. That really hurt.

They felt that I am never at home, which is not entirely true. I try to be here for them as much as I can, but it is impossible to split myself in so many ways. I am a grieving mother. Unfortunately my grief has taken me away from my sons and that is unforgivable.

I could see Richie was holding back tears but I never said anything or moved to comfort him. I didn't want to interrupt the flow of grievances and let them talk while I listened and in doing so, I began to understand their anger and feelings of helplessness, which are much the same as my own. I could see that we were all lost.

Tom didn't say a thing until it was almost over, when he simply told the boys he understood where they were coming from. 'I felt the same way when my mother and father split,' he said, which made them both look up with renewed interest. 'It is difficult and I will be doing my best to make it easier for you, but in a family everybody must respect each other.'

Mam broke things up by coming into the room to tell us that dinner was on the table and then taking the opportunity to have her say, supporting and affirming me.

This was the first time we had sat together as a family and tended the scars that Stuart's heinous act has visited upon us. For the first time in ages, we ate dinner and talked about normal things in a normal manner, even laughed and joked as if a huge burden had been lifted from our shoulders; the air cleared and time to move on.

We have to see how this thing with Stuart plays out.

My only concern now? I think Tom is getting itchy feet and would like to resume his London life before too long.

MARY

I dropped Junior home and knowing that the family meeting was going to be difficult, I disappeared into the kitchen, minding my own business and keeping right out of the way. This was a family problem and I was sure that Jen could work it out. I clattered away making plenty of noise so that I couldn't be accused of eavesdropping.

I blame myself for their situation because I haven't been able to give the boys and Jen the support I should have. Seamus got sick not long after little Molly's death and I have been preoccupied.

When I opened the door and announced that dinner was ready I overheard Tom's last few words - about how his own life had been thrown into turmoil when he was young and the need for respect all round - and decided to put my oar in. I sat on a straight chair next to Tom.

'Junior and Richie,' I said, 'you are my grandsons and you know that I love you. Right?'

'Yes, Nan!' they chorused as one. 'Love you too Nan!' A little bit of spark was returning. This was their routine answer that they had given since they were toddlers and first learnt to speak.

'Okay then. Now let me tell you this. Jennifer is my daughter and I love her more than I love you. Does that surprise you?'

'More than me?' Richie flung back, starting to enjoy our bantering.

'Yes, more than you, Rich! I have loved your mother since the day she popped her pretty little head into the world. It was love at first sight. Now, let me tell you about my daughter.'

They both sat back and waited patiently.

'She had four big brothers who adored her,' I explained. 'She was the smartest and prettiest girl in her class. Everybody loved Jennifer because she brought magic into any room. She was a good hurdler and could have run in the Olympics if she had wanted to, but she liked dancing better so that is what she concentrated on. She studied hard and got good enough marks to go to Cambridge and she became a successful lawyer.'

I waited for a few seconds to gather my thoughts.

'But then she married Stuart,' I continued. 'And, at first, it was good. You two boys and then Molly came along and everybody was happy. I don't know what went wrong but your mother changed from a happy, confident and smart woman into a person who did nothing for herself and everything for her husband and family. She gave up her work and became slowly isolated from her own family and her friends. Your Da didn't want to share her. He wanted her all to himself.'

I leaned forward. 'You see, that's what you boys are doing. You want your mother all to yourselves. You don't want to share her with a man who can help her to be happy again. You are making your Mam your victim.'

I stood up and begged them to give their mother a chance, and that they may even find that my Jennifer, their mother, will return to that happy, smart lady who is fun to be around.

'Now, dinner is ready,' I said. 'And I want you to eat every last skerrick.'

'Why is that Nan?' said Richie.

'Because you can't make decisions on an empty stomach.'

RICHIE

When I got home from school, we all sat in the lounge room, looking at each other, not really sure of where to begin. Mam started and went on about how we don't respect her. That made me sad and I cried a bit but I don't think anybody noticed. She wanted to come up with a solution that the whole family would be happy with. That was good because it gave Junior and me a chance to tell Mam how we feel. We just want things to go back to how they were.

We want Mam to stay and look after us. The house is always empty and only Aunty Wen wants to be with us. She is always here. Mam never is. She is always up at Molly's grave, or with her friends meditating, or seeing some lawyer about important papers.

When Nan came into to tell us dinner was ready she told us that she loves Mam even more than she loves us. That is a surprise because she loves us heaps.

All Mam ever thinks about is Molly. She thinks that one dead child is better than two live ones.

JUNIOR

Mam talked about respect but our football coach says that you have to earn respect. I know I bully Mam. But because I don't want to end up like Da, I will try not to do it.

I told her how she had chosen Molly to go to London with her and Tom and couldn't care less about us boys. That she didn't even talk to Da about it. And then everything went wrong! Molly died, Da was put in jail and Mam was always somewhere else.

We are always being teased at school about Da being put in jail and it is fuckin' horrible. When we see him he says bad things about Mam all the time. Grandma has been kind but Grandpa is fuckin' crazy and says things about the family that are not nice.

I told Mam that I think that Aunty Wen loves us more than she does. But in the end I said that Richie and I will be cool with her decisions. 'Just one thing, though,' I pleaded. 'Please don't make us change school and go to London.'

Anyway, when Da comes home Tom won't be able to stay here because it's Da's house and he won't want a fuckin' jerk like him around.

TOM

The last thing I want is to make Junior and Richie uncomfortable in their home. I know how that feels and it is not good. It won't be long until they are grown up and have lives of their own; they will go their way and we will go ours and they won't care what their mother gets up to. However, she needs me here at the moment and I will not leave unless she asks me to, but in the meantime I shall try to make it as easy as I can for Jennifer's sons.

At the meeting, the boys unloaded all their baggage from the previous months. It soon became apparent that their anger and aggression masks their fragility.

I moved off the couch and sat in an upright chair so that I could speak. I told them that I was sorry and that I knew it had been really bad for them and that I had no wish to add to their stress and make things worse.

I think I know how they feel because I also felt helpless and abandoned at their age. Not for exactly the same reasons, but something similar and I felt very alone and unloved. 'It wasn't anybody's fault,' I said, 'it was just the way things were because the adults around me had made decisions that affected me badly.'

If the boys don't want me here, that is sad but Jennifer needs me here at this time and I will be waiting for her to ask me to leave before I do so. It is about time that Jennifer stopped being the victim and demanded some happiness in her life. The boys have no right to stand in her way.

The family meeting cleared the air a little.

JENNIFER

Since our little family conference the boys have settled down and accepted that Tom is staying here with me whether they like it or not. I know they will get used to it.

Things seem to be working out. I'd forgotten just how good sex influences your whole wellbeing and I feel great. I still think of Molly every day but I have lost that overwhelming sadness that grabs you around the legs and drags you down into the mud so that the effort to do anything is almost insurmountable. Some hours of some days I am almost happy.

I am very busy of late keeping all the plates in the air, Da is ill and Mammy needs help, I have been seeing a solicitor regarding the divorce and I like to visit Molly's grave every day just to ensure she isn't lonely up there by herself. Sometimes it is after dark when I get home but Tom is there with the boys and sometimes Wendy drops by and brings a meal so everything on the home front is taken care of and they all seem happy.

But you can't please everyone. I suggested Tom start up an African drum group in the old summerhouse at the family home but Kevin put a stop to that, saying he didn't want to disrupt the neighbours' amenity. Some people just never grow.

Part Eight

STUART

H ere is the state of play. On the good side of the ledger, I am out on bail, can go to work, and am allowed to play golf. On the bad side I have to report to the Garda three times a week, am staying at Mam's, which is a trial as I haven't lived at home since before I got married, and only have limited access to my lads. I see them just once a fortnight and even then I always have somebody looking over my shoulder.

They were a little wary at first and were having difficulty trying to comprehend that I could do what I have been accused of. But blood is thicker than water and it has been up to me to reassure them and build on the strong bond we share. After all, we have kicked a lot of soccer balls together over the years, spent many enjoyable afternoons in the garden and mucked around in all sorts of fields and parks with hurling sticks. They always knew that my business limited the amount of time I could spend at home with them, but accepted it was all for the good of the family.

Our relationship has gradually become more solid and the visits seem to be going well. At our first awkward meeting someone needed to break the ice, and where I struggled the social worker shone.

That woman is so good at taking the edge off things. She is younger than the boys' mother, and dresses in a way that is not necessarily fashionable, but red hair has always attracted me and I like the splash of pink dye that slashes like a scimitar across her forehead highlighting her blue eyes and flawless skin. Her build is slightly plumper and more rounded than Jennifer's, who with her dedication to Buddha, yoga and eating nothing of any real substance over the years, is now as thin as a stick of celery.

Social workers are funny people. I am convinced that somewhere in Dublin there is a school teaching 'Social Worker Make-Speak'. Her instructions are delivered in a flat, even-handed manner via a multitude of bureaucracy-gone-mad, politically correct phrases that seem to loopily cover every issue. But she is able to take command of any situation, and being a single mum with a teenage son, has a good idea of the workings of the young male mind and is able to build a bridge, providing me with a much needed link to the lads.

In many ways she is a thorough professional, but in others tardy and forgetful, and rarely with you in the present, rather on the phone solving some hare-brained personal problem. She will chat merrily with her clients about matters that vary from proper diet and hygiene, to feeding the dog, how to get the television fixed and what forms have to be filled out to get the dole. Her phone rings constantly, and she blithely answers without any discretion at all, speaking of the most personal of things. 'Vaginal warts?' she said to someone one day. 'I know a very good doctor in the system who can help.'

She is always rummaging around in a giant purple leather bag that seems to contain enough food, implements and technological devices needed to maintain a Third World country, all the while puffing away on a damn cigarette.

But when we meet up with the boys she is good, very, very good. On the first visit when I opened my front gate, I stood for a moment, simply taking it in and admiring my house. Orla slipped her arm through mine and patted my hand, commenting upon its grandeur and my well-tended garden. When she went inside she was even more impressed by my modern furnishings, artworks and other home comforts. I liked that.

Junior is downright surly to her most of the time, difficult and non co-operative. Richie tries to be pleasant but he is such a sissy that he annoys the hell out of me. I realise I can't buy my way back into their hearts, but the odd gift here and there does not hurt my cause, and Orla has proved inspirational in her choices as she seems to know what young boys like.

She has advised me on re-building my relationship with the boys via focusing the conversation on what they are doing at school, how their sports are going, the latest games on the computer, their friends and so on. She has taught me the art of asking open-ended questions, avoiding those that elicit a simple, mumbled 'yes' or 'no' answer.

She and Mother seem to have hit it off and after each visit when we return home she usually stays on for a chat. Mother loves the company and likes to boil the kettle, make a cup of tea, and get Orla's view about how the visit to her grandchildren went. The pair greet and farewell each other with a hug.

Under my bail conditions I am not allowed to deliberately seek Jennifer out, but on one occasion my visit unintentionally went well over the allotted time and, as we were leaving and Jennifer was returning, we collided in the front garden like two rogue asteroids in space.

Jennifer behaved very badly and I am pleased that Orla actually got to see what I have had to deal with over all these years.

My little social worker is sweet and I am pleased the judge insisted she keep an eye on me. She is completely non-judgemental. I like that.

JENNIFER

The day I met up with Stuart when we shouldn't have, I just lost it. It occurred to me that he had absolutely no right to be visiting his sons after what he's been accused of doing. And here he was walking along the path of my garden talking and laughing with that red-headed bitch as if they had known each other all of their lives. Not a care in the world. It was so typical of Stuart.

Plus every time he sees the boys, he brings some gift or other. Which of course, after their initial uneasiness about the access, they have started to think is great. He's dishing out the largesse and buying their affection while I am doing all the hard work, caring for them and helping them to get through the tragedy that he has caused. It makes my blood boil.

We stared at each other for a moment, and then he apologized, saying that time got away from him.

I suggested that it was a pity that I didn't get equal time with Molly and he started on his typical 'Now, Jennifer' bit. Oh, that was it.

'Don't you dare fucking "now Jennifer" me!' I snapped. 'I put up with that shit for years. You have no right to say that to me. In fact, you have no rights at all, after what you have done. Now, get off my property!'

That did it! The phrase '*my* property' irked him and he showed it. He started to advance toward me, but instead of backing away as I once would have, I went for him, swinging my bag.

Then I felt a hand in mine, yanking me way. It was that Orla woman, the social worker! The cheek of her. I pulled away, screamed, 'Take your little bitch of a helper with you!' and stormed up the path into the house.

Before I slammed the door I looked around and there she was, comforting him and telling him that it was all right, that everything was okay, as if he was a schoolboy. He was lapping it up.

TOM

I am stuck in Dublin, away from my home, work and friends, with very little to do all day. If I go outside these walls, an army of sanctimonious souls make it quite clear that I am not welcome, that somehow I am to blame for a father murdering his daughter. They don't say it out loud, although one old bloke did the other day. I was going down to get a newspaper and walking past the community garden and he threw chook's shit at me and said, 'That's what I think of you, you little English prick. Go back to your own pig sty, fuck your own women, leave our Irish girls alone.'

I didn't tell Jen about it, as it would have upset her too much. But I have experienced a couple of instances like that so I stay inside mostly. I am a lover not a fighter!

Even in the house things aren't rosy. After the big family talk the boys now accept me but they still don't like me. I do my best and try to understand. I really do, but they come in from school all surly and ready for a

185

blue, as pubescent boys do, particularly Junior. The worst thing is that I usually have to cope with it by myself and that is not pleasant. Technically I am with Jennifer 24/7, and that should be awesome. But she is emotionally and/or physically absent much of the time. Honestly, she leaves the house most mornings and often doesn't get home until after dark. When quizzed she says she is tending Molly's grave, fixing up legal things for her divorce, or helping her mother with her Da who is quite ill. I hardly see her at all. If I offer to go with her she says 'no' because together we attract the vultures of the press so I am left at home to mope.

What would I do without Wendy? She understands the situation and pops her head in to say hello and have a chat. Sometimes we go out on the town after dark just to relieve the monotony. Even when she is home, Jen never wants to come along.

The thing is I don't need to go out to have fun; I want to hang out with Jennifer, and waking up each morning to my favourite person's face on the pillow next to mine is awesome and comfortable. I love it.

However, the boys see me as fair game and are hostile when she is not around and I am beginning to resent that I have put aside my work and commitments to concentrate on us and am receiving very little in return. This is not how it is meant to be.

STUART

Now things have settled down and the newspaper and television reporters realise that I am not the type to break my curfew by raging at Temple Bar nightclubs into the wee hours their interest has waned. Bored by my dull lifestyle, they have evacuated the street outside Mam's flat to look for a more exciting target.

Although the coming trial hangs over me I want to get my life back to as normal as possible under the circumstances so I have taken up an offer made by the Rector to resume my post playing the organ at Sunday service at St Patrick's.

At first I was reluctant. 'You and the congregation don't need to risk public criticism,' I told Iain. He gave that trusting, angelic smile of his. 'Let he who is without sin!' he chorused. 'It will be good for your image, Stuart. You will be seen as a man who truly loves his God.'

So one Sunday morning I sat on the comfortable stool in front of the massive, ornate keyboard, flexed my fingers and got ready to play. Any fool could see there was a mixed response amongst the congregation, with some showing an element of discomfort but Iain took the sting out by giving a wonderful sermon about the prodigal son, Christ's compassion for all people including the lowest of the low, and the need to give every accused person the benefit of the doubt until their guilt or otherwise is determined. I could feel the ice slowly thawing and a mild sense of acceptance emanating from the pews.

Musically, it didn't take me long to get back into the swing of things, with just a few errant notes and chords here and there, mainly on 'Lift High The Cross'. My efforts to play well, combined with the soaring sound of the organ's mighty pipes, swept me away from my daily troubles, launching me briefly into a place of personal salvation and heartfelt redemption. After service Iain intoned quietly to me, 'This will bring tremendous long-term benefits, Stuart, you will see.'

Unfortunately one of the Sunday papers tumbled to my weekly performance and had great fun with the headline 'Little Molly's Dad Pumps Up His Organ', accompanied by a photo of myself snapped by some spiteful zealot on his cell phone. He managed to capture me at a moment of musical delight, my head thrown back in sheer ecstasy. For a few hours I was the laughing stock of talkback radio. Best ignored and prepare for the trial.

JENNIFER

What a joke! A photo of Stuart on the front page playing the organ at church, for God's sake. The sanctimonious bastard! He is the laughing stock of this town.

After the debacle of us meeting in the garden, we have changed the routine so that the boys meet him at the Sunday service and then go to Moira's for the roast. Not only are the visits now weekly, the social worker has requested that they expand things a little, proposing they go to the park to fly a kite after lunch this week. They are always pushing the boundaries. Secretly, I don't really mind as that gives Tom and me 'together time'.

STUART

Jennifer regularly makes it clear that she never wants me to have anything to do with either of our sons again. But the law has determined that I can see them and it is not in her province to prevent that happening. It boils down to a matter of principle - I am legally and morally entitled to see my children and therefore that's what I shall do. It is good for them to be away for a couple of hours from the controlling, poisonous approach of their mother and that little skunk she sleeps with.

Junior is quite happy with that but Richard is difficult to engage with, preferring not to see me at all and when he is with me he hardly says a word. That is okay. Even if he doesn't say much, he can at least observe that I am not a crazy man, but his calm and devoted father.

This week, Orla suggested that it might be beneficial for the lads to be out in the air rather than being cooped up in their grandmother's flat. 'After service why don't we meet in the park near your home and they can fly a kite?' she proposed.

Sounded good to me and so in typical style, I dutifully went to the local toy store, spent quite some time selecting a reasonably-priced kite which I felt would suit our needs and happily arrived with Orla at the park near our home - only to discover that the boys had brought their own kite, a considerably more ostentatious model than the one I had brought for the day's entertainment. In fact it was about four times the size, in the shape of a giant flying fish and had thick rice paper decorated in brilliant splashes of red, green and purple, with six long tails flying off the edges.

'What's all this?' I asked as they approached. '*I've* brought the kite!'

'Well, we brought this one, Da,' said Junior, 'just in case you forgot.'

'Me? Forget! Don't you dare say that! I have never let you boys down, never. If I say I'm bringing a kite, then I bring one. See! I've got it here. It's just what we need. That's too big, it will never get off the ground.'

Orla held her hand up in a stopping motion as I advanced towards them. 'Stuart,' she said in a soothing, conciliatory tone. 'It's okay! We've got two to play with now. Twice the fun.'

Her eyes were warning me to calm down.

'Okay,' I said, 'Fair enough.' I backed away.

But something about the design of the boys' kite, the look of it, the colours, it irked me. I motioned towards it.

'So, where did you get this, then? It must have cost a fortune.'

The lads shuffled uncomfortably until Richard provided the answer. 'Tommy, he brought it for us when he and Mammy came back from Thailand …'

'What do you mean, Thailand?' I said. 'Don't you mean New Zealand? She was supposed to have gone to New Zealand. I bought the ticket for her!'

There was silence as the boys both stared solemnly at the ground.

'Well,' I said, 'what's going on? Did your mother go to New Zealand? Or Thailand? Come on, tell me what happened!'

Silence. I moved closer. 'I demand to know! I am your father. Now tell me.'

Richard burst into tears. 'Oh, for heaven's sake, you little pansy,' I snarled. 'Grow up.'

'Well, Da,' Junior suddenly weighed in. 'If you really want to know, Ma changed her ticket and got off at Dubai and met Tommy there and then they flew on to Thailand together, where his mum lives, and they went up the hills somewhere and stayed in some shitty little village and hung off every word of some guru during the day and then screwed each other's brains out during the night. It was a real fuck-fest I bet you.'

Orla gasped, and I didn't know whether to laugh at the colourful explanation or scream blue murder at the content. The next bit made the decision for me. 'Then, on the way back,' Junior continued, 'when they heard you got charged with murder, he didn't get off the plane in London, he came over here and now the fecker is living at home with us. Drives us crazy, he does.'

What the hell? She had told me she had finished with that little smart-arse and that he would never come near any of us again. Now, here is Junior telling me the bastard has set up camp in Dalkey! In my home! In my bed! The thought of him hijacking my family seared a hole in my brain.

I couldn't help myself. I grabbed the kite and started ripping it to shreds, tearing at it like a madman, stripping it to pieces and stamping on the colourful bits of rice paper as they fluttered to the muddy lawn. And when I finished snapping the bamboo struts, I hurled the pieces as far away as I could.

Richie was cowering behind Orla, shaking with tears. Junior kept his distance, but slyly gave me the thumbs up. At least someone is on my side.

'That's what I think of that home wrecker,' I shouted and moved towards Richie.

'You tell that mother of yours if she fuckin' well goes anywhere near that fuckin' little prick I will kill the both of them. And you as well!'

I grabbed each of the boys by the shoulder, and pushing them in front of me so their feet barely touched the ground, I began marching them swiftly back towards home. 'Better still, I'll tell her my fecking self!' I growled.

Orla moved swiftly to stand in front of me, blocking my way, pleading, 'Stuart! Stuart? Stop! You'll break the conditions of your bail. They'll put you straight back into jail!'

She grabbed my left hand and pulled me a couple of paces away and then gently guided the boys to the edge of the park and watched as they crossed the road and headed for home. I was fuming so much I was hardly aware of this until she came back and stood in front of me. 'Stuart, what are you doing? If you keep going like this, you are writing yourself a one-way ticket back to hell.'

We stared deeply into each other's eyes and then Orla suddenly took my hand in hers and began caressing it gently. The soft gentle touch of a woman, something I had not experienced for such a long time, proved irresistible. I suddenly took her in my arms and kissed her fully and firmly on the lips. She didn't resist and kissed me back.

In a few minutes I lost all control and suddenly a moment of astonishing physical and emotional bliss caught me unawares, my messy pent up lust exploding everywhere like a randy teenager.

To my surprise, Orla did not walk away. She stayed and we spent a long time in each other's arms and I think we both know that if the opportunity presents itself we could be lovers.

ORLA

Wow! That was a bit unexpected! I never thought I would ever be involved with an old fuddy-duddy like Stuart Hoare. He is not my type. Dennis, for all his faults, was a more macho, physical kind of type. As you would expect of a merchant seaman. Rough, tough, sparky. Trouble was, he could get too rough sometimes and that's what brought things to an end.

But Stuart? He reminds me of my Da - good looking, dresses well, can be entertaining and is solid. My mother never understood Da. She was constantly on his back about his drinking and the poor fellow was always under the pump.

I like Stuart's sturdy, steady approach to life and the way he has handled this dreadful thing that is hanging over him - in complete control of his perilous situation. Until this afternoon in the park, that is, when he totally lost it with the boys. That frightened me and I could see that the lads were scared as well.

The whole thing could have gotten out of hand. That's exactly how awful things in families happen! My training took over and I quietly talked him down, taking his hand and making him look directly at me.

After the boys were over the road and safely on the way home, he would not let go of my hand and sort of pulled me into an embrace. I could have backed away but the funny thing was I didn't want to. It was somehow romantic there in the park with nobody around, just him and me. I was turned on, so I kissed him back. He's obviously been on rations for quite a while because the next thing I know he's groaning in ecstasy. Awkward!

We went back to the car and I drove him home. He never said a word about what had happened and neither did I. When we got there I had a cuppa and a chat with Moira as usual. She asked me about the boys and the kite flying and I was non-committal about the scene in the park. My next challenge? Should I include it in my report?

JENNIFER

We had a kite at home that Tom had brought from Thailand for the boys so it was a good opportunity to try it out. Apparently, all was going well until Richard announced that the kite was a gift from Tom - ah, from out of the mouths of babes - and Stuart went right off his head.

The lads were petrified but the social worker stepped in and took control of the situation. Somehow she stood her ground and didn't let him intimidate her, managing to calm him down and getting the boys safely back to us.

She must know how to handle him. But there will be no more outside visits. That man can't be trusted.

TOM

There is no way I can live here. They hate me in Ireland, calling me the vermin that destroyed a family. The press hassle me and I am locked up in this house on the hill with no way out. It is like living in a bubble, made worse by the fact that the O'Briens are in and out of the place all day, every day, making it clear to me that I am just a hanger-on, that Molly was no relation of mine.

As well, things are very strained between the boys and me. I get along famously with Richie, but Junior positively despises me and shows it at every opportunity. I know you shouldn't let a teenage kid dictate to you but I can't help thinking of my younger days and how hard I found it to be nice to Mum's boyfriends, so I can empathise and don't blame him. Nevertheless it can be very unpleasant and he keeps trying to turn Richie against me. Poor Richie, he loves to chat to me when there is just the two of us, but he goes all quiet when Junior enters the scene.

Work is the other thing. My gigs are mainly in London and that's where I have to be to earn money. There is nothing much for me to do work-wise in Ireland and I get bored. There are only so many movies you can watch on Stuart's big television!

But it seems it will be a fair while before Stuart's case comes to court so I figure I will have to tough it out here in Dublin and support Jen until she feels comfortable, and then I think it is better that I go back to London, work during the week, and just fly over for the weekends. I shall talk to Jen and do whatever she thinks, but she will probably agree with my view as she has enough on her plate without having to look out for me.

The worst part is that Jen mostly refuses to come with me if I venture into town for a night out. She can't stand the attention we seem to attract, so most times Wendy comes with me. She is a great bird, so much fun to be with and with no strings attached. I almost feel as if I'm dating her. Have to be careful not to overstep the mark.

WENDY

Poor Tom. He really is trying to do the best by Jen but it is very difficult.

How can I explain? They came back from Thailand and the boys played up, didn't want Tom there and were very rude to him, especially Junior. Jen stuck to her guns and wasn't going to let them control her like Stuart used to. But they have learnt the game at the feet of the master and even though they agreed to back off, it was only a matter of time before the whole horrible scenario exploded again.

One night I dropped in on the way home from work expecting Jen to be there but she was up in the hills at Molly's grave. I left the car out the back and came in via the rear entrance so they didn't hear me for a while. Poor Tom was copping it from Junior. He was giving him a mouthful of cheek with every second word a swear word, really nasty stuff.

Tom was taking it, gently trying to calm him down but just being run over completely. I couldn't believe it! I dropped my keys noisily on the table and they looked around, surprised. 'Who do you think you're talking to, Junior?' I asked horrified. 'Tom's in charge when your mother is not here.' I have never had any reason to speak crossly to either boy as they love and respect me and the feeling is mutual so he didn't like me pulling him up.

'Tell him to go back to where he comes from,' he sneered, pointing at Tom. 'I don't want to see his ugly face or hear his pathetic music when I come home from school ever again. He thinks he owns the fucking place! This is my father's house, not his!' And he stormed out.

I turned to Tom. 'How long has this been going on? Where's Jen? Does she know this is happening?'

After that incident I have taken to dropping in after work on a regular basis. Jen is never at home but my presence seems to calm the boys down and they don't attack Tom when I am there. It's almost like a pack dog mentality that they have. Now I drop in with some sort of treat or the other, or to bring a meal and stay for dinner. Tom enjoys the company. It must be very lonely for him with Jen out of the house all the time.

STUART

After years of Jennifer's coldness I am smitten by Orla's warmth, her generous proportions, the lavish and passionate way she does everything, her impetuous willingness to become lost in the moment, the sexy throatiness of her laughter.

Even the smell of the cigarettes on her breath, normally something I would find repulsive, does something for me. I find the whole package the intoxicating essence of a woman who lives out there on the edge.

Between this and my isolation I am developing very strong feelings for her. Feelings I try to push to the back of my mind because I am in enough trouble as it is without becoming romantically involved with my social worker. God almighty, imagine if that gets into the papers.

At night in my lonely, single, boyhood bed I shut my eyes and think of her. And being a healthy fifty-something man, I sometimes dream of her. Perhaps she is growing fond of me?

TOM

When Wendy stumbled in on the argument with Junior she couldn't believe what she was hearing. I told her it goes on most nights. This evening it was over the music I was playing in the lounge room but it can flare up about anything - where they throw their bags, what's for dinner, whether there are snacks in the fridge.

'Does Jen know about this?' she asked.

'I have told her that they come in from school angry and unhappy,' I said. 'But she thinks it is part of the grieving process and that they will slowly get over it, especially if I am gentle with them.' I suddenly felt resentful now that I had verbalised it.

'I must say that it is getting me down,' I continued. 'I think it is unfair of Jennifer to leave all the agro to me, to make me Mr Bad Guy. By the time she gets home they are as nice as pie. Butter wouldn't melt in their mouths!'

Quite frankly, Jen has no idea. I don't want to make mountains out of molehills so I keep most of the bad behaviour to myself.

Wendy understands that I am struggling and so it is a great circuit breaker when she drops in on her way back from work. The boys obviously love and respect her and she knows how to get the best out of them. It must come naturally to her, as she doesn't have children of her own.

Sometimes she stays and shares a meal and I open a bottle of wine from Stuart's expansive cellar. He sure knows how to live the good life. Jen always knows when Wendy has eaten with us, as she can smell the wine on my breath when she comes in. She doesn't drink so is sensitive to the aroma.

ORLA WHITE

I know this is crazy but I have always liked a bit of adventure and after that incident in the park I pretty much let Stuart lead me where his passion dictated. On the other hand, it is fun teaching this old man a few new tricks and somehow desire creates desire.

Moira and Old Richard are always early to bed so I have taken to popping in after dinner and we are assured of privacy. They never suspect a thing and our precarious situation heightens the thrill.

There is an important distinction, though. Stuart is in love with me but I am merely having a fling. I saw what he was capable of that day and as I work with those types all the time, I am very wary of him. I'm not stupid!

STUART

I enjoy the thrill of the chase and the dangerous possibility of discovery, and each morning I wake up longing for the moment when I will see Orla again. She teases me with the promise of what is to come, using her friendship with Mother to linger at our dinner table while she discreetly puts her hand on my thigh and rubs me and makes me hard while at the same time chatting to my oblivious parents.

She sometimes even visits in her own time. I feel so liberated as I anticipate her next arrival, what we will do and how we will do it. The madness and the naughtiness is disarmingly alarming. What am I doing? Me, Stuart Hoare, organ-playing pillar of the Church of Ireland, businessman, financier, having an illicit affair with my Government-appointed minder right under the very noses of those waiting to send me to jail for a dreadful crime. We fully understand that we will have to be careful because if word gets out she will be severely disciplined for her lack of professionalism, and at the very least taken off my case, if not fired.

'Ah, if only the Rector could see me now,' I said one day as we lay spent on my single bed.

She winked and chirped, 'He'd probably join us.'

This outrageous suggestion was sacrilegious to the core and the deeply embedded and devoted Christian in me jumped to my friend's defence.

'Iain is happily married to Leila and would never countenance having sex with another woman!' I stuttered indignantly.

'Who said it would be me he would be shagging?' she added, a snort of laughter echoing through the tiny room.

'Orla!'

'Well, half the time he's in a dress …'

This woman shocks and excites me and has brought me to a heightened place of joy while I adapt to my new, albeit uncomfortable circumstances. If I can maintain this balance until the trial begins I feel I will be okay.

Meanwhile, it is truly written that the law grinds on inexorably, mired in tradition, rooted to the past, tripping itself up on absurd processes set in concrete. Delays, depositions and determinations have all conspired to push the commencement date further and further back. Who knows, the whole thing may be thrown out of court, saving everyone time, energy and money.

The bonus to these hold-ups is that they nettle Jennifer and frustrate her camp. She is anxious to get this all done and dusted, to see me flung in jail with the greatest of haste so that she and her little drummer boy can get on with their nasty little affair.

They don't know that I am enjoying a world of sexual delight of my own!

Part Nine

FINBAR MCMAHON

At last, Stuart Hoare has been arraigned to appear before a judge and a twelve-person jury at the Central Criminal Court on August 16th on the charge of murder. The trial will be held in the Criminal Courts of Justice chambers in Parkgate Street.

'Stuart,' I warned him, 'there is little room to manoeuvre when it comes to the penalty for murder in this country. The sentence is mandatory. It's life, and life means life.'

'You mean, I could be in there until I die?' he said. 'What about probation?'

'No date is set for probation at sentencing. Instead the prisoner's future is left in the hands of the Parole Board who may review a case like yours after seven years. Maybe then you might get some relief.'

For the first time, the situation Stuart faces has finally come into focus for him. 'You never know how these things go,' I warned him. 'All sorts of things come in to play and although it's not necessarily fair, it is the system.'

'The truth will come out,' he hissed.

'The truth? Truth is like mercury, or quicksilver as some call it,' I said. 'One minute it is solid, the next it's liquid. Fill a beaker with it, and the surface bends. Pour some into your hand and it slips through your fingers …'

What we need is a top-notch barrister, and although several top-quality silks put up their hands for this job, I know that Fionnoula Nolan is the one for the job. I recognise fully that Stuart Hoare is an olde-worlde man's man, but think of the shock value that a woman will be conducting his defence! We are, after all, defending pretty much the indefensible.

STUART

The weepy Dublin sun crept through the grimy window of McMahon's tiny office in an unfashionable old chambers building that had once been ear-marked for demolition but saved from the wrecker's ball due to the dire economic straits in which the whole country finds itself. Frankly, it was a mess - thick legal tomes stacked high on tables, his desk cluttered with papers, depositions and letters. Piles of manila folders stood between him and me, encircling his desk like a moat designed to keep his clients at bay.

A brusque tapping on the door was followed by a tornado blowing into the room. About five foot two, sallow complexion, the blackest of hair setting off her dark eyes, early thirties at the oldest, she extended her hand in greeting. 'Fionnoula Nolan, your barrister for the trial.' Taken aback, I battled for words but that didn't worry her.

'I will be frank, Mr Hoare,' she continued. 'I'm not here because I necessarily think you are innocent. I am here to put all my skills into developing a case for the defence that will get you the best possible outcome.'

She said plenty more, mainly about what a challenging brief it was and how Jennifer had availed herself of a ruthless winner-takes-all counsel named Flannery to support the state prosecution team. She then set up an appointment in her chambers, and was gone, just as quickly as she had blown in.

I was left sitting, staring at the piles of manila folders, alarm bells ringing.

McMahon noticed and mumbled something about me feeling perhaps a little deflated because a woman would be handling my case, that I didn't trust her because I am only comfortable in a man's world.

He hit the nail on the head. I have lived my life entirely within the male domain. The women in it have always been there to do as I wish, to see to my needs, to make my life easier. I don't really trust women to do the important jobs. They are incapable, hormonal and unpredictable. Women are too flaky to be barristers. Besides, I would not be in this mess if it wasn't for a woman.

I stared at the folders in front of me, thinking.

'Change your perceptions Stuart, and get used to it,' said McMahon. 'Miss Nolan is among the cream of our rising young barristers. Top of her class at law school and already an impressive track record. To use your oft-quoted analogy about leadership, this time around you be the first officer, and let her skipper the boat.'

I absent-mindedly touched the top folder with the toe of my shoe. It slid sluggishly down, almost in slow motion, bringing the rest of the pile with it, like a melting glacier down a stony mountain valley.

McMahon watched it, in an almost dream-like trance. 'There you go,' he said calmly. 'That's what is going to happen to your case if you don't take her advice. It will collapse before your very eyes.'

FIONNOULA NOLAN

God, what a meeting. I had to tell him to stop going on and on about his wife making him do it. 'Mr Hoare,' I interrupted, 'no one's going to buy the "my-wife-caused-me-to-do-it" angle! And if you think you are being painted as the devil himself now, wait until the Jennifer & Flannery Show goes live in court, with colourful reports every day in the media.

'Every little detail, every moment where you have been the less than exemplary husband, every little nuance that indicates you dislike your wife, any situation suggesting the slightest intimation of violence will be paraded in court.'

I suggested he lay low and try not to attract attention, as unfortunately any publicity is liable to work against us. Much of the public do not like him at this moment. 'We are running the risk of being tried by media,' I said.

I sense that he thinks that I am incapable of doing this job. But actually, I am his best hope. If he trusts me, my team will get the required outcome for him.

'My advice is that we bargain for a lesser charge with a view to you pleading guilty to that,' I said. 'It will give us more negotiating power.'

The man was not for turning. 'I am not admitting guilt to anything!' he yelled.

I pleaded with him, reminded him that he was the last person to have anything physically to do with Molly before she went over the edge. He had her in his arms! I begged him to cop manslaughter, admit he did it, and get a much lighter sentence that will almost certainly be further reduced with good behaviour. 'Out in five, by my reckoning,' I said.

But he is obsessed with his wife's paramour. 'That little bastard!' he kept saying. 'He fucked my wife on *our* bed!'

Saints preserve us. Just do as I say!

STUART

Obviously I do not relish the prospect of going to prison for any amount of time so I swallowed hard and controlled my emotions and asked Fionnoula that I have time to think about it and talk to family and friends.

Orla and Mother both came down on the lawyer's side. As for Father, it made me sad to think that this was an opportunity to show him that I am not the disappointment of a son that he long considered I was, but unfortunately the Alzheimer's means he is not capable of taking it all in. Nevertheless, from an idiot's mouth, occasionally comes sense. In a rare moment of lucidity Dad said I should 'stand boldly before the court martial, son, and take it a like a true soldier.'

That was it. I knew what I had to do.

I reckon we will make a good team, my sublimely talented young lawyer with a brilliant career in the making, and me, a man who has everything to lose, but also everything to gain. That's two exceptionally good reasons why together we are going to take this right down to the wire.

Our next meeting was pretty brief. 'Ms Nolan,' I said, 'here are your instructions. It's murder or nothing.'

DEFENCE LAWYER, OPENING ADDRESS

Stuart Richard Hoare is a man of exemplary character who has lived his life according to the good book and has never, in his fifty-plus years, attracted the attention of the authorities. He is a well-regarded businessman in this town, a church-going citizen, responsible father of three young children, a community minded man of the highest credentials. It is completely out of character for him to conspire to commit such a heinous act. Stuart Hoare is innocent of murder. His daughter's death was a horrible and unfortunate accident. He did not deliberately throw Molly over the bridge to her death.

At worst Mr Hoare was distracted and inattentive, failing to realise the risk he was taking with his daughter's life. His actions may have been careless, unforgivable even, but they were not deliberate and therefore he is not accountable to the charge as writ.

We will argue that little Molly Hoare's death was an accident. Simply an accident!

Stuart Hoare got out of the car because there was a hold up in traffic and because he needed respite from the constant barrage of criticism and nagging coming from his wife. He was upset and distracted by the emotional events of earlier in the day - starting with the shocking revelation that his wife was leaving him - when he took his young daughter from her car seat to breathe some fresh air with him.

They were on the narrow footpath of the bridge when Molly asked him to play Catch Molly, a game that he had played with her since she was an infant. In this game, he held her in his arms and pretended to drop her, catching her at the last minute. She enjoyed the adrenalin rush and always begged for more. There were puddles on the road on this day and that made it all the more fun. Catch Molly before she fell into a puddle and got wet!

Unfortunately, when he was distracted, she accidentally slipped out of his arms and onto the road beneath.

We will present evidence to the court that Stuart Hoare has never been physically abusive to the children. He has always been a good father, an upright citizen and a pillar of his local church. We will call witnesses to testify to this fact, people who have known Stuart Hoare for many years.

We will also present to the jury a psychologist who has diagnosed Stuart Hoare as having been in a state of 'fluctuating dissociation' at the time of the incident. When he dropped Molly he was upset and in a hypnotized state and not responsible for his actions.

We plan to prove to the jury that Molly Hoare met her death following an unfortunate series of events that were perhaps avoidable, but which nevertheless resulted in a horrible, dreadful accident.

PROSECUTION LAWYER, OPENING ADDRESS

We will argue that Mr Hoare deliberately and knowingly threw his daughter over the bridge in order to extract revenge because his wife was leaving him for another man. Stuart Hoare has had a long history of violence towards his wife and we will produce hospital and medical documents to prove this.

Several witnesses will attest to Mr Hoare's strange behaviour after his daughter had fallen. When everybody else was in panic and rescue mode, he was in no hurry to reach the injured child. He took time out to punch his rival for love, breaking the man's jaw and shattering his eye socket before calmly making his way down to the motorway and his daughter. These are not the actions of a man who has just seen his beloved daughter fall to her likely death. Stuart Hoare showed no emotion at the scene, even cadging a cigarette from a bystander.

On the day the Garda took him in for questioning Mr Hoare seemed devoid of all remorse. He felt justified and vindicated. In his statement he actually said, 'I have shown that bitch that she should never muck around with me.' He is a cruel and calculating killer.

He believed that he owned Molly. That she was his child to do what he liked with. He believed that he owned his wife and that she needed to be punished for breaking up the family.

We will present testimony of people who will confirm that he had in the past made serious threats of seeking revenge against his wife should anything disrupt the marriage; that he saw his relationship with his wife and children as one of ownership. It was only after he had spent a cold, lonely night in a prison cell with time to consider his situation that he modified his story and made it out to be an accident.

The defence has rustled up a 'psychiatrist of last resort' who will attempt to vindicate Mr Hoare's actions saying he was suffering a case of fluctuating disassociation and was temporarily insane at the time of the incident.

However, we will produce three of our own highly regarded professionals who disagree with this diagnosis and maintain that the defendant is capable of horrific actions and knew exactly what he was doing. They will attest to the fact that Mr Hoare presents as a borderline psychopath, a person who is so emotionally bereft that he can function as if other people are merely objects to be manipulated and destroyed without concern. That depiction aptly describes Stuart Hoare's actions before, during and after the incident on the motorway bridge.

In explanation, there are approximately twenty criteria used to assess a person's level of psychopathy. They include aspects such as emotional shallowness, glibness and superficial charm, a grandiose sense of self worth, lack of empathy, a tendency to boredom, thinking more with the head than the heart, being self-absorbed and constantly driven to win. In other words, they understand what another person may be feeling, but they do not feel it themselves.

Corporate professionals often score highly on the test, but that is not to say they are out-and-out psychopaths, rather that they lack moral scruples and are indifferent to other people's suffering. This disregard for others helps them achieve their aims, and that is what we are saying about Stuart Hoare.

According to the measures Mr Hoare presents as a borderline psychopath. All his actions on the day in question indicate that he is unable to empathise, he is shallow in his emotional response to others and has little ability to reflect on how his actions affect others.

We contend that Stuart Hoare deliberately and wantonly dropped Molly Hoare over the bridge into traffic below in order to cause pain and grief to his wife Jennifer Hoare who was leaving him for another man. He is guilty of murder.

THE JUDGE OF THE CENTRAL COURT

There is no middle ground in this case. When everything is presented, the jury will have to decide whether it was simply a tragic accident, a heartbreaking mishap, or a deliberate act of vengeance taken out by an angry father against his wife.

Was Stuart Hoare mad? Or was he bad?

That will be the jury's duty to deliberate.

STUART

Each day I dress in a good suit, silk shirt and blue tie and ensure my shoes are clean and sparkling for my appearance at the trial. I need to present as a fine upstanding citizen, a successful and well-respected businessman. I keep my head high and endeavour to hide my emotions, never looking Jennifer's way. This may be interpreted by the jury as a sign of respect and in some way as significant. However, to be perfectly honest I do it because she makes me sick; I simply can't bear the sight of her.

The O'Brien's gun counsel Flannery loves nothing better than to label me 'murderer' but who can take seriously a legal hustler whose nickname around the hallowed halls of the legal world is 'Flash'.

My astute lady barrister ruthlessly objected to Jennifer's accusations of negativity in our relationship and diminished them by keeping up the attack even when the aging judge upheld objections. The bitch soon discovered that re-telling isolated incidents involving differences of opinion does not constitute a massive case of domestic violence. Individually cited, they come across as trifling and querulous - a roll call of minor complaints, events and attitudes that surface in thousands of families across Ireland every day. 'He insisted I come home early from parties,' which was an important issue to her, only seemed a querulous, inane complaint to those not in the full know.

My counsel further brought to the court's notice that Jennifer and Tom were former university lovers whose re-kindling of their relationship on Facebook had split the family. When Jennifer argued that they did not 'split' the family, Fionnoula calmly and succinctly spelt out the obvious.

'Mrs Hoare, you were taking your five-year-old daughter with you to set up home in the East End of London, leaving your two teenage sons behind with their father. One parent in England, one parent in Ireland; one child in England, two children in Ireland. If that is not splitting the family then what is?'

Ah, Jennifer. No comeback on that one!

Because of legal requirements, the pre-trial reporting of my case had been confined to the basics, but now it was officially coming out that the reason we were on the M50 that day was because Jennifer was leaving me. This was the first time the public was hearing the heart of the matter and the court stirred noticeably. Ms Nolan paused and stepped back to let it sink in before the judge was compelled to call for quiet.

She went on to point out that even members of Jennifer's own birth family had rallied around me and agreed to help me with the wellbeing and care of our two sons while she was living 'the rock star life in London.' That the two grandmothers had offered to take turns at cooking the evening meal and keeping the lads' school clothes in good condition. Usually, she pointed out, the two opposing sides in a marriage breakdown follow their divided loyalties, so this was most unusual, if not extraordinary.

When questioned about the crucial moment when Molly went over the edge, Jennifer had to agree that she never actually saw it. At the time she was stressed and trying to clamber out of an unfamiliar car and admitted that at that stage she could not dare construe that I would do such a thing deliberately.

Then Ms Nolan went for the jugular, questioning Jennifer's personality and posing a series of questions about her background. Many of these were objected to by the prosecution or ruled as inadmissible. But the gallery, the press and the jury still got to hear the killer phrases that Fionnoula wanted them to hear, starting with, 'You grew up in the well-to-do suburb of Blackrock, did you not?' She then followed up with references such as 'father a wealthy entrepreneur,' and 'attending an exclusive private school,' and going on to study law 'in the leafy halls of one of the great universities of the world,' adding that the family was so well-to-do that it could afford for her 'to board at one of the premier student colleges at Cambridge.' She pitched a line that 'unlike most students, who wait on tables, slop out kitchens or pull pints to buy their books and pay for the gas, there was no need for you to work to sustain yourself while you were studying, was there?'

Across a few minutes, Fionnoula had cleverly constructed an image of a poor little rich girl, a spoilt princess who was doted on by her father and brothers, one who was used to getting her own way and never capable of compromising. Throw in the 'rock star' reference and Jennifer was suddenly looking very vulnerable.

The gallery, the press and the jury had heard exactly what the defence wanted them to hear and when Jennifer finally lost all composure and started screaming hysterically about how unfair the trial had been to *her*, Ms Nolan's job was all but done.

The tide had turned and Jennifer's innocence had been washed away on a sea of tears, leaving behind very little sympathy for her case.

I have to admit Ms Nolan was good, very good.

JENNIFER

By the time Stuart's case finally started Da's heart was playing up so Mam opted to stay with him and look out for the boys while I sat through the endless and often gruelling days in court.

Taking the stand was difficult but I knew I had to do it for Molly. I objected to Stuart being referred to as 'your husband' because in my mind he is no longer, and he will never be again.

The prosecution led me through the questioning as gently as possible but the defence was nowhere near as kind. The irony of it all is that Stuart is having his sideshow run by a woman. And a tough, independent one at that!

She is relentless. 'Limiting ourselves to the events of the day, Mrs Hoare, the simple fact is that the reason you were on the motorway flyover that day was because you were heading to Dublin International Airport, were you not? Leaving home and going to live in London with Mr Knight, the man with whom you were having adulterous affair?'

Well what could I say? No, because I liked his bongo drums?

She dwelled endlessly on the marriage break-up and my part in it, questioning me relentlessly about how I provoked Stuart, suggesting that I ambushed him when he returned from golf on that fateful day and that I had given him no room to manoeuver.

She attacked me over my supposedly privileged background, making out that the O'Brien clan was filthy rich and that I had always got my own way in everything. She proposed that I had split the family in two by taking the daughter and leaving the sons; that even my family had felt so sympathetic towards Stuart that they offered to help care for the boys when he was at work.

I kept trying to tell the story of our abusive marriage and make the jury understand how difficult it had been. But even when I did gain a little traction, his fancy female barrister was right in my face, portraying Stuart as a poor misunderstood creature who is really a nice guy!

Sometimes I was unable to stop myself from standing and screaming objections to the lies spewing from Stuart's camp and mostly I ended up in tears. As the days dragged on I sensed the tide turning against me but felt powerless to do anything about it. I came away each afternoon feeling as if I was the guilty one and that poor Stuart was the victim.

The whole thing is unfair and horrible, more like the 1916 Easter Rising than a court of justice. The accused is getting the royal treatment while the victim is left out to suffer in the cold like a pauper.

Then the inevitable happened. Da found one of the newspaper reports so upsetting that his heart went into unnatural rhythm and he landed in hospital in intensive care.

WENDY

I am afraid that this court case is making Jennifer bitter and angry. The defence is doing their best to make her look like the home wrecker and Stuart as Mr Squeaky Clean Businessman of Dalkey.

I know for a fact that the marriage was long over because of his history of physical, sexual and emotional abuse. Fine upstanding Christian man indeed! Witnesses at the golf club overheard Stuart and his friends discussing what they would do if their wives ever left them. Stuart actually said that he would deprive Jen of

Molly as she belonged to her and the boys belonged to him. That man can only see things from the perspective of ownership. He is disgusting.

Poor Tom. He really is trying to do the best by Jen but it is difficult. She is so tied up with all that is going on that she totally neglects him, hardly even knows he is here. He is standing aside and giving her all the time she needs, wary of sitting in court to support her as it only serves to inflame her situation. So his days are long and tedious and my advice to Jen would be to get this case over and done with and not keep Tom waiting for too long because a good-looking man like him will be snatched up if she dilly-dallies. I think he is gorgeous and have got to know him pretty well in the last year. The way I see it is that he has been very patient.

Since Seamus has been in hospital, I have been seeing to the boys a bit more. They are great and I pretty much let them do what they wish, as long as I am around to keep an eye on things. What their mother allows them to do is another matter, but I don't think it's my job to set the rules, rather simply keep the ship sailing smoothly while Jen is otherwise occupied. She is exhausted at the end of each day and goes straight to bed after dinner.

TOM

I stayed on to support Jen through the trial but I only seem to be in the way and complicating things. Each night she comes home from court exhausted, pleads tiredness, withdraws to the bedroom and leaves me with Wendy. Talk about sending the lamb into the lion's den!

Wendy has been an almost full time carer for Junior and Richie lately, running them about and organizing meals. She is unable to conduct a relationship for herself as she is too tied up with Jen's situation so we have been enjoying each other's company.

The sexual energy between us is palpable, but Wendy laughs it off and calls it tantric sex. 'The sex you have when you are not having sex, darling,' she says. The idea is to channel all the sexual energy that we would normally expend during an orgasm back into our bodies. This builds an even greater reserve of energy and we become more connected to the universe. 'A great and noble theory!' I say, as I pour her another one of Stu's classic reds. 'It's a win-win situation!'

I have never delayed the sexual act before and I must say, I am enjoying this new celibacy thing. For me it's the best of both worlds. We are supporting Jen as well extending our exploration of Buddhist yoga.

Sometimes I think we are having too much fun while Jen is going through the pain of the trial, but life is there to be lived and enjoyed.

Still, it might all end soon. I have to go and give evidence next week.

STUART

Yesterday in court Orla was wearing the beautiful gold Lancaster watch that I gave her as a surprise gift. She is here every day in her professional capacity as social worker on the case. It is good to look over and see her.

When Tom took the stand he stated he had little or no recollection of anything from the moment he began to drive up the flyover until he woke up in hospital several days later. I did my job well! However, under questioning from Flannery he ventured that he has a recurring dream about a man throwing children over a bridge and the prosecution attempted to link this, suggesting that after having witnessed a chillingly awful event he has buried it deep in an unreachable spot in his subconscious. 'The dreams are actually what he witnessed,' they proposed.

This was pure conjecture, and Ms Nolan firmly objected and made it clear to the jury it was unprovable psychological poppycock. Looking at him, with his hip hair and rock star clothes, I thought, 'Nobody in their right mind would believe this Peter Pan.'

Other witnesses proved to be either unreliable or ultimately withdrew their evidence. My lads saw nothing and to save them the stress they were not called, while Kevin was distracted by his cell-phone and the accident involving the elderly couple and the motorcyclist. The bikie similarly saw nothing and neither did the husband who was more stressed about the damage to the grille of his Mercedes.

It transpired that his wife, the lady who came over and exclaimed that I was 'the Devil himself', was convinced I deliberately threw Molly over the side, but under a barrage of questions, she on reflection now doubted herself as she was confused about 'the game' and what that all meant. This significant concession caused Ms Nolan to display a slight sliver of a smile.

Nevertheless, with a degree of confidence, Flannery called the prosecution's trump card, the knitting lady.

It is intriguing to see how the combination of the lofty architecture of a court room, its alienating language and legal eagles shuffling piles of papers and peering over their glasses can so often have a daunting impact on a witness venturing there for the first time. A judge and jury listening intently to every word you say and the inference that a man's whole future hangs on your every answer can be overwhelming. The constant request to give simple 'yes' or 'no' answers and not provide any elaboration can prove unsettling, the lack of opportunity to embroider an answer with detail frustrating.

Under this pressure, the knitting lady ultimately could not trust herself to swear to what she saw. Three times she started her answer by saying, 'Well, it sort of looked to me as if …' Response by response, her evidence slowly fizzled like a deflating balloon into nothingness.

So, after days of evidence, it all boiled down to my recollections. The gallery buzzed with anticipation as Ms Nolan rose to her feet to call me.

Then she said it. 'Mr Hoare will not be taking the stand.'

MCMAHON FOR THE DEFENCE

Flannery jumped to his feet and went berserk, castigating Fionnoula, her junior, me, the doorman, anyone, for devising a 'devious legal ploy designed to ensure that the people of Ireland will not be privy to the information they deserve to know.'

His spectacular performance was curtailed by the judge who advised him that as an experienced and respected member of the legal fraternity he should be well versed in the vagaries of court practice and must abide by them. Flannery eventually sat down, banging files on the desk and gravely muttering dark threats.

The reaction rolled like a clap of thunder around the courtroom. What a scenario. After days and days of testimony the only person who really knew what happened on that flyover was not going to testify under oath but instead present an unsworn statement to the court.

A masterstroke by Fionnoula, it meant Stuart could have his say but not be subjected to a cross examination that might take him down dangerous, dark alleys that could colour the jury's view. The judge solemnly advised them that his statement would be quite legal but would not carry the weight of sworn evidence. 'It should therefore be treated with extreme caution,' he intoned gravely.

Then, just when peace was finally restored, pandemonium erupted again when Ms Nolan stood to read the statement on Stuart's behalf.

It was Jennifer's turn to go crazy. She leapt to her feet pointing in her husband's direction, shrieking, 'Why isn't he reading it? He should be reading it! I demand he reads it!'

This spurred the rest of her family to weigh in. 'The weak fecker,' Kevin yelled, brandishing his fist. His brothers joined in, a cacophony of cries echoing through the chamber railing against Stuart's apparent gutlessness. 'You spineless bastard,' came the shouts. 'Be a man! Do your duty.'

Despite the best efforts of the tipstaff and his crew, the court plunged into disarray until the noisy mob were unceremoniously nabbed, silenced and frog-marched out into Infirmary Road.

Jennifer was crying, her fancy lawyer had been sidelined, several members of her family had been evicted and we appeared to be left holding the trump card.

After all that fire and emotion, the reading of the statement was something of an anti-climax but it did hit a chord. You could hear a pin drop.

SWORN STATEMENT - STUART RICHARD HOARE

The death of my daughter, Molly Hoare, was an unfortunate accident, which I truly regret.

On that drizzly afternoon of Saturday April 25, 2009, my wife, Mrs Jennifer Hoare, our five-year-old daughter, Molly, my wife's husband, Mr Kevin O'Brien, and myself were travelling in Mr O'Brien's car from our home in Dalkey to the Dublin Airport.

The reason for this journey was that my wife was leaving our marriage of seventeen years to go and live in London with another man, Mr Thomas Knight. She was taking Molly with her and leaving our two sons, Stuart Junior, aged thirteen years, and Richard, aged eleven, in Ireland for me to look after.

I accompanied Molly in the back seat of the car as I would not be seeing her again for some time.

The trip was a stressful and emotional one as I had no prior knowledge of Mrs Hoare's plans and had only found out about them when I returned from playing golf that morning.

After driving via some major roads and various side streets, we were about to get on to the M50 via flyover number three when we came to a halt. I saw that there had been an incident involving a car and a motorcycle up ahead on the flyover and traffic was at a standstill while we waited for it to be cleared. It threatened to make us late on our journey.

We waited in the car but my wife continuously complained and blamed me for the delay even though I had no control over the situation.

In order to take myself away from her incessant nagging I decided to exit the car and wait outside on the road. I unharnessed my daughter Molly Hoare from her car seat to take her with me for a breath of fresh air.

It was raining lightly and there were puddles on the ground so in order to keep her entertained I began a game that she and I called Catch Molly.

This is a game where I pretend to drop her and arrest her fall at the very last moment so no harm comes to her. I played this game in varying forms with all three of my children when they were small. For its safe execution and pure drama it relies on the child's trust and my excellent reflexes, honed on my years practicing martial arts. It is a game the children love.

We were playing happily when the air was shattered by a sudden and extremely loud shout from Mrs Hoare. I lost concentration at the crucial time for the briefest of moments and accidentally dropped Molly who fell to the motorway below sustaining injuries that ultimately lead to her untimely and tragic death.

It was an awful accident.

I have thought of the dire consequences of my actions every day since and after having spent many hours reflecting painfully on that day I now understand that by engaging Molly in this game and in this fraught situation I was foolhardy. It was a dangerous thing to do and I am deeply remorseful.

I unreservedly apologize to my wife for my actions, to my sons, Junior and Richie, to all of the Hoare and O'Brien families and to the broader community and the people of Ireland.

I want my sons to know that Molly's death was a dreadful accident and that I am so sorry that my carelessness has deprived them of a sister they truly loved.

I wish to apologise for the pain and suffering that this accident has brought my wife, Jennifer.

I also apologise for the physical pain and suffering incurred by Mr Knight as a result of a blow I delivered to his head in the heat of the moment. In my defence I must point out that at that time I considered that he was as much responsible for Molly's circumstances as I was, as he was the reason that we were there on the flyover. If he had not chosen to take my wife to England with him we all would have been safely home at that time. He needed to be punished. I did not intend to kill or maim him. If I had, I would have hit him harder.

By admitting my guilt and relating my own personal recurring sadness, I submit myself to the wisdom, judgement and mercy of the court.

I swear that the information I have provided is true and complete.

Stuart R. Hoare.

FLANNERY FOR THE PROSECUTION

This shameful presentation purports to be the truth but I have no doubt it is a flimsy tissue of lies.

I am disillusioned at the way this case has been conducted and I have loudly castigated the shoddy undermining of the due processes of the law and complete lack of integrity the defence has shown in denying both the court and the public the right to know the absolute, untainted truth behind this distasteful episode.

Ms Nolan is new to the profession and if this theatrical performance is indicative of the quality of graduate coming out of our law schools, then I cry for justice in this country. She cleverly choreographed a completely entertaining production for the jury, playing them like fiddles.

As for those O'Briens! By creating undignified chaos in the sanctity of the courtroom they turned all and sundry against them, and when Ms Nolan finally got to read the statement for the accused, it seemed that Stuart Hoare had suddenly gained a whole lot of credibility.

THE JUDGE INSTRUCTING THE JURY

There is no middle ground in this case. There are only two possible scenarios:

1. Was Molly Hoare's death a heartbreaking accident and will this father live with deepest regrets for the remainder of his life as the result of his moment of foolishness?

2. Is Molly's demise a deliberate act of vengeance by an angry husband in order to extract revenge from his unfaithful wife who dared to leave him?

This is what the jury must determine.

JURY FOREMAN

As foreman I am right at the centre of the so-called Trial of the Century and it is my grave responsibility to make sure all members come to a unanimous decision. We have to determine whether Stuart Hoare did deliberately throw his daughter to her death. If he did then he is guilty of murder and must be sentenced accordingly. But if we have any doubts then we must find him not guilty and he is then a free man.

After our first count of heads about half the members said they had more or less made up their minds but wished to have time to talk it through. The others were convinced of his guilt and wanted to hang him tomorrow. I doubt that they fully, actively listened to what had been laid out before them by the witnesses and the judge.

Unlike the string-him-up group, I have listened to every word, clinically considered all angles and respectfully weighed up every aspect of the case. From that, I am convinced that Stuart Hoare did not mean to drop Molly that day. I am a conservative thinker and inclined to be old school. In fact, I went to Stuart's old school …

Not that I was there at the same time as Hoare was, I must add. If I had have been, I obviously would not have been allowed to sit on the jury and would have excused myself. He's a bit older than me but as a member of the Old Boys' Committee, I can tell you, he passed through those grand old halls without attracting the interest of the school historians. He left no lasting impression and failed to achieve anything that has become part of the college's story. But no matter what his achievements, and whether we like it or not, he is one of us and we should do the best by him. It is a code of honour and who knows, I might need similar support myself one day.

JURY WOMAN

And I thought we would be in there for thirty minutes, tops!

We argued it up and down for hours and slowly but surely, even the most insistent of us who thought he was guilty began to get worn down under the pressure from that damn foreman. He just wouldn't see our way.

From a woman's perspective, I am convinced that Hoare is as guilty as hell. He did it to seek revenge against the wife and wreck her chances with the boyfriend, who incidentally is one cool looking dude.

But the foreman kept arguing that there was not one person who could genuinely and definitely state that they saw the actual moment when the little girl went over the edge, except perhaps the old lady whose car had knocked the bikie. But Hoare's clever legal eagle punched too many holes in her story so she began to doubt herself and eventually all she could say was, 'I thought I saw it.'

The knitting lady was the same. The defence made her so unsure of herself. I believe that she saw it but just couldn't bring herself to commit to that. You know what?

I bet that poor thing lives with an abusive husband, too. No self-belief at all, scared of saying something that might impact on this bully boy forever.

Our foreman kept running with the theme that there was a man's life at stake and he was suffering enough with the loss of his little girl. That all the evidence was circumstantial and no one could definitely say they saw him do it, so he should not be punished any further.

Eventually the red-faced, pot-bellied electrician from Palmerstown down the other end of the table stood up and said, 'Oh, for feck's sake, let's give the poor bastard the benefit of the doubt. Now, who's for a pint?'

JURY MAN

How the effin' hell did we end up picking this feller as the foreman?

Characters like him amaze me. They turn up wearing a snazzy suit, carrying a leather briefcase and talking with a silver tongue, naturally assuming they will take charge.

This bloke went through every witness statement, every medical report, every police account, detail by detail, point by point until people's eyes began to glaze over and a couple of the smokers started to develop the edgy, nicotine-starved look.

I was all for knocking it over in the first hour, sending Hoare off to jail and getting the hell out of there. For me, every hour away from my business is losing me money. It's tough enough in the sparks game at the best of times, but these days when the economy has slowed up so badly it is an absolute nightmare.

It had been obvious to me from the start that the bloke did it deliberately to shaft his pretty little redhead wife and bugger up the devious plans of her fornicating boyfriend with the Monkees haircut. You could see that a mile away.

But hours later we were still at it.

So when Mr Smart-Arse Foreman said, 'Let's go through this again,' I swapped sides. 'You are right,' I said. 'This Stuart feller is not going to do anything bad again. It was just one of those terrible one-off things. By gee, thirsty work, this business, isn't it?'

JURY WOMAN

At the mention of the phrase, 'Who's for a pint?' I have never seen a bunch of people move so fast to give their vote, pick up their stuff and get out of there, the smokers leading the way.

JENNIFER

As we sat in the stuffy courtroom awaiting the verdict I could tell that Stuart was very anxious because he kept adjusting his tie, shooting his cuffs and swallowing hard, all the while staring hard at a point somewhere in front of him.

Up until now, despite what he has done to me over the years, I have always believed that Stuart could never conceive doing such a bad thing to our little girl. But as a result of this court showdown I have been having second thoughts, particularly after I had to listen to the appalling things that he and his team insinuated about me.

And then, when he was so gutless that he could not even stand up to cross-examination under oath and personally tell the world what really happened, I knew deep down in my cold, broken heart that he did it deliberately. Knowing him as I do, he loves the spotlight and would have taken the stand if he wasn't afraid of being exposed.

STUART

When the jury retired to consider the verdict I don't think I have ever felt more nervous in my life. I tried to put a lid on it, but they were out for hours and when they finally came back into the courtroom I was a nervous wreck and the atmosphere was electric.

I braced myself, deliberately squared my shoulders military style and held my head high, just like Father would have wanted me to.

The judge asked the foreman, 'Have you come to a verdict?

'Yes, we have.'

'On the charge of murder, how do you find the defendant?'

I was truly grateful that Kevin had been banned from the court room. On hearing those two words, he would have destroyed it.

JURY WOMAN

It was only when the foreman stood up in court to deliver our verdict that I realised that he and the defendant were wearing the same suits, shirts and ties, with their shoes as shiny as all get-out. They could have been twins.

STUART

While all about us went crazy, with Fionnoula congratulating her team and the gallery babbling away in an excited reaction, Jennifer and I briefly found ourselves together in a small annex to the side of the court.

You have to give her her due. She was shocked, but still very gracious, even giving me a perfunctory kiss and telling me that she was sorry that I had had to go through all of this but at least the air was cleared and now we could put this awful episode behind us and get on with our lives. A bit shallow coming from the woman that caused it all!

I thanked her and did what I considered the right thing and told her that I would be returning home the next day. 'You may continue living in the house if you wish,' I said. 'But if you do you will have to forget the Englishman and be my wife in all respects.'

That changed everything. She spat at me like a Kilkenny cat, saying that I just wanted her to stay on as the cook and housekeeper, iron my shirts and have dinner ready when I get home.

That was it. There's no way she will stay under the same roof as me again. Ever! And I told her so.

To be honest I don't give a damn any more. The boys will be happy to stay with me, and who knows what may happen. New beginnings I say! Out with the old and in with the new.

I stepped outside into the soft rain as a free man, to find myself surrounded by friends, family and supporters as well as being hounded by opponents and the raucous rolling ratbags of the media.

'You must be happy with the decision?' came a strident voice.

'Were you surprised how quickly the verdict took?' said another.

'Stuart, what's it like to be a free man?' came a third.

Stupid, inane questions! Of course I am happy. Of course it feels good.

My first inclination was to clam up and ignore the howling wolves but when I was almost past them and about to step into the car, I stopped and indicated that I would say something; share my wisdom so to speak.

'No man wants to be incarcerated in a permanent cell of regret, inside the prison of a tortured mind,' I said. 'Contrary to your assessment, I am not a free man. For the rest of my days I will be shackled by the fact that my daughter is no longer alive and I played a significant role in the events that led to her demise. That is the life I face. It is not the life of a free man.'

I flopped into the back seat and shut the door. 'Wow,' said McMahon, as he fired up the motor and edged slowly through the throng. 'Where did that come from?'

I pulled the piece of paper from my inside pocket that I had been memorizing for days. 'I got Buchanan to source it from an out-of-work writer he found in the pub,' I said. 'He was good, very good.'

JENNIFER

I respect the court's decision and was prepared to wave the olive branch but he would have none of it. I crossed the courtroom to congratulate and support him but he rudely brushed me off telling me that he was coming back home and if I did not plan to be a proper wife to him then he would give me twenty-four hours to get out. 'The lads will stay with me,' he declared pompously. 'As was decided on the day you left me to go with that feckin' little smart-arse.'

That's it. End of story. The sensible thing to do is make the move London, pronto. That's what we planned to do before this sorry saga began so that is what will happen now.

When I got home Tom had already decided to go and had his bags packed. He said he was anxious to open up the house and get back to work and normality as soon as he could. 'I know you have a lot of things to do, Jen,' he said. 'So you can follow me at a later date, when everything has calmed down.'

I will go and spend a couple of weeks with Mam while I settle the boys and make arrangements. 'It all seems so sudden but I have sort of known it was coming,' I said. 'So in some ways it is not a surprise.'

The good thing is that in London nobody will know me, nobody knows my history and nobody will judge me and I can go anywhere and do anything. Tom and I can be together at last. I am free.

The Press - editorial

The 'little Molly on the bridge' story has captured the public's imagination and they haven't been able to get enough of it.

We have carried many stories examining the case and its aftermath, delved into every aspect of Stuart Hoare's history from primary school days on and even trawled through his tax, Garda and business records, interviewing anybody who knew him - friends, acquaintances or associates.

Many people have lost a lot of money through the crash of the Celtic Tiger, the bad decision-making of our government and the appalling mismanagement of our banks. Hoare was one of those, his Tallaght development a disaster, a monumental project that went broke, although he has other strings in his bow to fall back on.

Stuart Hoare is a dull character that has been set apart from the rest by being charged with a dastardly deed and perhaps this fact alone prompts us to ask, 'How could an ordinary man do such an extraordinary thing?'

It appears he didn't. Stuart Hoare has been exonerated and is free to go and get on with his life, hopefully never to be heard of again.

His wife is the more interesting one! Redheaded, educated, privileged, beautiful, a mother in a lovely house in an exclusive suburb. It appeared that she had it all; everything she needed to have a good life.

And yet she was prepared to give it all away to run off with a dope-smoking, middle-aged second-rate drummer from England.

Now that's a good story!

LOVER, HUSBAND, FATHER, MONSTER

Part Ten

TOM

It is now impossible for me to be here with Jen in Ireland, living in the family home under constant scrutiny. The Irish are strange buggers. It is all about emotion, never logic, and they absolutely hate me.

Stuart was very smart playing the 'murder or nothing' card and he is feeling smug and vindicated. It seems that he will now return to normal life, reclaim his castle and take up his business dealings as if nothing has happened. Hardly fair.

Jen and I decided that I should leave for London immediately while she goes to her mother's place to tie up any loose ends, see that the lads are okay and get her mind focused. I fly out tomorrow. She will follow when she is organised, and although we will miss each other, the time will pass quickly until we can be together again.

Once I arrive in London there will be a lot of catching up and reclaiming of my own old life to do. I look forward to being in my own digs where I can be who I want, do what I want, and nobody will care either way. I will get back to work and continue with my music, hopefully drawing deep on my recent experiences to write a pile of original material to increase my street cred.

JENNIFER

Stuart gave me twenty-four hours to vacate the house. I did it in half the time. To avoid seeing him I left early the morning after the verdict and went straight home to Mam's.

I quickly realised that Da was very ill. He finds it difficult to get out of bed in the mornings and is often confused with his thought processes. He ingests a plethora of medicines and drugs, has to wear an incontinence pad and has become a very fussy eater. On top of that he is a very grumpy patient.

'I knew he'd had a health scare,' I lamented to Mam over an early morning cup of tea, 'but I thought that he had given up the cigarettes and the drink and he was all the better for it.'

'And he was, lovie,' Mam replied, 'but Molly's accident knocked the stuffing out of him. He'd been perfectly healthy until Stuart did what he did.'

The following night, while we were watching television together, my oldest brother Patrick completely set Da off kilter.

'You know I have been staying with you for some months now,' he said nervously.

'Of course, darling,' said Ma. 'When you came down from Galway I have never seen you so worn out and stressed. The rest here is doing you good, isn't it?'

'Yes, and the reason I felt so bad ... it ... it ... it will all come out in the open tomorrow.'

'What do you mean, Paddy?'

He looked down and clenched his fists. Tears began to well.

'I'm giving evidence to the Ryan Report on Child Sexual Abuse.'

Ma and Da looked at each other as if he had just said he was going to catch the next rocket to Mars.

'Darling …'

'No! Ma, Da. Listen. I have to tell you this. When I was an altar boy there was a newly ordained priest named Father Gerard. He used to take me sailing after the eleven o'clock Mass every week. You remember that?'

They both nodded slowly.

'We always came back home to Blackrock for Sunday night's tea,' he continued. 'At first nothing happened but then … then, he started touching me and rubbing up against me and it sort of gave me the creeps so I tried to keep out of his way, but you and Da liked him and kept inviting him back, so I was sort of trapped. I couldn't say anything about it.

'Then, do you remember when he took me on the St Patrick's Purgatory pilgrimage to Station Island where we had to walk across stones in bare feet and pray for three days? There was a group of us but somehow he managed to arrange it so that we were separated from the rest in the dormitory and I was in a tiny little room with him. That weekend was the worst of my life. He raped me several times. I was so ashamed. Remember how I came home bleeding and told you I had fallen and hurt myself on the rocks?

'He had me petrified and although I tried to keep away from him as best I could he always seemed to entrap me. That was when I stopped going to Mass, remember? And nothing you or Da could say could convince me to go with you. That bastard felt quite at home here and was always catching me unawares and doing terrible things to me that have haunted me all my life.

'Now the psychiatrist says I have to tell you what happened to me or I will never get better.'

Having let it all out, Paddy slumped forward crying uncontrollably and that only served to make Da explode. He thought men who cried unmanly. Red in the face and struggling for breath, he showed not one skerrick of sympathy but instead accused Paddy of making trouble. He was so angry he reverted to the dialect of his childhood. 'Why are ye telling me all this nonsense now?' he yelled. 'Why didn't ye tell me when it was happening? Because you've made it all up, that's why! Ye have made it all up to excuse the way ye are, Paddy! You're a feckin' communist, trying to bring the church down! Doing the work of the Protestants! Shame on you. Shame!'

Poor Paddy. He couldn't tell Da at the time because he knew he wouldn't be believed. And now, after all these years when he had finally summoned the courage to explain it, he was still being called a liar. That said it all. About his family, about the Church and about the state of Ireland.

Da took to his bed fuming, and never really recovered.

MARY

That damn Stuart, he has escaped scrutiny, gotten off unscathed and come up trumps. He gets to resume his life, while poor Jennifer has been thrown out of her home and had her children taken away from her. We are all very angry about it because in our eyes he is as guilty as hell.

It's funny how things work out, though. She is here with us until she joins Tom in London and it seems that God has taken care of me by sending Jennifer when Seamus is so sick. I know it is ridiculous, but he blames me for both Molly's death and for Paddy's situation. That is difficult to deal with. He says that I encouraged

Jennifer to leave Stuart. 'If you had have been stronger then none of this would have happened,' he keeps saying.

As to Patrick's situation, Seamus' view is that as the wife and mother I was in charge of the family's moral upbringing and I failed miserably. 'All this time has gone by and Paddy hasn't said a word,' he said. 'So, why is he bringing it up now, when he said nothing while it was supposed to be happening? He just wants to destroy everything. The church, this family, that priest's good name.'

'How could he tell you?' I demanded. 'He was a child then, and now when he's a man in his fifties you still don't believe him. It's ruined his whole life, busted his marriage. I'm his mother. I believe him. That evil man was welcomed into our family and he abused our trust. I feel bad because I should have known. I should have protected him and I didn't.'

All of this makes Seamus a difficult patient to look after as he harbours grievances about me and the way I have carried out my mothering, and that is difficult to take, so having Jennifer here is something of a blessing.

JENNIFER

Paddy's devastating revelations have made it almost impossible for me to get away to London, as Da is now quite ill, even more truculent then ever and extremely difficult to handle. My mother needs me, so I stay.

At least, that is what I tell Tom when we Skype every day. But deep down, I know the real reason that I stay is because, well, I just can't find the wherewithal to get up and leave. An enormous lethargy has taken over me, sucked the energy out of me. I seem to have settled back into an almost mundane domesticity in the secure womb of my childhood home.

As well, it is just so hard to leave my boys and my darling Molly. Every day I tend to her little grave and then walk the paths of the Dublin Hills that we so often trod together. In a valley, adjacent to an old restored orphanage that is being used by a Retreat Group, a creek babbles and bubbles its way over smooth yellow rocks and oval stones past an old military cemetery. My walk often takes me across the ancient moss-covered bridge, where I open the wrought iron gate and go inside and stand in front of the neat rows of plaques that declare here are the mortal remains of German airmen and sailors who perished on Irish soil in the Second World War.

I read the tributes and think how sad it is that these boys, some of them only eighteen years old, died so far away from home and loved ones. But also how beautiful it is, that here in Ireland more than sixty years later, their graves are well tended and their memories kept alive in this beautiful rose garden. Nothing could be sadder than these young lads dying prematurely - some as a result of wayward planes crashing, others washed up on shore from sunken boats - but the Irish people have converted their tragedy into honour, doing what we do best and telling their story. The people who lovingly laid them to rest in this alien country did not know them but they too had sons, and so they honoured them.

Were the young men frightened when death came?

Were they so different from my Molly?

How did their mothers grieve?

Did they have the same black hole burnt into their heart like I have?

Terrible things have always happened but it's the way we deal with them that renders them noble or tragic. I have vowed to convert the evil that happened in our family to good, to take the tragedy of Molly and ensure that her story is told. I don't quite know how I am going to accomplish that but I have noticed that Mam and the boys listen to my ramblings and don't push them aside.

WENDY

We were out together after our meditation session when I broached a subject with Jen that has been worrying me. I wanted to know what was going on in her mind. 'Jen, have you shut Tommy out completely? It's been ages now since he went back to London and you show no inclination to go and join him. Is it over between you two?'

She denied it, saying that it was because she was just so busy. Then she said she had no time for Tom at the moment and that no matter how hard she tries, she still somehow blames him for what happened to Molly. She knows this is not logical, but she can't help thinking it.

I told her to step back and listen to what she was saying. How can she blame Tommy? It had absolutely nothing to do with him. I begged her not to let Stuart dictate her relationship and warned her that it would give that bastard great pleasure if things didn't work out between her and Tom.

Getting pretty agitated I pointed out, 'That is what motivated Stuart to kill Molly. He wanted to destroy you Jen! Don't let him do it! You were unhappy in your marriage long before Tommy came back on the scene and you would have left Stuart anyway. He was abusive, for God's sake. How can you blame Tom? He is a victim, an innocent bystander. It's cruel thinking like that!'

My advice to Jen is not to keep Tom waiting for too long. He has been very patient, giving her all the time she needs, but a good looking man like him is bound to be snatched up if she dilly-dallies.

That is why I don't feel guilty about the feelings that seem to be developing between Tom and me. We have been thrown together by our situation so I have gotten to know him pretty well and I think he is gorgeous. She has sort of pushed me into being the 'surrogate Jen'. I consider I have been keeping him warm for her until she is ready.

JENNIFER

Wendy didn't hold any punches and told me exactly what she thought. She doesn't seem to understand, and thinks I should go and live with Tom in London pronto. When she suggested that Stuart still controls me I felt sick, as I know I need to release myself of him altogether. She even quoted Buddha, probably from one of her self-help books, but it rang true.

'All life is impermanent, Jen,' she said. 'Every existence eventually comes to an end, and must be followed by a rebirth somewhere else. If you deny that, you are neglecting the final solution to your suffering. Surely Tom is the one who can heal you.'

I hear what she is saying and I agree with her. I must remember that all things have a reason and a season and my time to mourn will soon become my time to heal. Perhaps Tom can help that process. I will phone him.

TOM

Hooray, Jen has finally made the big decision to come to live in Barkers Road. After I hung up last night, I couldn't help but jump around my flat like a schoolboy at the end of final term.

I love my little place, which, although not in the most salubrious part of London, has a great multi-cultural feel with lots going on. I am near to my main studio and it is always simple to get my stash when I need it so I feel sure that Jen will grow to love it too.

WENDY

I hope I am doing the right thing here ...

MARY

Well, I guess she had to go. This on-again, off-again relationship - bear in mind, they first got together something like thirty years ago - has to be resolved one way or the other.

They have faced some mighty trials and tribulations over the years, the pair of them, with happiness always being snatched away from the last minute, often in the most horrible of circumstances.

As Jen headed off to the airport, I clutched my rosary beads and prayed fervently to all the saints that this time it would all come good.

TOM

Wow! It is awesome being together and it surprises me how good it is to get home from work to an orderly house and to have Jen and my favourite dinner waiting for me. Sunday mornings are easy. There is a Zen-like comfort in tackling chores together and the joy of just chilling out and perhaps going out for brunch or a movie. Life is different with Jen here. I don't need to go out to have fun; I can have it at home just hanging out with her.

Nevertheless, even at my age, I don't really understand women. Why are they so hung up on cleanliness? My lifestyle is pretty random and I suppose sometimes my housekeeping is a bit haphazard, although I reckon I do make an effort at tidying and cleaning. I certainly excel at picking everything up off the floor every now and then and making it disappear into the spare room. But still Jen reckons that my place is a mess. If she only knew! By the same token, if it makes her feel more comfortable to clean then it's fine by me.

JENNIFER

Being together is our greatest joy. It is blissful to be so in love. Having said that, I get pretty lonely when Tom is working - and a lot of his gigs and session work is at night - so all I ever seem to do is wait around for him while I do housework. Because the house is small and old, and Tom leaves his clothes where he drops them, it becomes untidy very easily and so I am always stepping over things, which is very annoying.

He tells me that he did a big clean up before I arrived. But from my perspective, it was only a surface job and this is still very much a bachelor pad.

'Underneath this so-called semblance of order lies two decades of decay and decadence,' I said. 'The carpet squishes when you walk on it and the windows haven't been cleaned for donkeys' years. That's why you have to have the lights on during the day.' He looked at me as if I had just outlined the Theory of Relativity.

So while he is at work I don the rubber gloves and systematically tackle the grot build-up. It keeps me busy as I go about trying to turn his house into our home, a project that keeps my mind and body occupied and helps me overcome my sadness and sense of dislocation.

I cleaned the windows, took down the mildew-ridden curtains and made new ones. I also discovered there were good floorboards under the carpet. So I ripped the carpet up, oiled the boards and put down a couple of throw rugs and it has all come up a treat. I got rid of piles and piles of junk, bought new towels and linen and did a fair bit of painting and decorating. I am pleased with the results and think our little place is becoming a very cute and cosy love nest.

Only one more thing to do - move those drums that dominate the entire lounge room!

TOM

There are lots of things about the way I live that irritate Jen and she does tend to go on about it a bit, so I am a little out of my depth, particularly when she says something like, 'Tom we need to talk!' That frightens the daylights out of me.

The place is starting to look stylish, like an Ikea store. Curtains on the windows, rugs on the floor, new bed linen. But Jen doesn't really like my stuff or the way I arrange it. She has moved the television out of the bedroom and put it in the lounge and got me to move the drum kit into the spare room! Fair go.

JENNIFER

I know Tom is a rock 'n' roll bachelor but surely a man in his forties doesn't need to drink to excess and smoke weed every time he does a gig? I get a bit impatient with him when he comes home high as a kite and wants to play sex games for hours on end. I'm too old for that.

TOM

Jen is having trouble separating from her boys. She spends a good hour on Skype each night talking to them. That annoys me a bit because we only have the tiny kitchen and one small living area, and they are interconnected, so it means that I can't really enjoy watching television or even pick out a tune on the electronic keyboard while she is on-line.

Lately she has picked up a bit of conveyancing work, which gives her money to get out and about and keeps her brain busy, so she doesn't dwell on things as much. However, it seems to me that while her body might be in London, her mind is still in Ireland with the boys and Molly.

JENNIFER

When I finally left Dublin for good I was still unsure that I was doing the right thing by everybody. But what I do know now is that it is wonderfully blissful to be away from Ireland and all that is happening there.

In Dublin I could not go anywhere without people hassling me. In London I am just another face in the crowd. I am free! I now understand how movie and pop stars feel when they get to a place where they are not recognized and can just be themselves. The media has not come near me since I landed. Tom shows me around his patch, and sometimes takes me to his gigs, or the theatre, or to meet friends. When he is working during the day I visit the museums and galleries.

Wendy has been over a couple of times and we have a grand time together. That girl is so random she gives me confidence. But London is not Dublin and a lot of it is still foreign territory to me, to the extent that I'm a little afraid to go out by myself at night. There are a few pubs along Barkers Road, but some of them are not the most savoury of places.

TOM

We have settled into a comfortable routine and life is uneventful, but pleasant. It inspires me to have Jennifer here. She complains about my marijuana smoking but it doesn't do any harm, just makes me mellow, and more

244

sexy! I am writing some really good original music. They say that any publicity is good publicity and my music career has taken off again. Big time! The television show that I had made in Dublin stood up well and is being considered for Britain, America, and Australia. They want me to do another series. Who says drummers are dumb?

The boys will be over later this month so I will finally have to move my drums out of the spare room into the garage to make way for a couple of beds. Not fair. It's bloody cold out there!

JENNIFER

It's been a while since the boys and I have been together even though I have been talking to them nightly. I can't wait for them to be over here for their mid-term break.

I bought a bunk bed and am having it delivered next week and I plan to take them all over London town and give them the time of their lives, poor mites.

After the re-decorating bills came to light, Stuart went off his nut and cancelled my credit card. So until the divorce settlement comes through, I only have the couple of thousand euro that is in my personal trust fund. But I now have a little part time job working for on-line lawyers, with the promise of more to come, so money is not so much of an issue any more. All will be settled soon and I will know where I stand.

Then perhaps we can move out of here into a better neighbourhood.

STUART

At last, over the last few months my life has been getting back to something approaching normal. That is not to say that things have been without their problems.

After the court case I was working very hard to catch up on business matters and was therefore not getting home until late most nights. I did not appreciate that the lads were running amok, particularly Junior, so when I was called up to the school regarding his behaviour I thought I'd best do something about it.

Problem solved! I got myself a live-in housekeeper.

Orla White.

Well, why not? She already knows the lads well because she has been our case social worker through the difficult times when all that nasty business was going on about Molly.

And secondly, she understands me.

I pay her tax-free money under the counter, as she wants to keep her job with Social Protection. For a small amount of cash, plus free board and lodging for herself and her son, all she has to do is be here after school, cook the evening meal and keep the place tidy. It is a good arrangement and I love it, as it is beneficial for my equilibrium. You have heard of friends with benefits? In this situation I have a housekeeper with benefits, so to speak!

Now, I go to work and can concentrate on the job at hand, the boys head off to school and are behaving themselves, and of an evening there is somebody here for them. I am better off without Jennifer. The sex is certainly better! But you cannot keep that woman out of the picture all the time. When I realised that she was still putting things on the credit card I stopped it, but not before she had spent thousands of my dollars on prettying up little drummer boy's crappy little East End flat.

She insists that not only is the divorce going ahead, but she is going to take me to the cleaners as far as the property settlement goes. Can you believe it? She says she will get half! I am very angry and will fight it tooth and nail. From my perspective, she left me, so she should get nothing. Never mind that the boys are living with me and I am picking up all their bills.

DETECTIVE BRYAN KELLY

At first I thought it was a joke and I wanted to brush them off.

'It's about the Molly Hoare case,' said the voice on the end of the line.

'You're a bit late, now, madam,' I said, 'the fellow got off scot free and is back living the life of luxury in Dalkey.'

'Yes, I know, but my son has something I think you ought to see.'

'See?'

'Yes, he was there that day. On the flyover. With his camera …'

'Your son? A camera? Put him on the line, will you?'

LOVER, HUSBAND, FATHER, MONSTER

Part Eleven

STUART

O ut of the blue, the coppers have turned up at my business, arrested me and charged me with murder!

They didn't even give me time to go home to pack a bag. I was allowed three phone calls to sort things out. The first I made to Mother who sobbed and sobbed to the point where she couldn't speak. There was no way she could look after Junior and Richie in her state so I had to eat humble pie and put the second call through to Mary O'Brien and ask her to pick up the boys and see to them.

And the third? Signalling Buchanan, who sprinted off to his office to get my lawyer on the go, I placed the last call to Orla. 'If you value your government job and your sanity, pack up and leave the house immediately,' I said. 'Jennifer will be on the next flight out of London, the O'Briens will be swarming all over the place within the hour and the bastards will be swilling champagne and celebrating all night. You won't want to be there.'

MARY

Stuart has been arrested! I couldn't believe it when it first it came through on a news bulletin, but then five minutes later he was on the phone telling me it was true, and that Moira was too upset to do anything, and would I take care of the boys until he could make some other arrangements. No asking how Seamus was getting on since I last spoke to him, or anything like that. But then again, that's Stuart through and through - everything is always about him.

He wouldn't give me a straight answer to my questions, but mentioned something about an incriminating video and that he was going back in jail.

I telephoned Jennifer immediately and she got on the internet to see what she could find out and to book a ticket home. She couldn't get one tonight but will be here first thing in the morning. I picked up the boys and took them to their own home as they have all their things there.

It was a bit hard explaining it to them, particularly as I am in the dark about most of it myself, but they have to be told by family. It's a hard world out there. Wendy came in after work, as she had heard the news on her car radio, and set up the Skype so we could talk to Jennifer.

None of us can believe it.

WENDY

When I heard the news about Stuart's arrest I decided to look in on the boys just in case. Mary was there with them and was all in a dither. The boys simply didn't want to know about it. They are overjoyed that their mother is coming back, but they seem to have forgotten the actual circumstance. Richie was helping Mary peel the spuds and Junior had headphones on and was listening to his music in the other room.

I phoned Jen and told her what I had heard, which came as an absolute shock to her as she had no idea about it. Apparently Molly's case doesn't make news across the Irish Sea. She immediately set up Skype and we had a long chat.

'There is no point in coming home tonight,' she said. 'I will stay, inform Tom of what has happened when he comes in from his gig, and come in the morning so I will be there for the boys when they get home from school tomorrow.'

'Jen, none of us can get our head around this news,' I said.

'Count me in,' she replied. 'I am just as shocked as you are. But we will know more when I talk to the Garda tomorrow.'

I shut the Skype and looked at the ceiling. There is a God! The bastard thought he had got away with it, but now it looks like he hasn't. I hope they put him away forever and he rots in jail until his last final moment.

Meanwhile Mary will stay the night with the boys, as I have to make an early start to go down to Cork for work.

JENNIFER

I am flabbergasted! I don't really know what it's all about. I prowled the net while waiting for Tom to come home and found something about the footage, but at about half eight it disappeared from the screen and was replaced with a sign saying there was an embargo on it. The Irish social media was just buzzing about it. Everybody has an opinion.

Tom came in and we talked it through. He will come with me to Heathrow in the morning as I have to be there by half nine.

'Are you happy, babe?' he said. Then he realised that 'happy' was probably not the right word.

251

'It's all very confusing and upsetting,' I said, starting to cry. 'On the one hand, it looks like Stuart will get his just desserts. But on the other, it is bringing back the awful saga that we had to endure and somehow had survived and which I thought had been put to bed.

'Now, here we go all over again. Will I ever get that man out of my life?'

TOM

Jennifer was sitting up for me when I came in from my gig. Her eyes were red and she had been crying. Wendy and her Mum had phoned to say that Stuart had been locked up again and she had spent the whole evening browsing the net trying to find out more.

She has organized a plane ticket to go home in the morning so I will catch the train from Canning Town out to the airport with her and come back home and wait until she calls me to decide what to. We shall have to be out of bed at the crack of dawn.

This is the freaky part. From what I hear about the footage, that constantly running nightmare of mine must be true.

JUNIOR

Da is in fuckin' jail again. I'm fuckin' sick of this. I just wish he would sort his fuckin' shite out. The good thing is that Mam is coming home. But she'd better not bring that fuckin' Tom with her. If she does I'm going to live with my girlfriend Maureen and her mother. I'm not staying in the same house as that fucker.

RICHIE

Nanna Mary came over last night and stayed. She let me help her get the dinner and I made an apple tart.

Wendy was here too and said it was the best she has tasted since her mother made them back in New Zealand. I am so excited that Mammy is coming home. She will be here when I get back from school. I had music practice but I will skip it and come home early. I can't wait!

PAUL SMITH - FILMMAKER

I have been out of the country for nearly a year on a trip that I had been planning for a long time but which nearly got derailed on the first day when I almost missed my plane because of an accident involving a car and a motorbike on the M50.

Fortunately, armed with my brand new video camera, I caught my flight with seconds to spare and made it to Antarctica to work on my dream project - at the Argentinian Research Station studying and filming emperor penguins.

After several months in Antarctica, I left for Australia and was having a good time filming the fairy penguins on Phillip Island when my sister called to say that Grandma had died and for me to come home for the funeral.

I arrived in Dublin last week, went down to County Clare for Gran's funeral, and came back home a few days ago. It being wet and miserable outside and having a few days to kill, I took the opportunity to go through the reams of footage I had taken Down Under and had never got around to looking at, on account of the sunshine and all of that. Nobody wants to be trawling through film when the surf is pumping.

'Start at the beginning, Paul,' I told myself, 'and do it logically.'

As it turns out, the first sequence was taken here in Ireland on the day I flew out. I'd come across an accident on a flyover. It was mayhem and so I got out and started filming, just to give the new camera a try. I stood back and tried to take in the whole scene, leaning against the car and keeping my hand steady as I panned around. But after ten minutes, I felt embarrassed about shooting pictures when so many people were either hurt or upset. A couple of people were obviously not happy, so I discreetly set the camera up on its tripod, widened the lens and simply let it run by itself while I sat in my car. I filmed until the ambulances had gone, the road was clear and we were on our way.

I took more than an hour's footage, but that's the good thing about digital equipment. You don't need to worry about the price of film.

If you watch it, you will see that fifteen minutes in, people in the various cars are getting agitated. They have places to go and are stuck. The bike rider is in pain on the road with people tending to him.

Then a sandy-haired man gets out of the back seat of a brand new BMW directly in front of the camera but diagonally on the other side of the road. He has a little girl with him whom he sort of jostles and plays with. You know, the game that some adults play with their little ones, where they pretend to drop them and catch them at the last moment. He does that three or four times and there is a juxtaposition of the seriousness of the accident and the joyous laughter of the little girl.

Then he moves away, carrying the girl with him, almost but not quite out of shot.

Nothing of significance happens for quite a few frames, probably thirty seconds or so, when suddenly a red-headed woman bursts out of the front seat of the BMW, screaming her head off and racing toward the man and the little girl. The driver of the BMW continues to listen to his earphones for a while, before the woman's screeching alerts him, and he too suddenly jumps out and rushes the same way.

I can't clearly recall what happened next because shortly after there was even more screaming and some bloke having his scone knocked off and people running everywhere.

But if you backtrack the footage and carefully examine the section before the woman jumps out of the car, up in the top left-hand corner of the shot, as clear as you like, you will see the sandy-haired man take the little girl to the side of the bridge and throw her over! It is quite deliberate, there on film. He holds her out, like a sacrifice, and then drops her.

When I saw this I could not believe my eyes and went back over it sequence by sequence. I called my sister and she looked at it.

'That is him!' she said. 'The Motorway Monster!'

I had never heard this phrase before. In fact I knew nothing about the case. Sensational as it has been, news of it never reached Antarctica or Australia.

We called Mam, she checked the footage out and straight away notified the police who came, had one look and said, 'That's the little Molly case, this changes many things.' And without much of a thank you they took my precious film away.

But by that time my sister had already put it up on You Tube.

NEW EVIDENCE EMERGES IN MOLLY HOARE CASE

A man has been charged with the murder of his daughter when new evidence came to light in the form of a documentary maker's film taken on the day little Molly Hoare fell to her death on the M50 motorway.

Previously unseen video footage shows Stuart Richard Hoare and his child, Molly, on the bridge of the No 3 flyover on the day of the accident.

Mr Hoare was accompanied by three security guards in court yesterday and sat behind glass, stony faced and staring blankly ahead as the charges were read out.

He has been charged with the murder of his daughter and remanded in custody until a new trial can be convened.

Previously, Mr Hoare was tried in front of a jury, found not guilty, and was free to leave the court and resume his life. However, it is alleged that this new evidence demolishes the defendant's case that little Molly's death was an accident, caused by a number of unfortunate occurrences, in particular the screams of his wife.

The filmmaker, Paul Smith has been out of the country on the Argentinian Antarctic Research Station in Antarctica studying penguins since the day of the accident. He returned to Ireland at the end of the season oblivious to the interest and public sympathy sparked by the Molly Hoare case. He discovered the forgotten footage in the editing room as he prepared his report.

Mrs Hoare has returned from London where she has been residing and sat in the gallery supported by family and friends.

Press report

Motorway Monster in court

Tired and upset, but impeccably dressed in a grey Armani suit, white shirt, yellow tie and smartly polished shoes, Stuart Hoare sat upright in court yesterday watching video footage which showed him deliberately and wantonly throw his daughter over a bridge onto the busy motorway beneath.

The presiding judge, Mr Justice Regan, advised the jury that this second trial of Mr Hoare was being held under the auspices of the Criminal Procedure Act 2010, which eliminated the long-standing double jeopardy rule and allows a re-trial of any murder case on the basis of 'new and compelling' evidence.

The judge instructed the jury to place considerable weight on the new 'and certainly compelling' evidence supplied by filmmaker Mr Paul Smith. He said the video provided irrefutable evidence that Stuart Hoare dropped his daughter with the intent to murder. In it Mr Hoare is seen deliberately stepping up, holding the child out over the railing, and throwing little Molly to her death. He does not look sidewards or backwards in response to his wife's voice, or any other stimuli, as he previously claimed.

The jury retired and returned a 'guilty' verdict after only forty minutes.

Hoare was sentenced to life imprisonment, the judge proposing that in the usual circumstances, at least twelve years of it would be served before admissions for parole would be considered. However, Mr Justice Regan deemed that if Mr Hoare receives counselling for anger management and for the recognition and treatment of narcissism and if ongoing psychiatric reports are favourable then the Parole Board could be asked to look at a case for release at the earlier date of seven years.

In delivering his sentence and recommendations the judge declared that he had taken into account that it is extremely unlikely that Mr Hoare will reoffend.

Mr Hoare was taken from the court, handcuffed and in the presence of two security guards, to begin serving his sentence in Dublin's Mountjoy Prison.

His wife Jennifer was in court, supported by family members, some of whom were still visibly angry. In a statement outside the court Mrs Hoare said that she was personally no longer angry but remained incredibly sad. 'Molly will live in my heart forever and I will always remember her,' she told reporters. 'The family can now pick up the pieces and get on with our lives. I am glad it is finally over.'

Part Twelve

STUART

Mountjoy Prison may be only a five-minute drive from the centre of Dublin but is a world away from reality and all hope, and not the sort of place a law-abiding fellow like me belongs.

Built 160 years ago, this dump is degrading to human beings. In the 1930s some cost-cutting civil servant determined the toilets in each cell were a waste of water and had them all pulled out. The result is that after four o'clock when I am locked up for the night and can't get to the communal toilet block I have to use a bucket. It sits under my nose all night until I slop it out next day. This cell stinks of my stink, and the stink of all those who have occupied it before me.

The jail itself reeks of murderers who have been hung by their necks, of republican patriots who have faced firing squads, of petty thieves high on dope and low on hope. Prisoners and officers alike are diminished by this hole, drugs leech their way into everything, cigarettes are the basic currency, and stand-over merchants call the shots. 'The Joy,' as it is laughingly called, is not a nice place.

Word went around when I first arrived that I was a 'rock spider', the lowest of low because I had harmed a child so I instantly became a marked man - isolated, glared at and whispered about. Little by little the tension built until I became petrified of all around me and living in a constant state of paranoia.

Then it happened. A group sneaked up behind me while I was going to the exercise yard and in an instant had a pillowslip over my head. I don't recall passing out but the next thing I knew I came to sprawled on the floor with a pain on the right side of my temple that soon turned into a crippling headache. A maniacal chorus of four or five thugs had ambushed me and done me over good and solid, taking turns to sadistically bang away at me until my innards were shredded and my backside was burning.

I was left to grope and stagger my way back to my cell and collapse on my bunk, the pain unrelenting. But what do I do? Ask for help? And if so, who should I ask? What do I say? Who will care? I am universally despised by the jailers and the jailed alike, so I don't exactly come from a position of strength. My hands are tied.

I am losing my grip on reality little by little as it becomes my tiny world. All I can do is hunker down, play the game and do whatever it takes to stay sane and alive.

I stoically count the days as I wait on the result of Orla's submission that I be granted visits from my lads. That is all I have to look forward to.

PRISON OFFICER STOKES

We are aware of the pillowslip incident as a couple of us actually saw it. But we knew from the moment he arrived that this fellow would be in for a bit of a pegging and it wasn't up to us to intervene. He was walking down the corridor and the slip was over his head in an instant and the blokes were wild and pumped up, so we left them to it.

This place is overcrowded, over-sexed and over its use-by date and we have enough problems keeping a lid on things. You have to pick your battles in this game and we certainly weren't going into bat for a fellow who killed his own daughter. 'It's a braver man than me who is going to argue with the tribal heavies over this one,' I said to my co-workers.

Hoare is a real mess, but he must realise that the only way to get through unscathed is to modify his behaviour, loose the hoity-toity attitude and try and become one of the crowd.

'To be perfectly honest,' I told my wife last night, 'I can't see that happening as he is a man who is totally full of his own importance, lacks emotional empathy and thinks he is better than everyone else in the place, us guards included. There is something very disturbing about him. But, not my problem!'

JUNIOR

I fuckin' hate visiting Da in prison but he fuckin' took the matter to court and we fuckin' have to go. Grandma Moira takes us and fuckin' Orla is always there as well. She left our place when Mammy came home as we didn't need looking after any more.

It must be fuckin' awful being fuckin' locked up. The first fuckin' time we went to see Da he was dressed in a tracksuit sort of thing and looked fuckin' awful, not like Da at all. He didn't say much and in the end, he got up and left us sitting there like fuckin' dorks. We thought he'd gone for a leak but he didn't come back. We waited and waited and Orla went to look for him and Grandma started to cry, so I said, 'Come on Gran, time to buy me a chocolate milk shake.' We fuckin' left and went to the Shelbourne, where Gran told us to have anything we wanted, that Grandpa was paying, so we did.

At least when the fuckin' court case ended and they led Da away, the nasty kids at school finally forgot about us and stopped all the fuckin' teasing. There are some nice kids too, and it makes you realise who your friends really are. I'm lucky because I am good at football and hurling and everybody wants me on their fuckin' team. Also I have lots of uncles who like to come and watch me play so I don't miss Da that much.

But Richie gets teased and sometimes I hear him crying in bed. I try to teach him how to throw the ball harder and how to use the fuckin' hurley but he's just not good at fuckin' sport. He spends most of his lunch times in the fuckin' library or the music room with other nerds. I just wish he would fuckin' toughen up. No wonder Da used to get angry with him and call him a fuckin' pansy.

One good thing is that we're not moving fuckin' house now that Da is in jail. Mam has taken it off the fuckin' market so that's grand.

Another good thing is that fuckin' Tom is over there in England and I hope he isn't coming back. God, that used to fuckin' piss me off. He'd turn up in the middle of the fuckin' night like a fuckin' crook and in the morning Mam would be all pink and rosy and fussing around him, making him fuckin' rashers and eggs and you could fuckin' just tell they had been fucking each other. They're too fuckin' old and it was yuk! It made me fuckin' sick.

I can't fuckin' wait to grow up and get out of here. I have told Maureen that as soon as I finish school I am going to get a flat in Temple Bar and she can come with me.

RICHIE

I don't like sport. I hate getting knocked over and I'm not like Junior, in fact I'm pretty un-co. I like going to the music room at lunchtime because the sporty kids and bullies don't come in there and pick on me. I hate them. They are always telling me that my Da is a crim who killed my sister. Mammy said to ignore them so I try to, but I find it hard not to cry and they seem to enjoy that. Best keep out of their way! I don't want to go on camp this year because I keep having accidents in my bed and I don't want anybody to know that except for Mam.

I've got a drum kit now, set up in the lounge, although Mum says she is going to move out the back some day. But my favourite thing is to play music on the piano because I can shut my eyes and think of Molly in Heaven. I sometimes write stories and poems for her and put them under our special posting rock in the back garden. That's where we used to put our pictures when she was alive so I hope she sees them at night when I am asleep. Tom says next time he comes over he will write some music for me to make the poems into songs. We started last time he was here.

I hated it when we went to see Da in jail. He looked awful in those old clothes, sitting there and trying to make conversation with us. He didn't know what to say. I didn't know what to say either, because there was a cop standing by the door listening to everything. Da always used to tell us what to do and how to do it, but now he is lost for words. It is really awkward.

Grandma prattled on about the shopping and the weather and what the lady up the road was doing, sort of talking for the sake of talking, and Da sat there silently looking at us really strangely. And then he got up and left and we waited but he didn't come back. That was a relief!

Granny told us that we could order anything we liked at Shelbourne's so I had a chocolate milkshake and a pink doughnut.

Junior really hates it when Tommy comes to our place but at least Mam doesn't cry so much when he is here. I think Tom is okay now and sometimes he can be cool like when he helps me write songs and shows me different riffs for my guitar and sometimes he plays the African drum while I play the piano and Mam sings. I like that because we're happy then.

When he is here, he helps me and the boys in our band and comes out to the garage when we practice. They all think he's cool, but I don't say that to Junior. He really, really hates him.

STUART

Those bastards have been inside my body. Now they are permanently inside my head. My life has become an ongoing state of total, permanent dread.

I live life continuously on edge, no matter where I am, the fear always hanging over me. Are they coming to get me again? What was that shadow? Did I hear someone behind me? Why is that fellow smiling at me? That man laughing over there? Is he sniggering at me, or somebody else?

It won't take much more to tip me over the edge and I will end up a mumbling, shuffling old lag, fearful, shell-shocked and totally devoid of all dignity and hope. Things that were once important to me are losing their value. They fragment, blur and exit via the ever-widening cracks in my mind as I battle for my sanity and fear for my physical safety. The events and people surrounding Molly's death have become almost dream-like, a vague memory from the distant past. That Stuart Hoare was another man in another time, a dream time.

My cellmate George tries to calm me down and give me survival tips and I couldn't get a better tutor. He is a decent sort of habitual thief who feels quite at home here. In fact, he says it is his home. Says he has forgotten how to live on the outside so that whenever he get released, before long he nicks something else and is back inside again.

'Keep a low profile, make yourself as small a target as possible,' he says. 'Invisible, if you can. Keep right away from the big feller, Battersby, and his stooges. My advice to you, old pal, is to hide in the library. Now there's a good place. Battersby doesn't ever go in there, says he's dyslexic, you know, can't read. So go there and with your education, you can find some good books to occupy your mind and stay out of sight. These fellers, nasty as they are, if they don't see you, they forget about you. The drug, it fogs their memories.'

The only thing George asks is that I do not go near the recycling bins, as that's his little hideaway. He spends his days there sorting rubbish and smoking cigarettes with a couple of like-minded buddies.

I took his advice and went and had a peek at the library, which turned out to be an absolute mess. Obviously at some stage, some do-gooder has endeavoured to provide mental fodder for the criminal classes by donating hundreds of books. But they are all over the place, in no specific groupings or order. I have taken it on myself to dust, sort and catalogue them. Plenty of work to do here!

Meanwhile, I never let my guard down until the heavy door clangs shut on my cell at night after lock down. Then we fill the hours before lights out lying on our bunks while George amuses me with yarns of his days in the IRA and his over-ambitious botched burglaries. 'Things never seemed to go as planned,' he ruminates. How much of it is true remains in doubt but he tells a good story and I believe I am growing fond of him. Weird! In turn, I read to him from the Agatha Christie series of crime novels I have unearthed in the library. He loves them. The funny thing is that my illiterate, kleptomaniac cellmate is not only my best friend, but probably my first real friend.

JENNIFER

What am I to do about Tom? Just when we were making a fresh start together in London, the new evidence appeared and since then life has become a confronting whirl of shock after shock for me. It has all been such a distraction that I have hardly had time to think about him, much less talk at length and decide on what we should do next.

When I rushed back from London that morning, my last words were that I would call him and we would decide when he would come over to Dublin. But when I got here, in the cold light of day, I realised that having Tom around would not be a good look and only bring back all the old bitterness - much of it misplaced - and muddy the waters. He is an innocent but nevertheless conflicting, divisive figure, poor Tom, and I feel really sorry for him. So I told him to stay where he is for the moment.

Each day brings a new challenge for me and as things pile up the likelihood of me going back to London to live seems to get further away.

When I do get a minute to Skype him, he looks so morose, and I notice that the flat is starting to slip back into its old bachelor ways. Behind him sitting at the tiny desk in the lounge, I can see crap piling up all over the floor. It won't be long before the drums are back in there.

'When are you coming back, Jen?' he implores. 'I miss you so much.'

'I can't say, darling. Da is not well, Ma is struggling to look after him, the kids are unsettled because their father is in jail and they hate going to visit him, and who could blame them? I wake up in the morning and my head starts spinning just at the thought of it all.'

'Well, let me help you, Jen. I'll come over and give you a hand.'

'No, I don't think that would be a good idea, right at this moment.'

Usually, he follows that statement with, 'Okay, maybe next week,' or 'Perhaps when your Da gets better.' But last night, he just stared straight out of the screen and said, 'Well then I fuckin' won't.' And it suddenly went blank.

STUART

In jail the drug is the kingmaker for the power-hungry and the panacea for the desperate.

'You must have someone on the outside who can get me something,' Battersby sneered at me one day as he held me against the wall with a gnarly hand around my throat. 'You mix in high circles. A doctor, a chemist, maybe? One of your golf club mates? Morphine will do. Sleeping tablets. Flu pills. Anything like that. I can mix it into something decent enough for these feckin' clowns.'

'I can't help you. Nobody I know would dare do something as risky as that.'

'Oh yes they would. Every man has his price. You'd be surprised what people will do for a few euro. Now I'm setting you a little task and I'm telling you, if you don't get some gear to me by the end of next week, you'll be regretting it.'

'Even if I could get hold of any, which I can't, how would I get it inside?'

'The woman that sees you every fortnight, the one that comes with those strapping lads of yours who I'm sure you wouldn't want to see hurt.'

'Mother!' I was horrified.

'No, you fuckwit! Not your fuckin' mother! The sheila with the pink hair, the bitch that puts it out there for you, the social worker! She can stick the gear up her arse, or up her fanny. I don't care how she gets it in, but I want you to get something, you hear?'

He let me go, stepped back, and a disturbing smile split his ugly face as he gave me a playful tap across the cheek. 'Come on, cheer up, there's a good lad. You haven't smiled once since you got here.'

I knew not to ask Orla to bring the drugs. I wouldn't put her in that position. I decided to ignore his threats, and cop it sweet so that he would realise he was wasting his time on a stodgy, immoveable old fogy like me.

A few days after the deadline had passed, I paid a horrible price for refusing to yield to his demands. They call it the Liverpool Kiss and he caught me in its careful construct. There was no need for discussion. He just walked up, his icy smile split his ugly features, and than, bang, the flat of his massive bony forehead came hurtling down from on high at full speed, smashing right into the bridge of my nose. Jesus Christ, it hurt. I went down like a sack of spuds. He walked away whistling. The medicos advised me that they would have to wait several days for the swelling to die down before they could straighten it out. Next day a photograph appeared of me on the front page of a daily paper sprawled on the floor in a pool of blood with the cheeky headline reading: 'Molly's Da nose what it feels like now ...'

The picture was far too clear for CCT footage. Somebody, probably a guard, had taken it and no doubt got fifty euro for it. Bastard!

I was further shocked when Orla turned up with heavy makeup masking a black eye to match my own. 'What's going on?' I said. 'Did they get to you, too?'

She looked vague so I changed tack. 'Did you slip in the bathroom?'

There was a moment's silence, and her bottom lip quivered. She looked down and whispered. 'He's back.'

'Who?'

She began to sob. The gears slowly whirred into place as I realised that her ex-husband must have returned to the loop.

Right there and then, with both of us injured and morose, it dawned on me that our relationship was a shell, a combination of professional visits and stolen moments with nothing in between. I didn't really know her.

JENNIFER

Da died. His funeral was huge because he was a well-known and much respected identity throughout the city. Friends and neighbours called to pay their respects in the Irish way and the whole gang came down from Kerry, all a bit older and greyer than they had been the last time I saw them en masse.

The Requiem Mass went on forever, with the grandchildren all doing a reading and the four boys and two eldest grandsons carrying Da from the church where they loaded him aboard a hearse and whizzed him down to his boyhood home in Killarney. He was finally laid to rest in the cemetery with his kin after what seemed to be days of pomp and ceremony. When it was all over we were exhausted and Mammy and I went home together. Mercifully Stuart was well out of the picture.

Now Mam is on a mission to pray for dear Da's soul, and to deliver him out of Purgatory and into Heaven before All Soul's Day. She is sure that if she can do that then he will forgive her all her shortcomings. Oh, well, if that is what she believes. In virtually the blink of an eye my child and my father have died and Mam has lost her husband and a grandchild. We have much grieving to do.

'We can only pray for the dead,' I said. 'We must look after the living.'

Perhaps in Heaven Da found the real truth!

MARY

The shocking events of the last eighteen months were very upsetting for my Seamus and, in the end that was what killed him. But I think the last straw was how upset the boys would become after visiting their father in jail. They hated the place and everything that went on there. Poor little darlings! Seamus was furious that the lads had to go through that and after they had relayed to him how grim it was, he vowed there and then that he would do something about it.

He shuffled off to his study, made a lengthy, muffled phone call to someone called Leo, hung up, came back and said to Richie, 'Only a couple of more visits, boys, and you'll never have to go there again.' Poor little Richie didn't know whether to think that was a good thing or a bad thing. Was Dad going to escape? Are they going to put a bomb under the place?

STUART

'Daideo has died,' Richie blurted as the two boys came in with Mother and sat forlornly in front of me in the jail's cold, cold visiting room.

'Now Mammy has Nan Mary staying at our place because she needs to be with us,' added Junior. 'She reckons the old house at Blackrock is haunted.'

That annoyed me. Jennifer back in residence in *my* home and now her mother moving in. It seems that I am Stuart, the great benefactor, that my home is their home, and everyone is welcome to bunk in. That really pisses me off. She didn't want to stay there and look after the lads before, did she? No, she was prepared to go off to lover boy's dingy bog hole in London. And now she is back playing lady of the house and has all the O'Briens coming and going as if they own the place.

But I could see that the boys were upset, as they loved their grandfather, the old scoundrel. Everybody loved him. Except me. Good old Seamus O'Brien, my long-running sparring partner, is dead. Extra, extra, read all about it. I couldn't have been happier but I showed restraint and didn't express my glee.

'That is very sad,' I lied, tongue firmly in cheek. 'I'm very sorry to hear that. Tell your Nan that I am sorry.'

That is not true. I ain't! May the Devil spit on his miserable soul. He's dead and I'm not, so I have won! Not that we ever acknowledged our hatred for each other; it was simply the underlying foundation to our relationship. Other people enjoy mutual admiration; we engendered mutual loathing.

We had the religious thing. He was Catholic; I was Protestant.

We had the education thing. He had left school at fifteen; I had finished high school and university.

He was a risk-taker; I preferred the slow and steady route.

He was from Kerry. I was not.

He fathered Jennifer. And, to his eternal chagrin, I married her.

My boys were sad and I was sad seeing them sad.

The little fellow started to sob. 'Daddy,' he said, 'we're sorry.'

'Sorry?' I said as tenderly as possible. 'What do you mean you're sorry?'

'It's all our fault,' he blubbered.

'It's not your fault your Grandpa has died. He was old. Old people die.'

'We know we should have stopped him,' chipped in Junior solemnly.

'You couldn't stop him dying Junior, only God could do that and it seems that he preferred to have the old man up there with him.' I couldn't help myself and continued, 'Although, after a few days, he will probably be sorry ...'

'No, what we mean is,' Richard sobbed, 'if Tommy had not been on the bridge that day, Molly wouldn't have fallen over.'

I drew in a deep breath. Wow. Is that how my little fellows think of it? That Tommy is the culprit. At least someone is on the same page as me!

'It's all our fault,' confirmed Junior. 'When he first turned up at home, we should have protected Mammy from him.'

The little bloke brightened up. 'Yes,' he enthused, 'I should have squirted him with my water pistol.'

'And I should have hit him with my hurley.'

'And pushed him out the door.'

'And chased him up the road.'

'And kicked him up the bum!'

They both started to giggle at the imagery, using inventive gesticulations and comic noises to show how they would have despatched him, before they suddenly calmed down, remembering that Seamus, the Pop who made them laugh, had died.

TOM

Once again, I am the biggest loser in all of this. The sudden appearance of the new evidence, followed by the re-trial and the jailing of Stuart - all of which I would have construed as something good for everybody - have combined to put me back into limbo.

Fuck, fuck, fuck. Things were starting to go really well when Jen was over here. Now she is back in Dublin, running around like a headless chook, and there does not appear to be a hope in hell of her returning to London soon, if at all.

I'm going to go out tonight in the West End with the express intention of getting extremely pissed and who knows what will happen?

STUART

A few days after the boys had visited, the portly figure of Monseigneur Daniel O'Farrell, Parish Priest of St John the Baptist, Blackrock, waddled into the visitors' room.

You could have knocked me down with a feather. The opposition? Here? It would have been very tempting to sneer my disgust, get up and start to walk away. But I didn't, as any visitor is a good visitor in this place. It breaks the monotony, so I put my hand out for him to shake.

'Stuart,' he intoned, 'I've got something you must hear.'

'I doubt it,' I said. 'You are the spiritual guide of the O'Brien family which harbours the shared disappointment that I was not hanged, cut into pieces and fed to the sharks.'

'That's where you are wrong. They are not all united in that consideration.'

I drew a deep breath and reluctantly invited him to sit down. I had never liked this fellow. Not anything to do with his Catholicism, just his over-bearing, smarmy attitude, and the way the family crawled in under his ample shadow and hung on to his every word. 'The Mons' they call him. In my opinion, being a Monseigneur is like being lodged permanently in the halfway house of the clerical wannabe. Too smart-arse to be a regular priest but not capable of cultivating the right contacts to become a bishop. But give him a few extra purple trimmings and a perky hat and it is enough to make him think he's a class above everybody else and the demi-god of his own little dung-heap, where he will stay forever.

'I come here because Seamus asked it of me before he passed onto eternal life,' he intoned in his pastoral voice. 'He was a very sick man you know, and he had very clear views on your circumstances …'

'Oh, I know that!'

'So you might be surprised to know that the day before he died he set things in train get you out of this hell-hole and have you moved to a more convivial place in the countryside.'

'You are kidding!'

'No, I am not. He instructed me to come and tell you that, seeing as you are family, he used his influence

274

with the bishop, his friend the Chief Justice and others to put in a word and get you moved out of here to a more humane place away from the riff raff and crowding of the Joy.'

'Well, I never …'

'On his final night Seamus called the Prelate of the White Fathers who once ran an old novitiate up on the border that has been converted into an open range prison. He went to school with Father Leo, so told him the whole sad story and they did a bit of plotting and called in a few favours. Then he made an even bigger effort and donned his best suit and got Mary to drive him up to see Iain, the vicar at your church. Over a few whiskies Iain said he was happy to help and would enlist the support of his bishop and of the local member who just happens to be a member of his congregation.'

'That is amazing.' I started to blubber.

'As you can see, you have both sides of the religious spectrum working on your behalf, so although we don't know the time frame, it will happen.'

Well, you could have knocked me down with a feather! Seamus, the old bastard. He did consider me family! Who would have thought?

Just think, I shall have a cell to myself, complete with television, and there will be no slopping out shit anymore as I shall have my own personal toilet. No doubt the food will be better as they probably farm their own and there will be plenty of fresh air rolling in from the Atlantic. No more media prying, no politicians exploiting me as a good reason for bringing back the death penalty, and but best of all, no Battersby and his goons threatening me.

God looks after his own and He is certainly looking after me! Alleluia! I will pray for the Mons, Iain and for the soul of old Seamus every day until I get out of here.

Jennifer is right on one count with all her Buddhist prattle. There is such a thing as karma.

'Having set all this in place,' added the Mons, interrupting my joyous reverie, 'the effort depleted Seamus completely and he died a broken man a couple of days later, God rest his soul.'

'And having done all this, did he forgive me?' I asked in anticipation.

'No, but he didn't forgive Mary or Jennifer either. He blames them for what they did in the build-up. He was a tough, self-made man, loyal to the faith and a profound believer in the highest of principals. He did not hand out forgiveness lightly.'

'Oh.'

With surprising agility, he stood up, shook my hand and turned to go. But not before he added quietly, 'Stuart, just be happy with what you've got.'

MARY

After the initial shock and grief of my husband's death I finally got around to thinking about me, and what I should do with the Blackrock house. I had to make the decision that faces all widows. Do I stay in the big family home? Or sell up and buy something smaller?

I was discussing my options with Jen when young Richie jumped in and begged me not to sell declaring, 'I love your house Nan. It's beautiful and it always makes me feel safe. I love the garden and all the birds, and Daideo's soul lives here. Please don't let somebody else live in it.'

What a sweet little boy. He is such a loving little fellow, not like his older brother who is well named - a junior version of his difficult, nasty father. That made me realise that this house, our family home, has been my refuge for over fifty years. 'You are right, Richie,' I said, giving him a cuddle. 'It is part of me. And of you! I would be crazy to sell it.'

Then I started to think a bit further. Richie loves the old place because when things have gone topsy-turvy at his home it has always been his safe harbour, his oasis to come to where he knows he will find security and help and love. What if we could possibly turn it into a place where any frightened child could come and get away from what is bothering him?

Jen has been talking about doing something to honour Molly's name. Then this could be it! Making the old house a refuge from the world, like it has always been for our family, a safe place away from brutality and violence. It is ideal for that sort of thing - the huge garden is beautiful and serene, there are five bedrooms and a large atrium, plus a big old family kitchen and several good living areas.

'Jennifer,' I said, 'there's plenty of room where we could make something good out of something bad.'

The idea excites me. I have plenty of money to see me out, and the old place is just sitting here going to rot. This way, it will enable me to continue to live in my home of fifty years while doing something worthwhile.

'Just think, Jen,' I said, 'Molly's name will live on, Paddy's demons will be expunged and Seamus' ghost will be laid to rest.'

JENNIFER

Sometimes Mam surprises me. She has suggested that we convert the Blackrock house into a refuge for victims of abuse and call it Molly's Place. I love it! It is a perfect way to remember her.

I realise that it will be complicated setting up something like this but if we start out small we can build as we get stronger. 'I can't sleep I am so excited,' I said to Wendy, 'and the plans keep going over and over in my mind.'

We have the building plus the skills and a dream to make Blackrock a place where abused women and children - and men - can go for solace, perhaps to do some gardening or just to sit and soak up the sun, talk and network with others, rediscover belief in themselves. Paddy is keen to be involved, reaching out to people like him who need a place for healing after all that the church has done to them.

'Wendy, just think,' I said, 'if we use the front three rooms, we can have one as a sort of refuge or safe haven for desperate people who need temporary housing to get them over a bump in the road, another for a meeting room and the third for an office.

'I don't expect that it will cost much at first and the family can easily cover the expense of coffee and biscuits. I will do a refresher course in Family Law so I can give free legal advice. I am excited and want to get it started.'

Since then I have been pleasantly surprised at the number of people who have come forward to help both physically and financially. Considering all I have been through, it gives one faith in humanity.

TOM

The heat generated by Stuart's re-trial finally calmed down and I thought I was getting somewhere with Jennifer; that she was ready to move back. But now she is preoccupied with this new touchy-feely, save-the-suffering-fucking-children project at Blackrock and so has found another reason to put off returning to London.

I began booking Friday night plane tickets in her name and insisting she get on the flight and at least come over and spend a weekend with me. But did she take up the opportunity? No.

The first couple of times I actually didn't mind as she gave Wendy her ticket and we spent the weekends out on the town. At least the little New Zealand pocket rocket knows how to have a good time.

Then when Her Royal Highness Princess Madam Jennifer Mary O'Brien Hoare, lawyer and humanitarian of Dalkey, finally did agree to come, you know what she did? She brought Wendy with her! That obviously was going to make it difficult to enjoy sex in this tiny house and, as a consequence, we didn't have any.

Just to rub it in, on the Saturday night, party night, Jen declared she wanted to stay in, as she was 'so tired from a busy week at her mother's place.' Give me a break. Wendy and I went out. I sometimes think I have more in common with Wen than I do with Jen. We know each other well and I think she's a great bird who lives life to the full. It seems that Jennifer is actively pushing me away, almost as if she wants me to fuck Wendy.

We had supper and a deep heart-to-heart talk about Jennifer and me. Which evolved into an even deeper discussion about Wendy and me! In the dimly lit nightclub booth, the tantric heat we have been supressing somehow built to the point of no return, where our passions reached their ultimate bittersweet crescendo and in a fleeting, tawdry kind of way we had sex in a feeding frenzy of emotion.

After it was over we sort of stood up, brushed ourselves down and went home to where Jen was sound asleep in my bed. I didn't want to disturb her so I bunked on the sofa. They both flew out next morning.

Part of me celebrates the conclusion of our wonderful sexual dance while the other part bemoans what might happen next. Then again, what Jen doesn't know won't hurt her, so I won't tell her.

WENDY

Jennifer would not come out with us but encouraged Tom and me to go anyway, as she wished to stay in and Skype the boys. We had some tapas and enough margaritas to make us want to dance so we stopped off at a nightclub, one of those with separate booths and dark red curtains that look decrepit in the daylight but oh, so sexy at night. Tom spilled the beans about everything that is going on in their relationship and I'm afraid it has happened. I didn't mean it to, but we had a fair bit to drink and lost control and bonked a hurried bonk right there in the booth as the oblivious crowd boogied away to the sounds of Michael Jackson's 'The Way You Make Me Feel.'

The unspent emotion and pent up sexual energy that has been on a slow volcanic boil for months on end found its release. In my defence, we Buddhists believe sex is a natural human function that happens when we allow ourselves to surrender to the positive flow of energy that harmonizes, invigorates and releases. We simply enjoyed the moment and I see nothing wrong with that.

Besides, Jen has encouraged me to take her place in regards to Tom. From the start, I saw to his washing and his shopping in hospital, visited him in London when Jen couldn't go, picked him up from airports and ferries and partied with him and his friends.

She asked me to do these things for her because she couldn't do them herself. In my endeavour to be there for her and to help her and the boys through this awful situation I have virtually put my life on hold. In the beginning I was deliberately pro-active in taking over domestic responsibilities and caring for the boys but then my duties expanded in to taking care of Tom's needs as well. By simply being there for him, I feel I prevented Tom from losing interest in Jen and straying to another paddock.

We left early next morning to fly home and didn't talk much because Jen took the opportunity to catch up on her law refresher course and I slept. We picked up my car at the airport, I dropped her home and did a bit of shopping for the coming week. I felt awkward but I don't think that Jen noticed.

I have thought about it and decided that the relationship between Jen and me has become too interconnected, too intense, too incestuous. It is like we are a threesome - her, Tom and me. A trio that has to be broken up one way or another.

So I am getting out of the way and hotfooting it back to New Zealand. No matter how much I have enjoyed my time in Ireland, New Zealand is where I started out, it is where my remaining family is, and it is time to go back.

Jennifer and Tom are the couple, and I am not going to make him choose. We were thrown into each other's arms and it is best for everybody if I am out of their way. I told Jen I was leaving and she broke down, sobbed and said she couldn't live without me, that the boys would be heart-broken, that her mother would miss me.

I felt sorry because she could not understand why I would leave at this stage and in trying to justify my exit I am afraid that Jen somehow kind of winkled the truth out of me ...

Perhaps it was because we are such good friends that I felt she deserved to know; perhaps it was just to relieve my conscience; perhaps it was because I needed to shut the door on this stage of my life forever. I don't know! For whatever reason, I took her hand and confessed to our betrayal, blaming myself and exonerating Tom, telling her that I came onto him, that he didn't stand a chance, that he still loves her. She seemed to take it well and we cried together, but for very different reasons.

Then when I got up to leave she offered to walk me to the car. She hugged me, waited for me to buckle myself in and, as she was closing the car door for me she paused, and intoned a cold, clear warning. 'Wendy, thank you for all you have done this past year for me and my boys,' she said. 'But you have completely and utterly betrayed me and I don't think I can ever forgive you, so please don't come near me or my family ever again.'

She slammed the door shut leaving me a gob-smacked and speechless. I turned the key and drove away. I'd been told!

Nobody holds grudges quite like the Irish.

JENNIFER

Wendy phoned the other day and asked could she come over to speak to me, which I thought was strange because she knows that she is always welcome. Even when Stuart was around and thrived on making her feel uncomfortable she still popped in whenever she wanted. Why was she suddenly asking my permission?

It soon became clear. Too clear. Heartbreakingly clear. She and Tom are having an affair!

Bloody hell. My lover and my best friend. I can't look at her. It will never be the same between us. She has totally betrayed me.

She says it was entirely her fault; that she had seduced Tom. That he always thought of me first and foremost. But she says that I threw them together. That I had left him out in the cold for her to look after. That I somehow wanted them to hook up. 'I am sorry, Jen,' she said, 'but it was inevitable.'

That is bizarre! I thought I could trust her to do the right thing by me. That she would look after Tom while I was grieving.

She says that our relationship has become a one-way street. That she does all the giving, and I do all the taking. That she has put her life on hold for me, while I see her as my alter ego, pushing her into Tom's arms. That a healthy man cannot be celibate and that as Tom was not getting sex from me, he had to turn elsewhere. She described it as a romp!

That's not how I see it. A romp is a bit of fun. This was not a romp, it was a betrayal. I shared my everything with her - my boys, my home, my life. I trusted her.

What does this say about Tom? I will speak to him, demand explanations. Wendy says that it was her fault, and perhaps it was, as I know she is promiscuous and has had many partners, none of them long term. She lives in the moment; she is impetuous, flighty, a free spirit. Obviously Tom was offered the forbidden fruit, nicely sliced and beautifully presented on a silver platter, and he couldn't resist the temptation. The weak-kneed bastard.

This could destroy our relationship but I am also acutely aware that if Tom and I break up then victory belongs to Stuart! So I will do my best to forgive Tom, clean the slate, pretend it did not happen and go on as before. It depends upon what he has to say.

This ongoing trauma that Stuart brought to our family has destroyed just about everything - my family, my relationship, my friendships. I meet people I have known since childhood around town and see the horror in their eyes as they turn away from me, not knowing what to say.

It has left me totally drained and heartbroken. I am no longer the person I was and it seems that it has affected Tom so deeply that we may destroy each other.

TOM

The fact of the matter is that I am a creature that cannot be caged. Wendy's a cool chick who simply lives in the now, not asking for or expecting anything. What happened between us was inexcusable and we both know that we betrayed Jennifer. I am sorry and am really afraid that I will lose my girl again, for good this time. However, there are extenuating circumstances that need to be taken into account.

Jen is almost dead from the inside out. She finds it too painful to admit that her daughter was a victim of patricide and somehow blames me for Molly's death. I have never put the blame on her and know that if I am patient she will heal in time, but I am in a difficult situation and I have no control over the outcome. That tragedy strangled her zest for life, but I believe I have been supportive and have never stopped loving her.

Now she is consumed by another mission. To make Molly's Place the centre for healing for the entire state of Ireland and quite possibly the world. She has no time for anything else.

I believe that her loss pushed me into her best friend's arms and that if we can get through the grief we can resolve this situation and our relationship may have a chance.

I deserve another opportunity but at the moment things look hopeless. Wendy's sisterhood with Jen is sullied and their friendship ended. Our nights on the town are over and she has fled to New Zealand never to return. Jennifer and I are left with the shell of a relationship.

Part Thirteen

STUART

Although the newspaper headlines scream 'Motorway Monster's Magnificent Manor' I don't care because I am here in leafy Loughan up in the north and, if I have to be locked up somewhere, well then compared to the hellhole I came from, I love it. This is 'low security', with the accent on the 'low.' The only thing I miss is the daily to and fro of business but dear old Buchanan holds the fort in Dublin beautifully for me and the money still slides into the bank.

The library here offers a computer course every Wednesday and suddenly a whole new world has opened up for me as I master Word and Excel and the wonderful challenge of the internet. So easy, so accessible! Why didn't I know all of this earlier? I could have brought my wife's seedy little chat-room affair crashing down long before it blossomed.

However, comfortable as I am, the fact is I am still in prison and I can't help contemplating the possibility of escape. It looks easy enough. The fencing is standard, no high walls, barbed wire or ready-to-shoot guards.

Blacklion, the nearest village is a mere forty-five minute walk away and just over the river and the border with Northern Ireland is the tiny hamlet of Belcoo. From there I could work my way east to Belfast where some docker might happily accept an envelope of cash in return for taking me to Scotland in his fishing boat. And from there, who knows? Europe? Asia? Maybe even sunny Australia? It's worth thinking about.

Frank, a veteran guard who has taken to sitting in my cell and having a smoke and a chat during quiet intervals, set me straight by pointing out that just about everyone who has elected to jump the fence over the last couple of years has been recaptured within a matter of hours by either the dog handlers or the helicopter crews using heat imaging technology.

'I would not be thinking of it if I was you, Stuart,' he says. 'The slog through sodden grass, the scramble around muddy lake edges and the slide down slippery riverbanks in pursuit of freedom is simply not worth it. You will be caught! Our mob takes escape from here as a murky reflection on our professionalism. Plus, we don't want to lose our jobs if the powers that be shut the joint down. It's the biggest employer in the area. It's personal like!'

'Well, it was just a thought.'

'Besides, Stuart, you have a name and record that excites activity; there's already all that shit on Facebook about you doing your time easy here. Best stay in your warm cell, lay low and serve your time. Pay your duty to society and go home after a few years a free man. By that time things will have moved on and they will be asking Stuart who? You'll be able to get on with your life.'

That's all very well for him to say but he's not locked up. He goes home to his own place at night. He's on the other side of the fence, so to speak.

Nevertheless, the summer sunshine brought my lads up north to see me in my new surrounds, such a long way from the confronting gloom of The Joy.

Don't know how old Seamus would feel about that, God bless him, but he was not counting on the persuasive powers of Orla. 'There are protocols to be observed in the follow-up to a shift as significant as this,' she said, nodding to the pile of folders in her arms.

My, how the boys have grown! Junior is beginning to talk in a deep voice and has a layer of fine hair growing on his chin. He obviously needs instruction from his father in the gentlemanly art of shaving but when I offered my advice he told me to 'fuck off' and to leave him alone. That hurt.

The whole visit was pretty painful. They brought a soccer ball and we had a kick on the lawn, but they were very half-hearted in their endeavours, hardly taking their hands out of their pockets. Very annoying. As for Orla, I am hurt and disappointed with her. Although every inch the professional, she never acknowledged our special ties and was evasive and distant all day. Her goodbye handshake - not a kiss - was cold and her farewell wave virtually non-existent. She is handing my case over to a local worker and wanted to finish her business and be out of here as quickly as possible.

It seems her redoubtable merchant mariner husband has sailed back into her harbour, berthed at her dock, handed over a string of worry-beads from Mykonos, a sari from Bangladesh and a carton of fags from Marseille, and she has fallen for the smooth talking bastard all over again. He obviously believes divorce is a piece of paper that means nothing. I agree. Jennifer deserves to learn the same lesson and I wish I could talk to this Dennis chap and get a few pointers from him. But what can I do? I am in jail.

ORLA

I made the trip with the lads because I needed to hand this case over to the local girl. I don't know what gave Stuart the idea, but he suggested that I get a transfer and move up this way to be close to him! He has this cosy picture in his mind of the pair of us moving into a little seaside cottage after he finishes serving his time and playing happy families together for the rest of our lives on Achill Island. Is he crazy? Or does he think I am? Just who does he think he is? The man is a self-centred loser.

I prefer my muscled tattooed sailor with not much money to any suave old crim who is rolling in it. That thing with Stuart was purely a petty dalliance that made my working life interesting when I needed to fill in some lonely days while Dennis was at sea. But now he is finding work on-shore and we are together again. We have put the past behind us and are trying to make a go of it once more, which makes my son happy. He needs a father's firm hand. I am finished with Stuart Hoare and once I dropped the boys back at Dalkey that was the end of that. Done and dusted.

I have been promoted at work and am now a manager, with six officers reporting to me. They say it is because of my exemplary service over the years, particularly my handling of the case of the Motorway Madman. They said I did it with a mix of professionalism and compassion. They don't know the half of it.

JUNIOR

I've told Mam to get a fuckin' grip; to fuckin' move on; that it's about fuckin' time that she forgot Molly; that

Molly is fuckin' dead and we are alive. When Molly died I was sad, but everything is still all about her and it fuckin' pisses me off. I wish she'd get over it! She's making life fuckin' miserable for all of us.

Nobody gives a fuckin' shit about me. I played really well in the county hurling team but the only person who came to watch me was Uncle Paddy. Uncle Kevin was going to come but then said he had to work that day. Mam dropped me off at the ground and said she had an appointment with some people at Molly's Place. She took off, taking Richie with her and didn't fuckin' come back like she fuckin' said she would. Wendy has gone home to fuckin' New Zealand and we won't see her for fuckin' ages, if ever. It fuckin' sucks.

I don't like being at home any fuckin' more. There are so many fuckin' rules. Maureen's mother has only got a small flat but she lets us stay up and have a smoke and a drink with her whenever we fuckin' want. She's cool but Mam doesn't like me going there. When my friends are at our place Mam makes them drink fuckin' soft drink, doesn't let them fuckin' smoke and makes them go home at fuckin' ten o'clock, just when the fuckin' party is getting started. That fuckin' sucks as well.

My friend Robbo and me have worked out how to get cigarettes for free while the fuckin' shopkeeper is not looking. We go to the Spar on the corner and I get the old prick engaged in conversation about what sweets I want to buy or lure him in to make a fuckin' chip butty while Robbo uses long cooking tongs to nick the fuckin' fags from behind the fuckin' counter. It's fun and we haven't been fuckin' caught yet. The fuckin' trick is to take only one fuckin' packet at a time, then he doesn't fuckin' miss them.

Da is in the fuckin' slammer up north and that sucks big time. I hate my fuckin' life.

RICHIE

Everyone dies sometime and it was Molly's turn to go to heaven before any of us. I hope she is having fun up there without me because sometimes I was mean to her and took her toys just to make her cry. I love my Nan because she knows that when I get angry it is because I am sad and need a cuddle. Mammy doesn't worry about me much because she is thinking about Molly all the time.

The best time is when I am playing my music and I can shut my eyes and see Molly dancing in Heaven. It seems a long time since I saw her and I hope it is a long time until I see her again because I don't want to die yet.

Junior and I went up to the country to see Da. We played footy on the grass and Da showed us his garden that he is making and took us to the library to play computer games. Da was cross because they were going to get another social worker and on the way home Orla said she is never going near that place again. It will be good if she stops taking us because we won't have to go then. Junior hates jail and so do I.

I got car sick on the way home.

STUART

Jennifer is white-anting me by telling the new social worker that the lads don't want to come to visit. So what does the silly bitch do, but come and ask me if there is anything else she can do? 'Is there is anything you need?' she says. There are plenty of things that I need and the most important one is to see my sons. 'And it is your job to make sure that this happens,' I say.

I am sick of the way the scheduled visits are growing less and less and how this slacker of a woman keeps telling me it is because the boys refuse to come and that she can't make them. I am supposed to see my lads every second weekend and I hate Jennifer for keeping them away from me because I know it is all her doing.

On the rare occasions my bitch wife ever lets them out of her treacherous claws, it has fallen to the ever-reliable Buchanan to chauffeur them up here. He sees it as part of his job description and I am sure that he also loves giving that new car of his a workout on the open road. He has turned out to be a truly loyal friend and business partner, never abandoning me and pulling off miraculous interventions, all the while somehow growing a business that many others would have abandoned long ago. I love that Audi of his. I get on the computer car sales pages and pore over the latest models dreaming of what motor I will buy when I finally get out of here.

As well, I have been putting my newfound computer skills to work, stalking the bitch and her drummer boy on Facebook. I am silently observing them and getting a handle on their routines. You can't believe it, can you? Despite the headline-grabbing circumstances they find themselves in, they still blithely put up snaps of themselves showing what they are up to in both Dublin and London. Not the happiest of times, it would appear, by the look of some of the grim visages.

From what I gather, things almost went to shit after Jennifer and Wendy went across to London for a weekend. Something happened and it looked like it was all over, red rover, and if that slut of a Wendy had something to do with it, I would not be surprised. But they appear to have got things going again. The last thing they need to know is that I am interested in them, so I make sure the mouse never goes anywhere near the 'Like' button.

I can smell freedom, smell life! I must return to Dalkey and sort this out.

Part Fourteen

STUART

Before you can say Arthur Guinness, I am over the fence and marching briskly down the road to resolution. Life is short; death is always lurking; it will get you in the end. So I must to do the things I need to do. Now!

I have never before hitched a ride, but with the generous help of local farmers on tractors or tray-trucks I make my way down to Drumkeeran, intent on getting through Lough Allen to Carrick-on-Shannon and the N4 to Dublin. The first couple of chatty helpers hardly listen to my implausible tale about the hire car breaking down, while my third chauffeur is less loquacious but more helpful, taking me as far as Dowra, where he has to turn off.

The next ride is not exactly the one I want. As I stride confidently out of Dowra, I see the unmistakeable shape of a prison van parked on the side of the road with old Frank leaning casually against the back door chomping on a sandwich and sipping from a mug of hot coffee. 'Well now, Stuart,' he says as I sheepishly approach, 'you appear to be suffering from an episode of the disorientation. You seemed to have gone out for a stroll around the grounds and unwittingly headed in the wrong direction.'

This old codger has taken a genuine interest in me since I turned up at the jail, discussing books and politics, playing me at chess, asking about my two lads, trying to work out where it all went wrong with me, all the while chewing through the smokes. Now I am lost for words.

He takes another sip from his coffee and looks up at the sky. 'By my estimation, providing of course we don't get stuck behind one of those feckin' farmers and their big-arse tractors lumbering along at two miles an hour in the middle of the road, if we get in the van right now and head back, we should be just in time to catch the lunch-time count. Which would be a good thing for us both, would it not, Stuart? We don't want me retiring with an escape on my watch, blackening my pristine record, do we? Might effect my measly pension.'

I nod slowly as he proffers the remaining half of the sandwich.

'Decision time,' he says. 'Do you walk past me and I blow the whistle? Or do you hop in the van, share my lunch and let me tell you all about my retirement plans?'

I follow his gaze to the sky, which is grey and starting to get dirtier as the wind blows in off Lough Allen. I look at Frank holding the sandwich in one hand and an old-fashioned prison issue whistle in the other. I walk up to him and take the food.

'You are right, Frank,' I say. 'I must have been hallucinating. A bite to eat will restore my sense of direction.'

On the way back, he tells me he is about to finish up after forty-seven years on the job and is retiring to a lovely little place right up on the tip of the north-west coast where he can hear the waves crashing on the rocks. 'I have spent a lot of time up there over the years and scraped together the deposit on the perfect little cottage and a handful of acres,' he says.

He drops me off just inside the gate and leaves me to walk up to the lunchtime check-in, as if I have been taking a healthy morning stroll around the grounds.

'Why?' I ask him before I head off. 'Why aren't you dobbing me in?

'I know what it's like when your trust is torn into little pieces, stamped on and flung right back in your face. I've had it done to me, too.' He hesitates for a moment, and some long forgotten memory of a powerful grievance rears up and brings a tear to his eye. 'But there were others who helped me out!' he continues, brightening up. 'It's all about passing on the goodness, the karma. Do unto others, all that stuff. Contrary to what many people think, Stuart, the world is a wonderful place.'

With that he drops the clutch and slowly chugs up the driveway, disappearing over the incline. Then suddenly the old van reverses back and stops near where I am standing pondering his words. Frank's balding head pops out the driver's side window and he motions me over.

'This is the situation. You want to get out of here and I want to retire in some degree of comfort. You have a prison fence to climb over and I have a financial hurdle to leap. If I can kill off my mortgage in one go, then I will spend the rest of my days in Paradise. In our own way, we both need help to escape.'

That last word makes me snap my head back.

'Be patient Stuart,' he continues, 'and we will formulate a plan which will get you to Australia and me to happy days on the sofa before a roaring fire. I don't think you belong here and I think I certainly deserve a debt-free last few years after a lifetime devoted to looking after some of the most miserable pricks Mother Nature ever spawned, yourself being the exception of course. We can help each other, but we must be careful and hasten slowly, covering all our tracks. Let's talk soon.'

Winding up the window and putting the old banger into first, he takes off, briefly spinning the back tyres and giving me the thumbs up.

TOM

She never wants to see me again - ever! And I am happy with that. In fact I feel very lucky to be out of the whole bloody nightmare. I don't know how I came to be caught up in that fucking mess. It just happened. As they say, it seemed like a good idea at the time. I would have been really happy to enjoy our affair, no strings attached, but Jennifer still has that Irish Catholic nonsense inside her head and wanted to legitimise everything.

I allowed her to talk me into standing by her side that day when she announced her intentions to that mongrel of a husband and then all that shit happened and I got carried along with the torrent, spluttering and choking, unable to escape. This last twelve months have been pure hell for me.

Wendy has been banished to her native New Zealand and me to my home in London, the message clear that neither of us are to darken Jen's doorstep again. A relief for all concerned if I say so myself!

STUART

Little by little we have been formulating the plan. We have determined that the day of Frank's retirement is the ideal moment for our scheming to reach fruition, and

Buchanan is the perfect person to source and deliver the money we need.

But first things first. A spot of spiritual cleansing is needed. After breakfast one morning, while everyone is concentrating on getting the day going, I quietly slip over the fence and strike out for the nearby Shannon Pot - ironically, the pond that is the source of the Shannon, the mystical river that was the focal point of our happy wedding ceremony all those years ago. I take my prison issue jacket off, get down on my knees on the grassy edge, cup my hands and reach in.

Splash, splash, splash. 'Let the icy waters from the womb of the Shannon give me strength to do what I have to do,' I say.

Splash, splash, splash. 'Let the biting winds scudding off Lough MacNean sharpen my mind.'

Splash, splash, splash. 'Let the last round of this ruthless battle of wills begin.'

BUCHANAN

I open the envelope post-marked Belcoo and carefully unfold the letter and begin reading. 'Holy feckin' Jesus,' I whisper to myself. 'The man's a madman!'

But still, he has thought of everything. And it is indeed a generous offer.

STUART

Even though the morning fog has long abated Buchanan still has his lights on full as he pulls up at the prison gate. The bored guard can't help but be dazzled by the magnificent late model Audi that hums away like a symphony orchestra as the snappily-dressed driver winds down the window and obligingly answers any questions. Yes, he is an associate of Mr Hoare. And yes, he is here to speak to him about an appeal that his legal team is planning. 'Is there somewhere private we could meet for a couple of hours?' he asks.

The guard obligingly shows him to a small meeting room just off the library and collects me from the vegetable garden where, as I feign work, I am humming the anthem of the slaves. 'Swing low, sweet chariot, coming for to carry me home ...'

It is Friday, the perfect day, Frank's very last one of dutiful, unimpeachable, trustworthy service across more than four decades. The chief warden apparently said so last night when there were drinks all round for the staff and a gold watch for the guest of honour at his testimonial dinner.

After ninety minutes of me and Buchanan involved in apparently serious discussion, Frank chooses exactly this moment to make his final departure from Loughan, taking with him a load of old books, personal papers, files and mementos that he has been cleaning from his office. He gives me the nod and it is relatively easy to slip quietly out via the library and scramble into the back seat of his old bomb of a Fiat, lie down and cover myself with a blanket. Frank carefully piles his load of memorabilia on top of the rug, revs up the old rattler and happily chuffs off down the driveway, waving to the guards who give him one last farewell tease, but who are otherwise distracted by the Audi.

The guards watch Buchanan in envy as he pilots his sleek yuppie machine majestically down the hill from the prison car park and through the gate, waving to them and thanking them, slowing to check the traffic before turning left and heading south for Dublin. Hopefully, the promised incentive of a full fifty per cent of the business will be ample reward for his discretion when he inevitably has to tell his story to the Garda. I know he will not buckle when they find out I have done a runner. He has too much to lose.

Little notice is taken of Frank as he passes out the front gate, turns the car right and heads north. Certainly no guard is around to witness the canny old retiree stopping five kilometres down the road, getting out, opening the back door and digging me out from under the pile of a career's worth of ephemera so I can join him in the front seat. My waxed-cotton trilby is pulled down low and my Donegal scarf wrapped high as he heads north towards his isolated little cottage up past Malin Head. We do not need to say anything, other than to chuckle. We have done it. Fooled them all.

Over the next few days, while all eyes look to Dublin, to Buchanan, to the ports, to the airport, to London, Belfast and Scotland, and to my carefully abandoned jacket discovered by the sniffer dogs at Shannon Pot, I am invisible, enjoying the simple pleasures of freedom - walking the rugged coastline, sitting on the rocks and staring out to sea, filling my lungs with the chilled North Atlantic air, picking up driftwood to jolly up the peat fire of Frank's warm, inviting kitchen. I am so far north, I can almost smell Iceland from here.

I wait, steadying myself to prepare for the next step in my plan.

JENNIFER

I open the door to two members of the Garda and my stomach sinks down to my ankles. 'Has something happened to one of the boys?' I ask.

It is about Stuart. He has escaped and they have come to warn me and offer me protection, they say. I knew it. I knew the bastard was up to something. Our marriage may have ended but we have been close enough to one another for all those years to build an undeniable predictive link.

They are here to search the house, examine the computers, check the phones and generally look around to ensure I am not giving him safe haven. As if!

My body immediately goes into at a state of hyper-alert, my heart pounding and my brain crashing into meltdown. I invite them in and allow them to carry out their task, glad that the boys are safe at school.

The boys!

What if he goes to the school and kidnaps them?

I voice my concern and the Garda offer to collect them and bring them home.

What if he comes in the middle of the night? Tonight, here, with me and the boys alone!

The Garda promise a security guard.

'There will be somebody here twenty-four seven, or until we apprehend him. He cannot escape the net we have set up,' they say.

Suddenly I am walking on eggshells again, and no matter where I tread or how gingerly I step, the cracks are appearing. Stuart will come to kill me. Or worse, the boys. His ability to conjure up psychological and emotional abuse has only scratched the surface. I phone Paddy, explain what has happened and ask him to sleep over here for a few nights until they apprehend Stuart. Mam is coming as well.

JUNIOR

So fuckin' embarrassing!

I come out of fuckin' school with Maureen and Eileen and there are two fuckin' big coppers waiting for

302

me. I think that they are here to take me in for shoplifting, and get a bit fuckin' scared and am about to deny everything when they tell me they have come to fuckin' escort me home. I tell them I knew my own fuckin' way home, and that anyway I have football practice and am not going straight home tonight. They take me aside then and have a word, telling me that Da has done a fuckin' runner and is on the fuckin' loose, and that they need to make sure that I am fuckin' okay.

What do they fuckin' think? That Da is fuckin' dangerous?

That's a fuckin' joke. I'm glad he's out because I hate that fuckin' place where he was. It fuckin' sucks! I hope they never fuckin' catch him and that he escapes to fuckin' Australia and fuckin' sends for me and we can do some surfing together.

In the end I have to fuckin' go with them because the fuckin' Principal comes up to us and tells me to cut out my cheek and to get in the fuckin' car and do as I am fuckin' told. 'Your mother is concerned for your safety and you are to go home in the Garda van,' he says.

I say goodbye to the girls and get in but slink down in the seat so nobody can see me through the fuckin' window. It makes me feel really crunchy.

RICHIE

A nice Garda comes to the classroom and tells me not to panic that nothing is wrong but Mammy wants us to go home with them tonight because Da is out of jail and might want to come and take us away with him. I don't want to go with him so I do as I am told.

They have to get 'Old Andy', that's the headmaster, to come and tell Junior to get in the car. He won't get in and is giving a mouth full of cheek and the girls that are with him are laughing because they think it is funny.

After we get in the van, the policeman tells Junior he is just like his old man and Junior says, 'Thank you.' Now, that is funny.

I don't want to go to school tomorrow. I want to stay with Mammy. I feel really sick and sweaty and my head aches.

STUART

Frank and I are living harmoniously like two old gay fellers. The locals are getting used to seeing us around and although they generally keep to themselves, they doff their caps if we pass them on the road and greet us politely when one of us goes into town for provisions.

They know Frank because they have seen him come and go on over the years - sometimes by himself, sometimes with his brothers, sometimes with his one and only son that he speaks little about - so they assume I am part of his clan and we do not contradict them.

JENNIFER

A week has gone by and they haven't managed to find him. I can't sleep. I am utterly terrified. I am scared that he is out for revenge; that either I or the boys, or all three of us, will end up dead.

I have been going to bed fully dressed ready for action, just in case he turns up. When I take my contact lenses out of a night I have my glasses on the table next to the bed at the ready. I am nervous.

Inspector Sean Shanley, who is in charge of the search team, puts his number into my cell phone and tells me that he is available 24/7.

'All you need to do is press the button and I will be by your side in an instant,' he says. That has made me feel safer.

But Kevin insists that I buy a weapon and comes with me to the gun shop. I purchase a little pistol decorated with mother of pearl inlay, small enough to keep in my purse or hide in a drawer. It could be called pretty if it wasn't so deadly.

STUART

I do most of the cooking and Frank is delighting in the culinary delights of a city dweller. Up until now he'd been living on spuds. It is his way to boil up the potatoes with their skins on and upend them onto a breadboard in the middle of the table. No knives and forks here. We help ourselves, cracking the spuds and lathering them with lashings of butter and a bit of salt. They taste terrific, particularly if we fry up some rashers to go with them.

But variety is the spice of life and if I can trap a few lobster and catch some fish, then the protein adds enormously to the meal. I also use Frank's shotgun to hunt hare and rabbits. That's one advantage of coming from a military family. Father taught me how to handle a gun and shoot accurately and you don't forget those things. Dear Frank hasn't eaten so well since his wife died.

JENNIFER

You can't remain in a state of high adrenalin forever and life is there to be lived, so I have resolved to stop being so paranoid and start to relax.

There has been a lot of speculation in the papers about Stuart's whereabouts, and despite the authorities saying that they are 'hot on his trail' and that 'an arrest is imminent', quite frankly, they seem to have no idea. The way I have to look at it is that with him a fugitive we are safer than we have ever been before. Surely he will not dare to show his face around here, as he knows he will be apprehended and returned to jail. And not the cruisey one either, but the Joy, and for a longer time.

With more than a fortnight gone and nothing having happened, I reckon the dog can sleep outside tonight, I will wear my PJ's to bed and the boys can go back to their own rooms. By my reckoning Stuart is probably miles away from this emerald isle and on his way to America or Australia by now.

He always talked about migrating Down Under, saying that the high euro would buy us a mansion in the sunshine and I must say, in the early days I agreed, saying that it would be good. But we had our parents to consider and I don't like the thought of all those sharks and snakes and spiders! So it was just a dream. Maybe now, with the Garda after him he might head that way. I certainly hope so.

I insist Richie go back to school today. He has been really uptight and weepy and not wanting to leave my side. He is worried about his father.

'Will he be okay, Ma?' he asks. 'Will the Garda shoot him if they catch him? Will he come home to live with us? Will they hang him when they take him back?'

I assure him that everything is going to be okay and that his Da is big enough and clever enough to look after himself. I paint him a picture of his father's life in Australia, surfing and riding horses and playing cricket.

STUART

We have one hairy moment when the priest from the local Catholic Church comes knocking at our door, expecting to be invited inside. Apparently it is that time of year when the parishioners make a pledge for the planned giving program for church coffers.

I answer the door and am about to put on my best Protestant voice and tell him to go to hell, that I am a Church of Ireland man and there is no way I'd give money to the papists. I want to tell him that I will count to ten and if he is still standing there by then I will get a gun and blow him to kingdom come.

But I hold back. If I cause a fuss, it could destroy my cover entirely. Word passes quickly around these parts. 'Come and see Frank next week,' I say. He disappears down the long drive without looking back.

JENNIFER

I knew it. The minute the police call off the guard on the house 'because of other more pressing commitments', weird things are happening and are getting me frightened all over again. First of all Buchanan turns up on my doorstep wanting to know if we are all okay, and suggesting that he will organize an all expenses paid holiday for us in Spain out of company coffers. That spooks me. Is it a Stuart trap? Is he in Spain too? And is he getting Buchanan to try and lure us there?

I decline politely, adding, 'I will let you know when we need a holiday and I will take the offer then.' No need to put Buchanan offside, as he has been very good with the company finances and never leaves us wanting.

Then a couple of days later a country bumpkin of a fellow turns up just as we are sitting down to dinner and when I answer the door he says he might have the wrong house number or the wrong street, but is this Mel Brown's house? When I answer 'no' he apologises for disturbing us and leaves, but not before turning around when he is half way down the path and taking a long hard look at me and the house.

Then I got to thinking about Facebook. I still use it a lot to keep up with family and friends as I am so busy with the boys and my work at Molly's Place. What if Stuart is reading my posts? What if he is stalking me and keeping track of my movements? The lads tell me he has picked up computer skills and has access to a government-issued iPad. What if he has learnt to use social media? How would I ever find out?

So I do a search. 'How do I know if I have a stalker on Facebook?' There are pages of it, most of it unhelpful but there is one You Tube post that seems to be on the money. I follow the instructions and lo and behold up come the numbers of all the people who have viewed my page in the last month. I patiently check them against their own activity. And there he is! Watching my every move. I panic and speak once more to the Sergeant.

'Mrs Hoare,' he starts to explain, 'You know our resources are stretched …'

'I know,' I say. 'I am ringing to tell you that we are moving out of the house today and staying in a city hotel for a week. After that I will spend a few days in London with Tom, er Mr Knight, while the boys go to Galway with my brother Paddy.'

'It is good of you to tell us, Mrs Hoare,' he says.

'And after I get back I will have extra security installed in the house and all the locks changed.'

He tells me that that is a good idea.

TOM

Just when things are settling down and I feel I have escaped the Irish nightmare - albeit with a slightly misshapen nose and a steel plate in my head - I get an anguished call from Jen, crying her heart out on the other end of the line. She is a mess. Stuart has escaped from the jail. 'I know that,' I say coldly. 'For some reason it excited the English press and it got a mention in the papers.'

Even though time has passed, she has got it in her head that he is about to turn up and do something malicious to her or the boys. She begs me to allow her to come over to London for a few days. 'Just to get away from Dublin and the danger for a while,' she says.

Danger? I know he's a fucking madman, but wouldn't he have shot through by now? Made it to South America like Ronnie Biggs? He's probably lying on a Rio beach with a pina colada and some big-boobed Brazilian bird in a skimpy bikini. And what about the Irish police? Can't those useless pricks do their job?

She says she forgives me - she forgives me, gee, how very generous - and that the family is worn out by it all and Wendy has gone and she has absolutely nobody else to turn to. Duh! And who caused all that shit, huh? Then the waterworks really start to flow.

'Oh, all right,' I say. 'Yes, yes, come over, if it will help you feel better.'

What can I do? I agree because I know, more than most people, what that mongrel is capable of. 'But I am providing refuge only,' I add. 'Nothing else.'

There is no way that I'd go back down the Jennifer track. I'm not that much of an idiot.

STUART

The time has come to stop fishing and hunting and make my final move before I get too comfortable and start thinking about staying here forever.

Frank says he will organise a car for me but I become concerned that he will be left isolated and without wheels.

I also wonder whether the aging Fiat, forlornly parked out the front, will make the distance I require it to travel.

'You won't be taking that old banger,' he tells me dismissively as he turns and opens the garage door to reveal the sensuous, unmistakeable curves of an E-Type Jaguar! 'Holy shit,' I say, drawing on my years of admiring classic cars. 'A nineteen sixty-four series one, four point two litre, regency red. An absolute icon! But … how?'

'A fifty-to-one shot at The Curragh twenty years ago,' he says. 'I bought it as a wreck from the deceased estate of an old English baron, spent all me spare time restoring it and have loved it ever since.'

He explains he used to drive it in the early days but not any more as he believes it would cause jealousy amongst his neighbours. 'Now is the time to put it to good use, Stuart,' he says.

I cook up one last meal baking a large salmon I hooked that morning, frying chips instead of boiling the potatoes. We open a couple of bottles of stout and say our goodbyes. I thank him and wish him well. Tomorrow he will awake to a new day, a new life, the first glorious moments of his comfortable retirement, funded by me, courtesy of Buchanan.

I ease myself into the luxury of the low-slung cabin, switch the ignition over and smile as the motor growls into life. This is more like what I am used to. My little excursion to Dublin town is going to right a lot of wrongs and nobody will be looking for me in a swanky Jag. I head south to Derry first and then point the nose of the beast southeast through Armagh to catch the motorway at Newry.

I feel as free as a bird as I cruise the magnificent machine along at just below the speed limit, luxuriating in the feel of the leather, the touch of the wood, the grandeur of the huge bonnet that stretches out in front of me. Frank is absolutely right. The smoky Fiat would have drawn unwarranted attention. Garda and media cars pass me both ways, either ignoring or staring jealously at the exotic lines of the classic coupe. Never at its driver. I am on a magic carpet ride and this is living!

The evening settles as Dublin hoves into view and I have to decide whether to take the N1 into the city, work my way across the river and get the Stillorgan Road and out to Dalkey, or to avoid the congestion altogether by turning off and taking the M50. I am reluctant to do the latter as it will mean I have to drive past the spot where Molly fell.

As the first signpost for Junction 3 approaches, I slow the car, drop back into third and then into second.

Yes? No? The decision is made for me. A duo of lumbering lorries alongside gives my ever-slowing vehicle little room to manoeuvre, and not wanting to risk damage by going for the gap, I stay in the exit lane and find myself on the M50 curving towards Blanchardstown and shooting underneath the overpass, right past the spot where Molly landed.

'God bless you, my little angel,' I whisper. 'Please forgive me.'

Tears hinder my view as my mind feverishly races, a mixture of emotions, memories and images of my girl child.

Reaching Junction 16, I regain my composure and exit for Wyattville Road, mind focused on the task at hand as I creep the Jag through Dalkey village and park it at the top end of our street. I lock the car and sit the keys on top of the rear passenger side tyre, as agreed, so that

Frank's brother Eoin can come by later, pick it up and return it to him.

It is dark. Just how I need it. The house is in pitch black. I know from my newfound interest in Facebook that my lads are at their grandmother's for the night and I am sorely tempted see them before I do what I need to do. But I resist. No need to complicate things at this stage. Jennifer will shortly be returning from her visit to that little bastard in London.

I have a key and I know how to by-pass the security system. My little red-headed wonder woman has no doubt changed the PIN, but it was me who had the whole thing installed just after we had bought the place and I know the over-riding master code. Some subtle switching here and there in the fuse-box, a few bulbs loosened, a bit of power flex I find in the cupboard under the stairs put to good use, and I am ready to go.

In the gloom, I make my way into the lounge room, pour myself a whiskey and plonk into my favourite chair, facing the door. It is grand to be home.

Home? What a fabulous sounding word that is!

Home. Happy. Heaven. What other comforting words can I think of that begin with 'h'? Of course, hearth.

I remember when we used to gather around the fire toasting marshmallows and taking turns at relating the happenings of the day. We did have some good times together, despite what Jennifer says.

JENNIFER

It is late when I finally get home after a turbulent few days at Tom's house. He didn't want me there, declared it was all over and gave me his bed while he bunked down on the lounge room sofa. He was cool to me all week, wouldn't discuss us, and even brought a lady friend back from the pub one evening. I could hear them whispering and giggling and knocking things over and doing God knows what while I was trying to sleep. So humiliating! But I am back and home feels good. Time to move forward with my two sons.

The boys and the dog are back from the country and are staying at Mam's for the evening. She will get them off to school in the morning and they will come back here tomorrow night. I have missed them.

I flick the hallway switch and when the globe directly above my head does not light up I move my hand across to the other side and tap the switch of the small reception room. No response there, either.

I begin to think that something may be wrong. Looks like the whole circuit has blown. There is usually a torch kept in the top drawer of the sideboard but I can't find it. As I close the drawer my hand brushes against the coldness of the little pearl-handled pistol. I pick it up and drop it in my handbag thinking that I will give it back to Kevin now that the danger period is surely over. Stuart must be miles from here by now.

As my eyes grow accustomed to the dark, I see a light glowing dimly at the other end of the hall near the kitchen. Strange! I must have left it burning all week. So that means there must be some power on. I go into the main lounge to try the light there. No result. Damn.

Suddenly, inexplicably, the reading light on the table in the far corner of the room turns itself on! How can that be? I stop, turn and walk over to investigate.

When I lean forward and attempt to fiddle with the switch I realise there is a power cord trailing from it. This thing has not lit up by itself. I look down at the cord and my eyes follow its course all the way to the other end.

And there he is, sitting in his favourite chair as comfortable as you like.

'Hello darling,' he says, his voice calm, chilling, snakelike.

I respond in a remarkably steady manner. I don't want to provoke him, as I know he is capable of murder and I am not ready to die just yet. I keep my cool. 'They said on the telly you were spotted in Scotland and heading for Australia. I was hoping that you had gone there and that you could make a new life for yourself, a new beginning. A life in the sunshine.'

'Oh, that was definitely not me,' he says, waving the glass of whiskey dismissively. 'There are a lot of portly accountants wandering the world. But there is only one who is Stuart Richard Hoare, husband of Jennifer, and father of Stuart Junior, Richard and Molly. And I am right here. Where I should be. In my own home with my own wife.'

I tell him that I divorced him, that he is not my husband any more, that Molly isn't his any more because he killed her, that the boys do not belong to him because they are ashamed to be his sons. He takes it calmly. Too calmly.

'But Jennifer, I haven't divorced you. Those papers you served mean nothing. They're just expensive legal clap-trap your pal Flannery prepared to add to his ever-increasing bill.'

I open my handbag, take out my lipstick and nervously apply it to my lips. He sits and watches in silence. I return the lipstick and scrabble around in the bottom of the bag amongst the purses, hand creams and power bills for my phone with the sergeant's number in the contacts.

Stuart does not move.

STUART

I watch with irritation as she rattles about in that huge bag of hers looking for her phone. It was something I found engaging when we first met, but not now.

I give her time until she finally locates the damn thing, presses some buttons, stares at it, tries again and tosses it on the carpet in frustration. Its blank screen lays face up, its battery as flat as a pancake.

Why am I not surprised? You could have bet a tenner on it. This is another indicator of her chaotic way of doing things - Mrs Flibberty Gibberty, darting from one place to another, never stopping still long enough to attend to the detail, unable to commit to one man, always on the move. I was good for her, giving her stability, making sure that the little things got done which allowed the big things to take care of themselves.

'Did you think that I had forgotten you, that I wouldn't come to see you before I left?' I say, in a measured tone, putting down my whiskey and leaning forward to pick up the phone. 'Is that why you didn't think it was important to charge this thing up? When I was here it was always powered, because I did it for you. We used to be so good for each other, Jennifer. You know that. I ran the business and you ran the home. And then you went off with that bastard drummer boy and ruined it all. You destroyed our family, you destroyed my life.'

JENNIFER

The phone on the floor irritates him, distracts him, causing him to pick it up like the gentleman he aspires to be and hand it back to me. But it is the gun I am really reaching for, and I take it out and point it towards him. I am terrified of its power, but maybe I can frighten him, send him on his way.

315

'You killed our child, our beautiful daughter. You murdered her,' I say, shaking with rage and emotion. 'Go away and never come back. Take a plane, go somewhere, Africa, Tasmania, any fucking where, just go and leave us alone. We don't want you in our lives. I promise I won't call the Garda until tomorrow at two, to give you plenty of time. I just want you to go!' I motion hysterically with the gun as I sob uncontrollably.

Stuart moves forward, calmly leans over and takes the gun from my limp hand. I submit, let it go.

He installs himself between me and the door, his legs firmly planted, knees straightened, leaning slightly forward, the ape-like posture he uses to invade my personal space and assert his supremacy. He grins his supercilious grin. I step back, but there is nowhere to go as I am hard up against the table in the corner.

'Me? Murdered Molly? That's not true!' he hisses. 'You made me do it. So I'm not going anywhere. This is my home. You are my wife. If I can't have you, nobody will!'

He flicks one leg out to the side, kicking at Richie's drums, breaking the big bass skin and sending the cymbals clattering. He must think the kit belongs to Tom.

I wince at the noise and instinctively put my hands to my ears. The house phone is on its cradle in the hall. If only I could contact the Garda, or Mam, anyone. I try to move towards it. He lets me past and then grabs me almost playfully around the waist, pulling me back against him. I feel his erection and am sickened.

I turn to face him, telling him he will have to do more time for breaking in here and accosting me. 'I am going to telephone the Garda,' I say.

His calmness frightens me.

316

'I'm not worried about that,' he sneers. 'I just need to set the record straight.'

I harness my terror because I know it turns him on. Thank God the boys aren't here to witness this. I withdraw into my inner self, and stare at him, keeping as calm and still as possible.

He mustn't know I am afraid.

STUART

A gun, hey? Who would have thought? My rootin', shootin', high falutin' woman.

She stands perfectly still and looks up at me, unflinching. She wants me gone, out of her life, but I'm going nowhere. I'm going to make sure she is mine forever.

I kiss her on the forehead; she squirms but doesn't try to move away. You have to admire her. The little redhead has got guts and her defiance both infuriates and excites me. I want her more than ever. I push my cock hard into her groin and the gun firmly against her heart.

She remains rigid, unyielding, still staring. Defying me. Hating me! Goddam, you little bitch. You fucking devious nasty little slut. Why can't you see sense? Damn you, Jennifer O'Brien, damn you. Just submit to me, for Christ's sake. Submit!

She makes me do it. I shake my head, shut my eyes, pull the trigger. Her blood spurts over the white rug beneath our feet, splatters the walls, ruins my shirt.

The silence of the darkened house is permeated by a single agonized, haunting scream.

She crumbles.

She is all mine.

THE END

LOVER, HUSBAND, FATHER, MONSTER

Lover, Husband, Father, Monster - The Aftermath
by Elsie and Graeme Johnstone
is the gripping conclusion of the trilogy, following
Lover, Husband, Father, Monster - Her Story
by Elsie Johnstone
and
Lover, Husband, Father, Monster - His Story
by Graeme Johnstone

OTHER TITLES

Other works by the same authors include:

- *Our Little Town*, by Elsie Johnstone. A snapshot of life growing up in a small fishing village across four generations.

- *Ma's Garden*, by Elsie Johnstone, a gentle tale about a young couple setting up home and launching a small-town newspaper in 1902.

- *Rainbow Over Narre Warren*, by Elsie Johnstone, the true story of a much-admired priest who built one of Australia's largest parishes through love, trust and respect.

- *The Playmakers*, by Graeme Johnstone, a novel exploring one of the great literary deceits of all time - did Shakespeare actually write Shakespeare?

- *Joan, Child of Labor* - the memoirs of ground-breaking Australian Labor Party politician, feminist, human rights activist and anti-Vietnam campaigner, Joan Child - with Graeme Johnstone.

All books are available as paperbacks or ebooks from amazon.com, smashwords.com, or through online and traditional book retailers.

For more information go to:
www.loverhusbandfathermonster.com